RUSHING IN
THE BLACKHAWK BOYS

RUSHING IN

THE BLACKHAWK BOYS

New York Times Bestselling Author
LEXI RYAN

Rushing In © 2016 by Lexi Ryan

All rights reserved. This copy is intended for the original purchaser of this book. No part of this book may be reproduced, scanned, or distributed in any printed or electronic form without prior written permission from the author except by reviewers who may quote brief excerpts in connection with a review. Please do not participate in or encourage piracy of copyrighted materials in violation of the author's rights. Purchase only authorized editions.

This book is a work of fiction. Any resemblance to institutions or persons, living or dead, is used fictitiously or purely coincidental.

Cover © 2016 Sarah Hansen, Okay Creations
Interior design and formatting by:

www.emtippettsbookdesigns.com

For Kimmi

About
RUSHING IN

In the football world, quarterback Christopher Montgomery is known for his cool-headedness, his determination, and his steely self-control. He's about to meet his match.

The favor seemed simple: Keep my new stepsister out of trouble for one summer.

I've never met Grace Lee, but Mom tells me she's a quiet and artsy college student with a troubled past. When I agreed to let her stay with me, I thought it was no big deal. I expected to share my apartment with a sullen girl who'd spend hours locked in her room.

I didn't expect a walking fantasy determined to make me lose my cool.

I didn't expect a woman with secrets so dark, so deep, I'd throw away everything if it would save her from the past.

Rushing in to do this favor is turning my life upside down—and not just because Grace needs her ass spanked. Keep her out of trouble? Grace is the trouble. And I want in.

RUSHING IN is a standalone novel and the second in The Blackhawk Boys series.

Football. Secrets. Lies. Passion. These boys don't play fair. Which Blackhawk Boy will steal your heart?

Book 1 - SPINNING OUT (Arrow's story)

Book 2 - RUSHING IN (Christopher's story)

Book 3 - GOING UNDER (Sebastian's story - Coming late 2016)

More Blackhawk Boys titles to be announced in 2017!

CHAPTER 1
GRACE

Before I met Dad's girlfriend, Becky Dupree, for the first time, my mom described her as "loose and easy—the kind of woman who likes cheap tequila and kinky sex with strange men."

Naturally, I decided Becky was going to be my new best friend. By the time I figured out Becky was nothing like my mom had described, she'd already won me over with her big heart and bigger hair. She's a native of Champagne, Texas, after all, and from what I can tell, half the middle-aged women in this city didn't get the memo that the early nineties died and took their Aqua Net with them.

My new stepmother-to-be might not like cheap tequila, as Mom promised, but she does like good coffee, which is why, even though I'm running a little late for our dress-shopping date, I'm stopping at the Common Grind before meeting with her.

Personally, I don't *like* coffee. That term is too casual and speaks nothing of my true devotion to the sacred brew. I *require* coffee. At this point, I may be more roasted bean than flesh and blood. And in the likely chance that this old-fashioned Texan's idea of the "perfect" bridesmaid's dress for me includes sequins or a big pink bow on my butt, I'd like something warm and comforting to get me through it.

I take a breath and push through the doors of the coffee shop where I worked last summer, my mind on my mocha and my mocha on my mind.

A blast of air conditioning smacks me in the face, and I lift my chin and take long strides to the counter, where I give my order to a greasy-haired guy I've never seen before.

"Two mocha lattes, coming right up." He takes my money, and I keep my eyes cast down, afraid to see who else is working today.

Unfortunately, the whole "see no evil" strategy isn't effective.

"I heard you were spending the summer in Indiana," someone says behind the espresso machine.

I force myself to meet the gaze of my former coworker. "Hi, Jewel."

"Did you run out of guys to fuck in Champagne?"

My gut churns with something as sour as spoiled milk and hot as lava. I don't like the feeling I get in the pit of my stomach when I'm in this town. The feeling I had when I was fourteen and my dad stopped looking me in the eye. The feeling I had when I was stupid enough to end last summer with a bang. I went to a party, drank too much, and exercised my consistently poor judgment.

I didn't think I was the kind of girl to sleep with a friend's crush, but though I remember very little of that night, my brain has supplied me with enough mental snippets that I know enough to regret. *Typical Easy Gee-Gee.*

The next morning, all the girls I worked with at the coffee shop treated me as if I were a walking STD, and it was like I was fourteen all over again. I thought Jewel would have forgiven me by now, but obviously I was wrong.

"Oh!" The greasy-haired guy at the register claps his hands then points at me. "You're Gee-Gee Lee! Damn!" He looks at his watch. "I have a break in ten minutes if you wanna head out back." He grabs his crotch. "You know what I'm talkin' about?"

Hot lava surges into my throat again. Burning. My reputation precedes me. Fucking wonderful.

"Not a chance," I mutter, but there's no sting in my words because my voice has gone small, and I hate that, hate it as much as this feeling in my gut that I lost myself last summer, that I slipped back into old habits, that I got drunk and let myself once again believe the lie that I'm only as good as the number of men who want me, the number of dicks I get hard. I hate that this town makes me feel like I'm the slut they decided I was when I was fourteen.

"Two mochas, was it?" Jewel asks before spitting into two cups. She snickers, and the sound makes my chest ache. She and I were never close, but by the end of last summer, I considered her my friend.

What I did with Isaac ended that.

I turn around, my quest for caffeine abandoned, and head for the door, moving fast enough that I can pretend I don't hear her mutter ugly words. *"Easy Gee-Gee."*

I'm not that girl anymore. I'm not *that girl anymore.* But I'm not sure of anything.

"Oh, honey!" Becky throws her hands over her mouth as I step out of my dressing room. "Oh, you just look so *classy,* sweetheart."

I bite back hysterical laughter. "Classy" is not a word people use to describe me, and to be fair, it's not a characteristic I've ever strived for. But from Becky, and after my encounter with Jewel at the coffee shop, it's the best kind of compliment. I like it more than I want to.

"You do look nice, dear," my father says, his thumbs tucked into his pockets. My dad's a big guy, a former police officer who keeps his back to the wall and always stands with his legs spread wide, looking as if he's bracing for a fight.

Becky steps up to me and takes my shoulders. "Do you think it covers too much?"

Since I'm the only bridesmaid, Becky decided she'd wait until I came into town before we picked out my bridesmaid dress. I secretly love that she's laidback enough to let me buy something off the rack for her big day.

Dad grunts. "If it were up to me, it would cover more."

Becky rolls her eyes. "She's a beautiful young woman, Eddy."

Dad makes a face and steps back, relinquishing control of the wardrobe decisions to his bride-to-be. I love that she calls him Eddy. Everyone—including my mom—has called my dad Edward for as long as I can remember. Occasionally someone will call him Ed, but I sincerely doubt anyone before Becky Dupree ever had the balls to call him *Eddy*.

I turn to the wall of mirrors to study myself. The simple black sheath dress is long and three-quarter-sleeved. It covers all my tattoos except the ivy on my shoulder blades. If I didn't already love Becky, I would love her now for giving me an opportunity to object to covering so much skin.

But this dress isn't about Becky wanting me covered up. She's never been like that. In fact, when she met me last October, I think she was downright delighted by my then-pink hair, crazy wardrobe, and loud personality. She's never made me feel like I need to tone myself down or cover myself up, and now she's doing what she does best with me—making it absolutely clear that she's not asking me to do it for her wedding, either.

"I think it's nice." It's *gorgeous*, but I'd have been happy to wear something that was less my style, as long as it wasn't God-awful lavender or bubblegum pink or covered with that itchy lace that makes my skin all red and blotchy.

Dad nods. "I'm glad my girls agree." He kisses Becky's forehead. "You have my credit card. I'll be in the golf pro shop when you need me. Take your time."

Becky watches him go before turning back to me with a

sweet smile. "Thanks for not giving your dad a hard time about this summer. We appreciate you agreeing to stay with Dash."

"It's not a big deal." I shift awkwardly. I don't want to talk about my summer plans, and I definitely don't want Becky psychoanalyzing my motivations for them. Dad asked me to stay with my stepbrother because he thinks I need a babysitter. I agreed because I don't want to live in Champagne, Texas.

"I told Eddy you're a big girl and you can stay at the house by yourself. I don't want you to think we were worried you were going to throw wild parties or something. But you know your dad. You'll always be his baby girl, and he couldn't stand the idea of you being alone here with no one around to watch out for you."

"Come on." I grin and nudge my soon-to-be stepmother. "Who *wouldn't* want to stay in rural Indiana for a wild summer while they're in college? Isn't that on every girl's bucket list?"

Becky laughs. "Blackhawk Valley is really pretty. I've seen it for myself. And Dash has a nice group of friends there. But it's no New York."

"Are you sure *Dash* doesn't mind me staying with him?" I already asked Dad this same question, and he was all, *"Why would he mind? Are you planning to make his life difficult? Make yourself useful, and no one will ever mind having you around."* The conversation ended there.

"I'm sure," Becky says. "I'd feel bad for asking the favor, but I think you two will get along."

I don't know much about my future stepbrother, and I haven't bothered finding out more. I know he's a football player, which is a strike against him, but not all guys who play football are assholes. Or so they tell me.

He's Becky's son, which is a mark in his favor, because Becky is one of the best people I've ever met in my life. Not only does she make my dad happy—which I honestly didn't think was possible—but she's also really fun to be around, and her goodness shines right through her smile.

But the primary mark in Dash's favor is that he doesn't live in Champagne, Texas, and on my list of requirements for summer housing, "Not Champagne" is number one. If my stepbrother is going to be my ticket out of the armpit of Texas for the summer, he's all right by me.

"I'll stay out of his way," I promise. "I don't want him to feel like I'm interrupting his life."

"He won't feel that way at all," she says. "Dash is a good boy and always has been. He's helpful and does what he's asked."

I swallow back a gag and paste on a smile. I don't want to spend my summer with an asshole by any means, but if he's half as sweet as his mom makes him out to be, I might fall into a coma from boredom before I even make it back to the city.

"He's sweet and thoughtful, too," she adds.

"He must get that from you."

"Ha!" She bumps my shoulder with one of hers. "I wish I could take credit for it, but I was just a single mom trying to get by. I think that's the way he was born. I really wish you would have come home to meet him this spring. He's excited to get to know you."

"Sorry about that." I shift my gaze to the sheer hem that lands above my knees. "I couldn't justify the time away from school." I turn around to avoid her eyes. "Would you mind unzipping me?"

She lowers the zipper halfway. "You'll get to meet him soon. He flies in tonight, but your dad said you already have plans?"

"I'm staying with Willow," I tell her. "But I promised Dad I'd be home in the morning so we could all have breakfast together."

"That sounds wonderful. I'll make pancakes." She grins, and I slip back into the dressing room.

When I've changed back into my clothes—distressed jeans and a strapless pink top—Becky's waiting for me at the register, chatting with a bright-eyed blonde. When I put the dress on the counter, the blonde looks at me and her eyes light up with recognition.

"I know you," she says. "Gee-Gee, right?"

My "friends" at the coffee shop today notwithstanding, I haven't been called Gee-Gee since I was fourteen. Hearing the name makes the acid churn in my belly. I lift my chin. "I go by Grace now."

"Oh my God! Your stutter is, like, all gone. That's amazing. I heard you were here last summer but I never saw you. You, like, totally disappeared after . . ." She shifts her gaze to Becky, then drops it to the counter before meeting my eyes again.

"We had to move for Dad's job," I lie. Even if a career move for Dad was the excuse we used, everyone knew why we moved after *that night*. If Dad hadn't wanted to come back here when he took an early retirement, I never would have returned. But he's a

Texas guy at heart, and this is where he belongs.

I stare at the girl's hands, willing her to move faster so we can pay for the dress and get out of here.

She doesn't move, and when I look up, she's staring at me and chewing on the corner of her lip. Is she wishing me dead, like so many other girls did back then, or is she trying to work up the courage to ask if I started a career as a call girl? A couple of people asked me that while I was here last summer. Apparently it was a rumor that circulated for a while.

God, I hate this town.

"Do you take Visa?" Becky asks.

"Oh, yeah. Sure we do." The girl snaps out of her inspection and gets busy ringing up the sale.

When we leave the store, Becky is too quiet, and she stops at a Starbucks kiosk in the center of the mall. "Do you want anything?" she asks.

"La-la—" *Fuck.* I take a breath and count out the syllables in my head before speaking them. "Latte with four pumps of caramel."

She's studying me. She doesn't ask if I'm okay or to explain what the cashier was talking about. I could count on one hand the number of days I've spent with Becky, but sometimes it feels like she sees me more clearly than my father ever did.

Right now, I wish she were as oblivious as everyone else.

CHAPTER 2
GRACE

"Oh, my God! Grace Lee! My favorite girl!" Willow Myers steps out into the dark, rainy night and wraps me in a hug so tight I can barely breathe.

"I missed you." I squeeze her back.

There's the kind of friend who makes you smile, who you always know you'll have a good time hanging with, one you can count on for a laugh and a drink after an exam sucked the life out of you. And then there's the kind of friend who knows you inside and out, who knows the secrets you never imagined sharing with anyone, who knows your ugliest pieces and parts and still thinks you're beautiful. That's Willow for me.

"I missed you too. Let's get out of this rain." She tugs me inside her parents' three-story brick home.

I spent a lot of time here last summer. Willow and I were practically roommates for all the time we spent together between here and Dad's house. Maybe this summer would have been the same had things played out differently. But last summer's stupid, drunken decisions brought my past back to haunt me, so instead I do everything I can to avoid long stretches in Champagne.

"How was your flight?" she asks as I toe off my shoes. "Have you seen your dad yet? What about your new stepmom? You said she's nice, but is it weird to know you're about to have a new stepmom when you're a grown-ass woman? Have you decided if you're going to call her Mom?"

I can only shake my head at the rampage of questions. We text incessantly, but Willow is nothing if not curious. "Good, yes, yes, kind of . . ." I struggle to remember the last question.

"Will you call her Mom?"

"Oh. No. I don't think so."

"I made us strawberry daiquiris," she says. "What do you say we have a proper slumber party?"

I look down at my clothes. It's raining so hard out there, I'm soaked just from the walk from the car. "If by 'proper slumber party' you mean change into our PJs and drink too much, I'm in."

She cocks a hip to the side and arches a brow. I've always thought she matched her name—long, dark hair and limbs that go for miles. She's a goddess, I swear, with beauty inside and out. This girl is the light inside the darkness I feel when I'm here. "Is there another definition?"

I follow her upstairs to her bedroom, taking my overnight bag with me. Willow pulls a pair of fuzzy pants and a Wonder Woman T-shirt from her chest of drawers, and I grab my sleep shorts and tank from my backpack.

Willow's parents are the kind of people who spend more time traveling than they do in their own home, and right now they're in Rome, so I don't have to worry about her dad seeing me wandering around his house braless.

I use her bathroom to strip out of my wet clothes, and through the bathroom door I can hear Willow singing, "Reunited and it *feels so good!*"

Once we're changed, we head back downstairs and to the kitchen. We pour our daiquiris into tall pilsner glasses before settling into the overstuffed cushions of her living room sofa.

"To braless PJ parties," Willow says, raising her glass.

I tap it with mine. "I'm pretty sure that's the name of a porno, but I'll drink to it anyway." We take long pulls off our sugary, slushy drinks. My chest fills with a warmth that is partly due to the proximity of my best friend and partly due to the irresponsible rum-to-mixer ratio filling my glass.

"I can't believe you're going to live with your stepbrother this summer," she says.

I shrug. "There's nothing that could keep me in Champagne for a whole summer, since you'll be off living the glamorous life in London."

She snorts. "Oh yes, changing diapers and wiping noses is oh so glamorous. Do you think I should pack my diamonds?"

Willow's a few years older than me and just graduated from Baylor. She's putting her art degree to as good a use as any and spending the summer in London. She'll be the au pair for some

RUSHING IN   13

Hollywood couple who's shooting a film there. The agency that vetted her and set her up with the job only told her the ages of the children and the length and location of the assignment. She won't find out who the celebrities are until she arrives.

"Think it's Brad and Angelina?" I ask.

"This couple only has two kids," she says. "Isn't Brangelina up to, like, forty-three kids or something by now?"

"Bummer. I was having fantasies of visiting you and getting to know Brad."

"Ha! I'm sure Angelina wouldn't let any nanny that close to her husband. Back to the stepbrother, please. What if he's a pervert or something?"

"Then I'll chop off his dick." I grin and take another drink. I can't imagine sweet Becky having a pervert for a son. "He sounds like a good guy. Becky says he volunteers with Big Brothers, Big Sisters and is a straight-A student. If he's anything like her, birds probably start singing when he walks outside."

"So you're saying your stepbrother is a Disney princess?"

I shrug. Maybe I should feel weird about committing to spend my summer living with some guy I've never met before, but I was already scrambling to find an excuse not to come back to Champagne between semesters. When Dad and Becky told me they wanted to travel around Europe for their honeymoon, I had the perfect excuse. Dad doesn't feel comfortable with me staying at his house alone—even if I am legally an adult now—so I jumped on the opportunity to live somewhere else.

I tried to talk my dad into paying for an apartment for me in

New York, but since I couldn't secure an internship or a job more "educational" than my usual coffee shop gig, he wasn't having it. Apparently, the idea of me living alone in New York terrifies my father more than the idea of me living in Champagne without someone keeping an eye on me.

"Either way, he's giving me a room for the summer. I'll get a job and keep to myself. Dad's happy, and I'm not in Champagne. It'll work out fine."

"I guess." She frowns. "I still wish I had a chance to meet this guy so I could feel better about your arrangement."

"To hear Becky talk about him, he seems practically perfect in every way."

"Which is he? A princess or Mary Poppins?"

"He's a football player." I grimace at that unfortunate fact about my new roomie.

"Now I'm picturing Mary Poppins in a football helmet." She draws her legs onto the couch and tucks them under her. "What's his name again?"

"Dash." What the hell kind of a name is that, anyway? It's as if Becky knew her son would become a football player and named him accordingly.

Willow swishes her drink in her glass, watching the slush swirl. "Dash what?"

"Dupree."

"Have you looked him up on Facebook?"

I give her a pointed stare. "You know how I feel about social media."

"I keep telling you to make a fake account so you can spy on people."

I shudder. "I'll pass."

"Oh well. I'll look him up later myself. Dash Dupree." She says his name as if she's trying to place it, and shakes her head. "I'll have to ask Robbie if he knew him in high school."

"Could be. They both played football at Towers, but the name doesn't ring any bells for me." Willow went to Champagne's Catholic high school, so she didn't know any of the people who tortured me at Champagne Towers. I went there less than three months before we moved to Maine, but my time there certainly made an impression.

Willow and I met last summer after Dad moved back here and she and I both had gigs at the local coffee shop. She was the very best part of being stuck in this city, and when my otherwise carefree summer ended in a shitstorm of my own making, she was there for me in a way no one else could be.

"Not all football players are assholes," she says.

"I will agree that Robbie is an exception," I say. Willow's boyfriend plays ball at Baylor and is really sweet, if a little dense. I knew him during my brief stint at Champagne Towers High School, and he may not have registered my existence, but at least he never mocked my stutter by calling me "Juh-Juh-Gee-Gee" like half the other guys on the team. "Speaking of Robbie, how's he handling your impending departure?"

She sets her drink on the coffee table and sighs. "He still hates it, but I keep telling him the summer will go fast. He'll be busy with football, and I'll be back soon enough."

We talk about college and our plans for the fall, and when the pitcher of drinks is empty, she makes us another, and soon we're giggling without reason and she's telling me about the time she and Robbie had sex in the locker room at Baylor and she ended up with foot fungus and a bruise on her ass in the shape of a locker vent.

"It's depressing that I'm so sexually deprived that I'm even jealous of sex that ended in foot fungus," I tell her.

"What about that guy you were dating when I came to visit on spring break? The one with all the tattoos?"

I shake my head. "He was hot but there wasn't much going on upstairs." To be honest, I knew that when I started dating him, but I figured I could handle a lower IQ in exchange for hard abs and barrel-sized biceps. I know it's clichéd, but I have a serious weakness for muscle, which probably explains my history with football players.

She arches a brow. "You are so picky. A guy doesn't have to be a genius to treat you right."

"Willow, one day I said something about my commander in chief, and his response was, 'I didn't know you were Native American.'"

"No!"

"I've sworn off pretty idiots, but I *miss* sex."

"My poor, horny Grace."

"That is accurate." I take another long swallow from my drink. I'm not sure if the sugar buzz or the alcohol buzz is going to hit me first. "Actually, 'horny' is a terrible word. Don't use it to describe me ever again, please."

"No kidding, but there's no good alternative short of calling yourself *randy,* and that makes me feel like I should be picking up men at the local seniors' club."

I wrinkle my nose. "*Randy* might be worse than *horny.* But whatever I am, I blame those books you recommended. Those books made me . . . what about *thoughtful*? It's the *thoughts* that get us in trouble, isn't it?"

"I prefer *thirsty.*" She nods, satisfied with her word choice. "You're *thirsty,* and who could blame you? Maybe your stepbrother has a hot friend you could entertain yourself with this summer."

I drain my glass and close my eyes, imagining bonfires and tattooed country boys with ripped muscles from bailing hay—or whatever they do in Indiana. Surely Dash has some good-looking friends who could entertain me. "God, it's pathetic, but I'm kind of counting on it."

Willow's phone buzzes and she grabs it off the coffee table and grins as she looks at the screen. "It's Robbie. He wants to swing by. Is that okay with you?"

I shrug. I'm all warm and fuzzy from the rum. He could bring a dozen friends with him and I probably wouldn't care. "That's fine with me."

"Are you sure?"

"You guys have two days together before you leave for London. Seriously, live it up. I was thinking about crawling into bed with my book anyway. I want to read the one about the fisherman again."

"You don't need to go to bed. Robbie and I can be together without screwing."

I cock my head and frown at her. "You want to tell me that you're half drunk and your boyfriend's coming over, and you want to sit out here and chat rather than jump his bones?"

She laughs. Willow's laugh has to be one of the best sounds in the world, full, and real, and unapologetic. "You know me too well."

"It's fine," I say. "Seriously. I'll sleep in your sister's room." Her older sister is out of town for the weekend, and I probably would have slept in her room anyway just to have my own bed.

"You're the *best*."

The doorbell rings, and I stand. "I need to use the restroom. I'll talk to you two lovebirds in the morning."

"Don't feel like you have to turn in right away. I have another pitcher of daiquiris waiting in the freezer and a stack of Christina Lauren novels on the kitchen island. I think the fisherman one is somewhere in there."

"God bless you," I call over my shoulder as I push into the bathroom. I pee forever—I really drank too much of Willow's mostly rum concoction—and wash my hands. I hear laughter, then feet on the stairs, and the *thunk* of Willow's bedroom door before I leave the bathroom. They're wasting no time getting down to business. Good for them. At least someone's getting lucky.

I planned on going to bed, but I like Willow's suggestion

better. Sleep never comes easily for me, so daiquiris and a yummy romance novel sound like the perfect way to pass a couple of hours.

Except there's a broad-shouldered dude sitting on Willow's couch, his head of shaggy hair bowed.

I groan inwardly. Muscle is my kryptonite. I'm seriously tipsy and *thirsty,* and I don't need to be tempted into bad choices with some jock Robbie dragged with him to his booty call.

"Hey," the guy says. "Sorry to invade your space like this."

"No worries." I say, then he looks up and my breath leaves my lungs in a rush when I see his blue eyes. *Damn.* It's one thing to be *thirsty* and have bits and pieces below the belt zipping ideas to my brain. It's quite another thing when my other organs get involved. Like my heart. And maybe my lungs, because breathing isn't coming very naturally right now.

I know this guy. He wasn't around last summer, but we went to the same high school when I was fourteen. Five years ago, before Dad moved us away from Champagne and away from my damaged reputation, and before *that night,* I knew that face and those stop-a-girl-in-her-tracks sweet blue eyes.

His shaggy hair was shorter then, his shoulders a little less broad, and he had smooth cheeks where tonight they're covered in stubble. But I would know the face of Chris Montgomery anywhere. A girl doesn't forget blue eyes like that, especially when they were the first she ever fell for. Especially when it all ended with a new life and a broken heart.

"Hey there," he says again, looking at me this time. He grins.

Holy shit, that smile. Those dimples send me back in time, and all the feelings come back in a rush. The high school crush that I didn't dare speak of. The boy who was so far out of my league I couldn't bring myself to talk to him. The ache I felt in my heart every time he was in the same room as me.

Chris Montgomery is fucking perfect. He's the guy that every girl in high school swooned over. All he had to do was walk by, flash those dimples, and wink, and girls would practically knock each other over for the honor of dropping their panties first.

He's hot. He's smart. He's some sort of football genius—or was back in high school. And he's a fucking gentleman.

He was always so kind to me—genuinely kind, not like other boys who'd tease and flirt but never bother to look me in the eye. When I was surrounded by guys who couldn't keep their eyes off my tits, Chris gave his attention to my face when he talked to me. To be fair, this only happened once, but I was fourteen and the contact required for falling in love was minimal.

I was so pathetic. Still am, apparently, because my cheeks heat and the room spins sideways. I feel like I'm fourteen again, still madly, naively in love with the boy who doesn't know I exist.

Only now I'm not that girl anymore, and we're alone in Willow's living room with a storm rumbling outside.

"Sorry to bother you. I only followed Robbie in so I could grab some paper towels, but the storm's really picked up, and I wanted to let the rain slow down before driving home." He holds up a bloody hand. "Any chance you have a bandage I could put on this?"

I was so busy with my trip down Memory Lane that I didn't even notice his right hand is wrapped in blood-soaked paper towels. "Oh my God! Are you okay?"

"It's not as bad as it looks, but I want to make sure it doesn't get infected." He actually smiles as he says it, as if the injury isn't even painful, despite what the bloody towels would suggest.

"I hope not."

"My coaches are going to kill me. If they had their way, I'd walk around with my hands in a glass case any time I'm not on the field."

"You still play football?" I'm so impressed that the words come out smoothly, without even the faintest hint of a stutter. I credit years of speech therapy. And alcohol. Even when my stutter was at its worst, a good, strong buzz made it all but nonexistent. (Let's file that under: Things You Shouldn't Learn At Fourteen—a pretty thick file in my case.)

"Yeah. I play at Blackhawk Hills University." He narrows his eyes and studies me. My stomach clenches, and I wait for him to recognize me as "Juh-Juh-Gee-Gee," or worse, "Easy Gee-Gee." I wait for his memory of *that night* to drain all the kindness from his face.

Instead, his grin stays firmly in place, his dimples greeting me without hesitation.

I force a smile, but it costs me. I don't like feeling this vulnerable, this dependent on another human's approval.

"Are you Willow's sister?" he asks.

He doesn't remember me. Maybe I should be offended, but

instead I'm just relieved. I guess I should thank my newly dyed black hair for his ignorance.

Yeah, or maybe you were never important enough for him to remember.

He points at me, his brow wrinkling in concentration. "Robbie told me Willow had a sister our age. Mary or—"

"Morgan," I say.

He extends his left hand—the one that isn't wrapped up in blood-soaked paper towels—and I take it, stupidly. "Nice to meet you, Morgan," he says. "I'm Chris. Robbie had too much to drink, so I gave him a lift. I wouldn't have followed him in if I realized he was going to disappear into his girlfriend's room right away."

I might not be the sharpest tool in the box after questionable amounts of rum, but a few things occur to me all at once.

One, Montgomery hasn't changed. He's still the sweet Southern gentleman with exemplary manners who looks out for his friends. Case in point: giving Robbie a ride here so he wouldn't drive after drinking too much.

Two, despite said gentlemanly traits and a history of keeping his eyes off my assets in high school, he's seriously struggling to keep focused on my face now. Maybe my tight, light blue tank is to blame, or the fact that it's a little cold in here, but he's definitely checking me out. And even after all these years, that's fucking *satisfying*.

Except for—three, he doesn't remember me. *Holy shit.*

Oh, and four, he thinks I'm Willow's sister, Morgan.

"Morgan." He narrows his eyes, as if trying to place a puzzle piece. I could help him, but I don't. "You kind of look familiar. Did we hang with the same people or anything?"

Only one night. I shake my head. "No. We ran in different circles."

"Well, it's nice to meet you, or meet you again." His grin is so genuine, and having those dimples directed at me feels so good I realize a fifth thing: I'd rather lie and pretend to be Morgan Myers than tell sexy Chris Montgomery who I really am. Especially when he's looking at me as if I'd make the perfect bedtime snack.

Would you like fries with that?

CHAPTER 3
CHRIS

Morgan's eyes give me a faint sense of déjà vu. They're this gorgeous emerald green framed by long, dark lashes. On her upper arm, she has a tattoo of cat eyes in the same color. *Those eyes.* We must have met at some point in high school. "I'm sorry if I interrupted your evening."

"You didn't interrupt anything." She pulls her bottom lip between her teeth.

I *really* like the way she's looking at me—all of me, like she loves what she sees and can't take me in fast enough. It's great for my bruised ego and by far the best part of my night.

Five minutes ago, I was irritated and wishing I hadn't let the guys talk me into that party. It had seemed like a good idea. Mom and Edward were having dinner with some friends who are in town for the wedding, and the stepsister I need to meet had plans as well. So I let the guys rope me into the kind of party I usually avoid—too much alcohol, so much weed you couldn't walk out back without a contact high, and God-knows-what going down in the upstairs bedroom. Sure, it was nice to see everyone, but I'd hoped that the guys I went to high school with had matured enough that getting together and getting trashed weren't their favorite pastimes anymore.

I wasn't at the party for more than an hour before those hopes came crashing down. And as it always does, too much alcohol led to fighting, and I cut my hand open trying to break it up. My *throwing* hand. I was ready to get out of there—there's no one from high school I care about enough to put up with that kind of bullshit. But then Robbie grabbed his keys and was talking about driving to his girlfriend's house, and the idiots weren't going to stop him.

It's raining so hard out there that it was difficult to drive even sober. I shudder to think what would have happened if he'd gotten behind the wheel. I've already lost one friend to a drunk driver, and that's more than enough for this lifetime.

But now I'm glad tonight's events brought me here, because Willow's sister is that killer combination of hot and cute. I'm not much for the rebound hookup, but after the ugly breakup I endured last weekend, having a girl this beautiful check me out feels damn good. Her long, silky black hair falls over pale shoulders, brushing the tops of her breasts, and her skintight sleep shorts show off her long, pale legs. I know she's dressed for bed and not for me, but *damn*.

Her pink cheeks turn red, and she heads to the kitchen and

opens one cabinet after another, only stopping when she finds a square black box.

Then, *boom*.

One second I'm ogling Robbie's girlfriend's sister, and the next we're in total darkness.

The oven beeps and the refrigerator cycles off as a loud clap of thunder bangs overhead and shakes the house. The windows light up, showing us a flash of the rain pouring down outside.

"There go my plans." Her voice comes from the direction of the kitchen, but I can't see shit between flashes of lightning.

"And what were your plans?" I ask.

"Reading and drinking until my insomnia cried uncle."

"I'm sure the power will come back on soon." Standing, I carefully move toward the kitchen and search for her silhouette in the darkness. I wish there was enough light to see her.

I hear the slide of a drawer opening and then a click. Light illuminates the hardwood floor at my feet.

"Flashlight," she says, holding the light under her chin. She grins, and it's a punch to the gut because it's a big, wide smile that takes up half her face and makes her even prettier. "I guess now I can read my dirty book after all."

I cough. "*Dirty* book?"

"So dirty," she says.

"Does that mean you dropped it in the mud or—"

"It means the characters have lots of hot sex." Her pink lips curve into a grin. "The good kind of dirty. Do you ever read dirty books, Chris?"

God, she's pretty, even holding the flashlight in a position reminiscent of someone telling campfire ghost stories. I want to kiss her.

How ridiculous is that? I want to kiss a woman I just met.

Okay, I'm a dude, and she's talking about reading a porny book, so I want to do more than kiss her. I want to slide my hand up her side and find out if those curves are as soft as they look. I want to keep grinning at her and see if her blush can go any deeper. I want to hear her say her name again. *Morgan*. God, it suits her. Sexy and cute. And then I want to hear her say *my* name.

"Do you?"

Oh, shit. I'm doing that guy thing where I'm too busy thinking with my dick to actually listen to what the pretty girl is saying. "I'm sorry. What?"

She laughs. It's a deep, rich sound, and it comes so naturally from her lips that I'm struck with the idea that she's one of those women who laughs in bed. "Do you ever read dirty books?"

"Um, I'm a guy. We usually . . ." I clear my throat, wanting to answer—God knows why—but not wanting to sound like a pervert. "Guys usually opt for the visual."

Grunting, she sweeps the flashlight down my chest, and if I didn't know better I'd think she slowed as the light's path crossed over my crotch. She brings it back to her face. "If you think women aren't visual, you'd be pretty shocked by my browser history."

"Dirty?" I ask, using her word.

"Tumblr is a beautiful thing."

It's official. I'm talking about porn in a blackout with the sexiest woman I've ever met. This night definitely doesn't suck anymore.

She sweeps the light across the kitchen and opens the freezer. She pulls out a blender full of red liquid before sweeping the light back to me, careful to point it at my chest and not my face. "Care for a daiquiri?"

Drinking in a blackout while talking about porn with the sexiest woman I've ever met definitely wouldn't suck either, but I shake my head. "Thanks, but I'm driving."

"Mr. Responsible," she says, pouring herself a glass.

I laugh. "Why do you say that like it's a bad thing?"

She overfills the glass, and it dribbles down the side. She licks the excess off with a quick sweep of her tongue before answering. "Trust me, it's not bad. There's a shortage of responsible men in this world."

I try not to grimace. She says *responsible* where Olivia used the word *boring*. *"Can you blame me?"* she asked. *"You never do anything impulsive. I needed to remember I was alive."*

I shove the argument from my mind and watch as Morgan puts the blender back in the freezer. She tucks the flashlight under one arm and carries the black box and her daiquiri to the living room. Yes, this is a much better train of thought than Olivia and the mind games she played spring semester.

In the dim light, I struggle to make out the sway of her hips in those short shorts, but I have a better view with the flashlight than without it, so I'll count my blessings. That said, I wouldn't complain if the power came back on right about now. Some sights warrant full lighting. Morgan's ass is more than worthy of a spotlight.

She sets her drink on the end table and the flashlight next to it so it's pointed at the ceiling. As she sinks into the couch, she pats the cushion beside her. "Come here. Let me take a look at that hand."

I almost forgot about the bloody gash. I'm perfectly capable of tending to my own wounds, but I obey, sitting next to her just to be closer.

She takes my hand in both of hers. "Is this your dominant hand?"

"Yeah." My voice is thick because her hands are soft and because I'm really fucking curious to know what she likes to look at on Tumblr. I open my palm as she unwraps the towel from around it to expose an angry red gash.

"Bummer. Can you make do with your left hand?"

"I can't throw for shit with my left hand."

She snorts. "Who said I was talking about *throwing*?"

Holy shit. Is she seriously asking me if I can masturbate with my left hand? "Is that an inappropriate question, or do I have a filthy mind?"

"Oh, it was totally inappropriate. Does that make you uncomfortable?"

I grunt, more intrigued than shocked. I've definitely never met a girl like her before. "It might if the lights were on."

She looks up at me through her lashes. "The lights aren't on."

I swallow hard. I don't want to read too much into her long

stares, but *hell*. "I know."

"What happened?" she asks, her gaze fixed on my hand again.

"Robbie got in a fight with a drunk idiot wielding a beer bottle. I stopped the guy from bringing it down on Robbie's head, and I got this in return. My coaches are gonna be pissed, but at least no one's head got busted open."

"Being a hero comes so naturally to you."

I laugh. "Trust me, there was nothing heroic about getting between a couple of drunken idiots."

"What were they fighting about?"

I shrug. "Who knows? Robbie's got a quick temper. Someone probably said something stupid that he took the wrong way. The whole party was like that. A good reminder of how much I don't miss this town."

"You and me both," she mutters. She sighs heavily. "Next time you can come over here and drink with me instead."

"I like that idea." I rarely drink more than a beer in a night, but hanging with Morgan and her sassy mouth while indulging in a few drinks appeals to me a whole hell of a lot.

She takes the black box off the coffee table and unlatches it to show the contents of a first-aid kit. I watch her in the dim light as she wets a cotton ball with hydrogen peroxide. She holds my hand in one of hers and uses the other to clean the gash.

I draw in a breath through my teeth, and she stops. "Does it hurt?" she asks.

"It's fine."

Smiling, she shakes her head as she finishes her task. "Of

course it is. Tough guy." She follows with antibacterial ointment before wrapping my hand in gauze.

"Now who's the hero?" I ask.

"You clearly don't know me." She's so careful as she wraps and secures it with white medical tape. "There." She lifts my palm to her lips and presses a kiss on the bandage. "All better."

"Thank you."

She meets my eyes and her lips part as if she planned to say something then decided against it.

"What?"

The flashlight flickers.

"Where's your girlfriend tonight, Chris?"

An image of Olivia comes to mind—her dark hair and eyes, that sweet smile that always struck me as innocent. I push it away. That's over. It ended dramatically and before it ever officially began. "I don't have a girlfriend."

She arches a brow and dips her gaze to my chest and slowly back to my face. "How is that possible?"

"Where's your boyfriend?" I ask.

"I don't have a boyfriend."

I grin and give her a similar once-over. "How is that possible?" She laughs, and I say, "No, seriously."

"Do you really want me to answer that?"

"I really do."

She grabs her drink off the coffee table and sips. Her tongue darts out to catch a drop from her bottom lip. "I fell for a guy once. I was young and stupid, and he was . . . better than Tumblr porn."

"High praise."

"I know, right?" She grins and takes another drink.

"What happened? How did falling for him bring you to tonight without a boyfriend?"

She lifts her eyes to meet mine, and something passes over her features, as if she's reliving a painful memory.

"He hurt you?"

She takes another sip, then another. "That's why it's called a crush, right?"

"If you want me to track him down and give him a piece of my mind, just say the word."

She throws her head back in laughter. "As entertaining as that prospect is, it's entirely unnecessary." Her expression grows serious as she brings her eyes back to meet mine. "I promise he's forgotten about me by now."

"I find it hard to believe anyone could forget you, Morgan."

She drops her eyes to my crotch. "That's not good."

"What?" For a second I'm afraid she's referring to the semi I've been sporting since she started talking about dirty books, then I follow her gaze and realize she's looking at my injury, not my crotch. Good. I think . . .

She puts her drink down and takes my bandaged hand in hers again. "It's already bleeding through. You might need stitches."

"It's fine."

Thunder booms outside and the flashlight flickers again, but this time it doesn't come back on.

"Sorry," she says, not releasing my hand. "The batteries must be old. I hope you're not afraid of the dark."

I turn the hand she was inspecting to squeeze one of hers. "I can think of worse times to be stuck in the dark." My voice sounds funny, thicker, as if something has a hold of my throat.

"You don't mind being here with a chick who'd ask you about your jack-off hand?"

"You're real. No games. I like that."

I can't see her eyes, but I hear her sigh. "Have you ever just wanted to be someone else for a night?"

Fuck yes. I don't know what being someone else means to her, but I can understand the sentiment. Ever since I started playing tackle football in third grade, I've felt the pressure of being the son of notorious Coach Colt Montgomery. As much as I love football, some days I wish I could play it without everyone else's expectations weighing so heavily on my shoulders.

"You probably think I'm crazy for asking."

"Not at all. I know exactly how you feel." I swallow hard. "You can be whoever you want with me."

"You promise?"

"I don't know, actually. Can we hold off until I get to look through your Tumblr porn? Whips and chains aren't really my thing, and if you were planning to take me to your Red Room, maybe don't be yourself until I get out of here."

She laughs louder now, but I can't see her so I have to imagine her face tipped up, her long, pale neck exposed.

I'm not sure what makes me do it. Maybe it's the storm or

the fact that she still hasn't released my hand. Maybe Olivia's accusations that she only cheated because I'm not spontaneous enough hit too close to home. Or maybe Morgan and I are just two people sitting in the dark who understand what it's like to want to be someone else.

For once, I don't know *why* I act. I just do. I lean in, cup her face in my good hand, and sweep my lips over hers.

CHAPTER 4
CHRIS

She draws in a shocked gasp, and I pull back, ready to apologize. Lightning flashes through the windows, and for a second I get to see her face. Her eyes are closed, her head half bowed, as if she's saying a prayer or making an important decision.

"Sorry, I—"

She reaches for me before I can finish, sliding a hand behind my neck and leading my mouth to hers again. I move slowly, and when my lips are just above hers, she whispers, "I can't believe I'm doing this," and then closes the final inch between us.

Her mouth is soft and sweet, and she tastes like strawberry daiquiris. When she opens her mouth and slips her tongue against my lips, I hear a groan I realize too late is coming from me.

Then it's a tangle of tongues and lips, and my hands are sliding up her sides. "I didn't expect this," I tell her.

"I know."

The last thing I need is Robbie telling her he suggested we hook up. She'd think I was a total asshole and came inside looking for this when I really just wanted some paper towels to stop the bleeding.

She leans back on the sofa, and following is the most natural thing in the world. As if she's mine and we've done this a hundred times. I love the feel of her under me, and love it even more when she draws her knees up on either side of my waist, and more still when I kiss her neck and she rocks her hips under me and makes the most amazing sounds.

She's wild and as unreserved as I guessed. She threads her hand in my hair and guides me to the sweet spots on her neck. She finds my good hand at her side and leads me to cup her breast. With every kiss, her moans grow more desperate, and with every touch her hand tightens in my hair.

I turn off my brain and move on instinct alone. I trail my open mouth over her collarbone and down and scrape my teeth over the swell of each breast as my thumbs find her nipples through the thin fabric of her tank top.

"Chris." She gasps when I run my thumb over her nipple. *Christ, she feels good.* "This is crazy."

She's right. This is crazy and completely unlike anything I've ever done before. Part of my brain knows that. "I can stop."

"Good," she says. "Don't. Not yet."

I groan in relief. Crazy or not, I need more of her before we put an end to this. I love the sounds she makes when I touch her, love the way she rocks her body under mine.

I slide a strap from her shoulder and pull at the fabric so I can taste her, and when my mouth latches on to her breast, she arches under me. "Yes. Please."

"You feel so good, Morgan."

In a blinding flash, the lights click back on.

Her eyes fly open. "Stop." She shoves at my shoulders, breathless. "Okay, we have to stop."

I sit back, take a deep breath, and scrape a hand over my face and wait for my body to redirect some blood flow to my brain. That moved fast. "Are you okay?"

Frowning, she pulls up her shirt, covering her breast and repositioning the strap. "I've just had too much to drink." She shakes her head. "I shouldn't have..."

Her words register, and I draw in a ragged breath. When I got here, I was so preoccupied by how hot she is and how much I wanted to kiss her that I didn't think about whether or not she was sober. And when I kissed her and everything went so fast, I only thought about getting closer, touching more of her, and eliciting more of those sweet, sexy noises. I didn't question whether or not that untouched pitcher of daiquiris might not be her first.

"Shit, Morgan. I'm sorry. I didn't think about how much you'd been drinking. I just thought..."

She straightens her shoulders and pastes on a smile that doesn't fool me for even a second. "It's fine."

"Don't say that if it's not."

"I'm not drunk, so don't beat yourself up. It's just... this is a mistake. You go home and give your left hand a try, and we'll pretend it never happened."

I flinch. I'm not sure if I'm more insulted by the fact that what we did is nothing more than a mistake to her or hurt by the idea that she could forget it so easily. Never mind her suggestion that I'll need to jack off to recover—okay, I totally will, but that's not the point.

"I don't need to forget this just because you wanted to stop. I'm sorry we got carried away, but . . ." I pull my phone from my jeans. "Let me have your number. I'll text you in the morning. When you're sober."

God, I sound like an idiot, but I don't want to walk away and let her go. There's something special about her. She's beautiful, but this is about more than green eyes and a smile that could knock me on my ass. I like her. She's ballsy and hilarious and unapologetic. She's so many things I'm not. She makes me want to learn the secret parts of her stories, the parts you leave out when you tell your closest friends.

She grabs my phone and programs her number, then stands and heads for the stairs. "I should get some sleep."

"Want me to tuck you in?"

She stares at me for a beat, and I wonder what's going on in that mind of hers. She was so open earlier, asking questions as if there wasn't a filter between her mind and mouth. I want that back. She drops her gaze to the floor and shakes her head. "If I had you that close to my bed, I'm not sure I'd make wise choices."

I groan at the thought of her making unwise choices. *Fuck.*

Walking away from her tonight shouldn't be so hard. This isn't like me. "That's fair."

I grab my keys off the end table and head toward the door, but stop when I reach the stairs. She's gripping the railing, waiting for me to go. When I step toward her, she licks her lips.

"May I kiss you goodnight?" I take another step closer, watching as she tugs her bottom lip between her teeth. "I promise to keep my hands in my pockets." I flinch. "Shit, now I sound like a weirdo. I don't mean hands in my pockets in the creepy way."

She had her lips pressed together, but they part when she bursts into laughter. "Don't worry. I didn't think you were going to rub one out while we were kissing." She squeezes her eyes shut and draws in a deep breath. "But still, I don't think it's a good idea."

I'm an idiot. "No problem. Sleep well." I turn to the door.

"No," she says, stopping me. "You can kiss me, but I don't want your hands in your pockets."

I turn back.

"I'd rather have them in my hair."

I stalk toward her slowly, tilt her face up to mine, and slide my hands into her hair. It's silky between my fingers and smells like lavender shampoo. Her lips part, and a fist tightens in my gut.

"You're so gorgeous." I skim her bottom lip with my thumb, and her eyes float closed.

"Kiss me."

"As you wish." I lower my head and brush my lips over hers.

When I suck her bottom lip between my teeth, she makes a little sound at the back of her throat, and I open my mouth over hers.

She tugs me forward by a belt loop, and in the next breath I have her pressed against the banister and one of my hands has left her hair and is sliding under her shirt. She's so soft and warm, and she arches into my touch like she wants to soak it up.

I break the kiss when I realize what I'm doing, and lean my forehead against hers. We're both back to breathing hard, but this time she's clinging to me instead of pushing me away.

"I'll call you tomorrow," I whisper into her hair.

"That's what they all say." She climbs up two steps and out of my arms. Her smile is a mask that gives me the distinct impression I could see her better before the lights came back on. "Goodnight."

She turns, taking the stairs. When she disappears into the darkness above, I let myself out.

The rain has slowed, and my mind is so full of Morgan that the short drive to Edward's goes quickly.

The house is dark, but Mom left the porch light on for me. I use the key she gave me to let myself in to her fiancé's house. I know I should start thinking of it as Mom's house, but that's still weird to me. Mom and I lived in the same two-bedroom cottage from the day I was born until I left for college. It's the place I'll always imagine when I think of home, but she sold it this winter when she moved in with Edward.

When I get to the guest room, I strip down to my boxer briefs and sit on the edge of the bed. What a crazy night. I left

Blackhawk Valley anxious to get away from my friends for a few days—because if you have a secret relationship with a teammate's sister, you don't get to complain to your friends after she fucks you over. And Olivia fucked me over good when I caught her with Keegan.

"It was just a kiss, and it just happened."

The way her hands were threaded into Keegan's hair made it look like a hell of a lot more than "just a kiss." Since everything went to shit last weekend, tonight was the first I've spent without thinking about the breakup. It's not like I'm heartbroken. Olivia didn't have my heart to break. But she did a fucking number on my ego.

Enter Morgan Myers.

I grab my phone. I know I told her I'd wait until tomorrow, but I can't resist. I find the entry for *Morgan* and compose a text.

> **Me:** *Thanks for bandaging my hand. And for the record, I have no intention of forgetting tonight. Despite what that first love of yours made you think, a girl like you would be impossible to forget.*

I throw the phone onto the bed and rub my temples. Thirty seconds later, my phone buzzes, and I can't grab it fast enough.

> **Morgan:** *Who is this?*

I frown. I know she didn't have my number, but I'd think it

would be obvious from my message.

Me: This is Chris. Is this Morgan?

The next text comes in seconds and makes my stomach sink.

Morgan: You have the wrong number.

CHAPTER 5
GRACE

It's the sunniest day in the history of sunny days, and at nine a.m. it's already so hot that the short half-mile walk from Willow's house to my dad's is enough to leave me sweating. I'm hungover, and even the slightest bit of heat makes my hangovers feel exponentially worse, so that's not doing much to help me love this town. I still don't understand why anyone would choose to move to a climate where the average temperature is only a few degrees cooler than the fire-and-brimstone hell my mom is so fond of describing to me.

My head is pounding. I'm pretty sure there's a toddler with drumsticks in there who's banging on shit for his own amusement. In my stomach, there's a war being waged between the half that I imagine as a used car salesman getting rid of inventory—*Everything must go!*—and the half that's more like the plant from *Little Shop of Horrors*—*Feed me, Seymour!*

"Grace!" Becky calls from the back of the house when I walk in the front door. "Good morning, sweetheart. Do you want some coffee?"

I love this woman. "Yes, please." I wander into the kitchen without removing my sunglasses. At least the house is cool, which should go a long way to help me keep the coffee in my stomach.

I settle onto a stool at the oversized island, and she tucks a warm cup of coffee into my hands.

"Late night at Willow's?" she asks quietly.

"Daiquiris" is the only explanation I offer, and because Becky doesn't have a stick up her ass like my father, she gives me a sympathetic pat on the shoulder.

"We've all been there."

I grab the sugar bowl and dump a few heaping tablespoons into my coffee. I couldn't sleep after Chris left, so I did the next most obvious thing and finished off the pitcher. I'm not typically much of a rum drinker, but I couldn't stop thinking about the way he looked at me with those dreamy blue eyes. And that goodnight kiss? *Hello, nurse.* None of that would have driven me to drink if my overactive brain hadn't insisted on replaying my memory from five years ago.

I take a small, experimental sip of coffee, and when my stomach doesn't reject it, I follow up with a long gulp. I love Becky's coffee. She gives the beans the respect they deserve and grinds fresh every morning.

"How's Willow doing?" she asks.

"She's good. Getting excited about her summer position."

"I'm sure she is. I can't even imagine a summer in London working for some Hollywood hotshots. She would have been welcome for breakfast, you know."

"She's got some stuff going on." By *stuff,* I mean she still has Robbie in her bed. The truth is, I left a note and snuck out before she got up. I'm not ready to talk about last night, and Willow would see right through me and know something happened.

Willow didn't go to Champagne Towers High School, so the only details she knows about *that night* are the ones I've told her. She knows about the quarterback who stopped everything before it could spiral out of control, but I'm sure she had no idea that my hero/former crush/the guy who broke my stupid fourteen-year-old heart was Robbie's ride last night. Hell, after living here all of last summer without ever running into him, I had myself convinced that I didn't care if I ever saw Chris Montgomery again.

Then, after only ten minutes of having those ridiculous dimples aimed in my direction, I was jumping him like the slut everyone in this town thinks I am.

I don't even know how it happened. I was buzzed at best, so I can't blame it on the alcohol. That level of intoxication doesn't make me do things; it makes it easier to do what I *want* to do. And last night, I wanted to do Chris.

I liked the way he looked at me, the way he laughed at my crude humor, and the way he asked me questions and hung on my answers like I mattered. And maybe I felt a little vindicated that he wanted me. Perfect Chris Montgomery wanted Easy Gee-

Gee.

Only he didn't. He wanted Morgan, Willow's sister. The power kicked back on as he said her name, and it snapped me right out of my fantasy and made me realize exactly how reckless I was being.

Bad judgment—that was what last night was. What was I trying to prove by making out with *the* Chris Montgomery?

The memory makes my stomach heave, and I close my eyes and exhale slowly. I'll never see him again, so it doesn't matter anyway.

"Only drug addicts and blind men wear sunglasses indoors," Dad says as he walks into the kitchen.

Oh, Daddy. I'm his biggest disappointment. When Mom and Dad split up when I was ten, Dad had dreams of getting custody of me and us having this idyllic father–daughter relationship. So he fought Mom in court and got custody—though, to be fair, I don't really think she fought back that hard. She never quite knew what to do with me. In fact, Mom and I are so different that if I hadn't seen the pictures of her carrying me, her belly round in late pregnancy, the exhaustion on her face, I wouldn't believe we were related at all.

Dad got custody, and Mom moved to Dallas. It turned out that Dad was still a workaholic, a police officer above all else, and he had no idea how to relate to a daughter who got boobs way too soon and who looked at boys way too often.

"Where are your manners, Grace?" he asks, scowling at my sunglasses.

"I forgot to pack them," I mumble, not bothering to remove the offending item.

Dad is not amused. "You missed breakfast—not that I was surprised."

"Give her a break, Eddy," Becky says. "You were young once, too. She and Willow celebrated a little too much last night, but they were safe, and it's not like she was hooking up with random men or something."

Nope. Definitely not random.

Dad stares at me and frowns. I'm pretty sure he's spent most of his life waiting for the day when I get knocked up or start turning tricks. Or both. He keeps me on a tight leash because he's convinced that without one, I'll self-destruct. To be fair, I haven't given him much reason to believe otherwise.

"Dash got in yesterday," Becky says. "He's taking a shower but he'll be down any minute."

Oh, yay and hoorah. I get to meet the goody two-shoes stepbrother today. *Joy*. Granted, this guy is saving me from a summer in Champagne, so I should be grateful, but this hangover isn't putting me in the mood to play nice.

"Oh! There he is!"

I follow her gaze toward the stairs, and in that moment my girlie bits do the cha-cha and my heart sends out a warning to my dancing ovaries with all the subtlety of a bat signal. He's beautiful, his broad shoulders covered in a fitted T-shirt that hugs thick biceps and is molded along a narrow waist. I can't exactly make out his six-pack through the shirt, but his rock-hard stomach and broad chest are as obvious beneath that shirt as my hangover would be without these sunglasses.

He walks into the kitchen and wraps Becky up in his arms. "Mornin', Mama."

Fucking crap on a cracker. I'm dead. *Dead.*

For one, this is the kind of guy who sees his mom and immediately pulls her into a hug, which—*come on*—is the sign he's one of a dying breed of men, for sure. And *two,* I know him.

After typing a fake number into his phone last night, I believed I'd never have to see his perfect dimples or look into those dreamy blue eyes ever again.

This can't be happening. This must be a nightmare. The guy hugging Becky is Chris Montgomery. Becky's son is Dash Dupree, a guy I've never met before. Why is Becky hugging Chris Montgomery?

He squeezes her tightly. "You look gorgeous in that color, Mom."

Becky giggles. "Save your flattery for tomorrow, Dash. I want you to meet Grace." She takes his shoulders and turns him around to face me.

Luckily, his back is to her so she misses the way his smile falls off his face as he looks at me. "Morgan?"

I try to swallow but my whole throat feels paralyzed. I can't speak, can hardly breathe. I know him. My soon-to-be stepbrother. My soon-to-be roommate. Last night's really bad judgment.

"Her name is *Grace,*" Becky chides. "I've told you that, Dash."

He grimaces and mumbles, "Right," never taking his eyes off me. There are no dimples for me now. Only disgust. He extends his bandaged hand. "Grace?"

Becky is watching, so I take his hand, and little tingles of pleasure shiver up my arm at the contact. My body is my biggest enemy right now, and though I don't normally beat myself up for the physical manifestations of a healthy sex drive, I'd like to lock my libido in a cage and throw it in the attic.

I pull away quickly and tuck my hands in my lap under the bar.

"Do you two know each other or something?" Becky asks.

Chris—or Dash, or whatever the hell his name is—just stares at me, directing all sorts of righteous anger in my direction.

"We went to high school together," I say. I watch Chris's eyes for that spark of recognition. *Nothing.*

I look a little different now than I did then—poked some holes in my ears, put some ink on my skin, changed the color of my hair more times than I can count—but I'm still the same girl he found in that basement, and he doesn't have a clue.

It's a good thing, Grace, I tell myself. But it's only good in the way that it's good not to get caught robbing a house when you know that at any minute, someone's going to watch the surveillance footage and you'll be found out.

"Oh, right," Becky says. "Grace, I always forget that you went to Champagne Towers for a few months. You know Dash? Why didn't you tell me before?"

"I didn't realize I did." My heart does that simultaneous

squeeze-and-expand thing again that really can't be healthy. It wasn't prepared for this. The knots in my stomach tighten around the pointed shards of my regrets. *What have I done?*

This is so bad. Like, push-the-*panic*-button bad. All my genius plans for the summer are turning to smoke before my eyes, and I keep waiting to wake up and realize that this is just a terrible nightmare.

I look to Chris. "When I knew him, he was Chris Montgomery."

Becky grins at her son affectionately. "Montgomery is his father's name, and I've called him Dash since he was three and would do sprints in the backyard. I've never seen a toddler move that fast. Let's see, when you were a freshman, Dash would have been—"

"A junior," I say. *I* don't need help remembering.

She turns to her son. "And you remember her too?"

His neck works as he swallows. "Not from high school, but we've . . ." He swallows again and his face contorts as he tries to contain his sneer, no doubt for his mom's sake. "We ran into each other at a friend's house last night."

Becky frowns at her son. She's not stupid. She can tell there's something going on between us, that something's wrong that we're not sharing. She forces a smile and turns back to me. "Are you ready for the excitement that is Blackhawk Valley?"

I laugh only because I know it's expected, but my mind races, replaying that night from my freshman year in high school on a fast-forward loop in my head right next to flashing images from last night. *Fuck, fuck, fuck, fuck, fuck.*

I remind myself that oxygen is important and that I need to take deep breaths. If I can just remember who and where I am, I can get through this. I can figure it out.

They call it a crush because it hurts. When I was fourteen years old, I never expected my crush on Chris to go anywhere, but I also wasn't prepared for how much it would hurt. I wasn't prepared to see him again, wasn't prepared for how greedy I'd be when he offered me those smiles last night, or how much I'd love the way it would feel when he touched me. I never imagined I'd end up his stepsister or that I'd spend a summer living with him.

I'm not sure the last part is going to happen anymore, judging by the anger in Chris's eyes.

"Are you ready, son?" Dad asks Chris.

"The guys are going to the tux shop to pick up their suits this morning," Becky says. She claps her hands together and grins. "I can't believe tomorrow's the big day."

Chris finally pulls those piercing blue eyes off me to smile at his mom. "I'm happy for you, Mama."

Dad steps between them and kisses Becky's forehead before whispering something in her ear that makes her giggle.

Her phone clatters against the granite countertop as it buzzes, and she grabs it quickly. "Sorry, it's the wedding planner. I need to take this. You boys have fun. I'll be right back, Grace." She taps the screen then presses the phone to her ear as she heads to Dad's study. "Hello, Patrice."

"I'll see you at the rehearsal tonight," Dad says to me. "It would mean a lot to me if you could be on time for once. And get rid of those damn sunglasses."

I'm so used to my father's criticism that it wouldn't even faze me if Chris weren't standing here, but something about him witnessing this makes my cheeks heat. Luckily, he has gone from full-on glare to avoiding looking in my direction altogether, so he doesn't see.

"Yes, Daddy."

"You could learn something from Dash here," Dad says. "He knew we had a full day today and woke up at a decent hour. He was coming back from a run before Becky and I had even made it out of bed. I'm hoping his work ethic rubs off on you this summer."

I watch them head out to the garage, and then I hide in the upstairs bathroom. I strip out of my clothes, crank the shower to its hottest setting, and attempt to wash away my hangover.

I feel trapped and exposed. Chris was never supposed to find out that I wasn't who I said I was last night, and he definitely wasn't supposed to be the guy I'm spending my summer with. It isn't just that I made out with my stepbrother. I mean, that's a clusterfuck all by itself. But the real problem is that I don't want to spend my summer—or any time ever—with anyone who knows about *that night,* especially not the guy who saved me from it. Chris may not have made the connection between me and fourteen-year-old "Easy Gee-Gee," but it's only a matter of time before he does.

I have to find somewhere else to stay this summer.

CHAPTER 6
CHRIS

"Then I'll ask for the rings," the preacher says, giving me a pointed look. "Put them somewhere safe but easy to access. You don't want them falling out of your pocket before the ceremony. I recommend the inside of your suit jacket instead of your pants pocket."

I nod. "I can do that."

"Just like when you'll give your mother away at the beginning of the ceremony, the exchanging of the rings is symbolic. It feels good to get it right and have everything run smoothly," the preacher says. "Your mom's counting on you."

My eyes drift back to Grace, as they've been doing since we arrived at the rehearsal. She's wearing this red dress with big white polka dots and red high heels. With the red bow tied into her dark hair and the tattoos peeking out from the low-cut back of her dress, she looks like sexpot Minnie Mouse. Last night I noticed the cat eyes on her arm, but I somehow missed the ivy that runs over her shoulder blades. It's so detailed it almost looks three-dimensional, and I want to trace it with my fingers and follow it to where it disappears beneath her dress.

And therein lies the problem.

"I'll say some words about your new family," the preacher says, "and speak to the importance of Chris and Grace's roles in this marriage and their new relationship as brother and sister."

Grace keeps her eyes cast to the ground but bites her lip at "brother and sister." I'm glad to see this mess she made is at least a little awkward for her. Whatever she was thinking last night, she's been avoiding me today. Her dad and I returned from getting our suits, and she was gone. She left a note for him explaining that she'd borrowed his old car because she had errands she needed to run. She promised to meet everyone at the church in time for the rehearsal.

I got here early, hoping we could talk before all the official stuff got underway. We need to sort out what happened last night. *I* need to know what the hell she was thinking. Only, she arrived five minutes late, and the minute she walked in the door we had to get started.

"This is typical," her father said. "Always late. Always in trouble. I'm counting on you to keep her out of trouble this summer, son."

I'm guessing the way I sucked her tongue into my mouth and felt her up last night wasn't exactly what he had in mind.

"Then the couple will kiss and begin the recessional," the

preacher says, and I realize I haven't heard a word since "brother and sister." "Edward and Becky, you exit first." Mom takes Edward's arm and they head down the aisle. "And Christopher and Grace follow."

"Not too far behind," the wedding planner calls, waving us into the aisle. "I want the photographer to get some shots of the whole family walking down the aisle together."

Avoiding my gaze, Grace takes my arm, and we walk down the aisle. Touching her reminds me of last night, of her skin under my hands on the couch, of the way she pulled me tightly against her as I kissed her goodbye.

The second we hit the church's vestibule, she turns away from me and heads to the exit.

I grab her arm before she can go far. "Grace." Her name comes out like an insult because—well, because if she'd told me last night that her name was Grace instead of lying about who she was, we wouldn't be in this predicament now. "We need to talk."

Mom's been so excited about us all coming together to make a new family. She'd be so disappointed if she knew the truth— that all I could think about standing across from Grace today was how she felt under my hands, the way she tasted, and the sounds she made when I put my mouth on her breast.

The only thought that wasn't full-out NC-17 was that Grace is a fucking liar. And, luckily for my sanity, I've been thinking about that a lot.

Grace stops and looks down at my hand on her arm and makes a face. "Fine," she whispers.

Mom deserves to be happy, deserves the perfect little family she imagined us becoming, and I can't help but think I fucked it all to hell last night. Except there was no fucking. Not that I was thinking clearly enough to keep it from going there had Morgan—*Grace*—been interested. But she stopped me.

Thank God. *Jesus.* It's hard to believe, but when it comes down to it, this could be worse. I've built a reputation in football and life in general for being cool, calm, and collected. That's who I am, but that wasn't who I was last night. Did I really let the bullshit with Olivia get to me so much that I needed to prove I could be spontaneous?

That has to be the explanation. Otherwise, I wouldn't have touched a girl I didn't know and wouldn't be in this twisted mess we're stuck in today.

"Dash?" Mom frowns and drops her gaze to where I'm holding Grace's arm. I release it. "Is everything okay?"

Shit. Above all else, I don't want Mom knowing what happened.

Sexpot Minnie Mouse smiles. "*Dash* and I just need a minute to talk about your gift."

I glare at her when she uses my nickname. Only my mom calls me that.

Mom's face relaxes. "Oh, you two! Don't you dare spend money on us!"

Grace lifts her palms, the picture of innocence, then scurries into the hallway.

I'm simultaneously grateful and annoyed. Grateful that my

mom remains oblivious to our drama and annoyed that Grace is such an accomplished liar.

I follow Grace, and she pulls me into a storage closet. The space is dark and barely big enough for us both. When she reaches around me to pull the door shut, her body presses against mine. Just like that, lust punches me in the gut.

This is what they mean when they talk about chemistry. Chemistry isn't the simple biological response of getting turned on when the moment is right. It's this powerful, undeniable attraction that has me hard even though the moment is all wrong. And *fuck* am I turned on.

Because she's so soft. Because she smells like springtime and lavender. Because even if she's a liar and the worst kind of trouble, I can't shake the memory of how good she tastes.

I don't know what she was hoping to accomplish with her lies last night, but I'm not going to be part of it. Even if I do want to kiss her again. Even if I'm dying to know if touching her could possibly be as good as I remember.

"What kind of game are you playing?" I ask, reminding myself who she is and that she can't be trusted.

"Game?" The word comes out in a low growl. "You mean the one where I don't tell my dad that his precious new son had me underneath him last night?"

"Are you trying to *blackmail* me?"

"What?" She makes another growling sound. "No, I'm trying not to ruin their wedding day, which is exactly what will happen if you blab about our *shared* momentary lapse in judgment."

"*My* lapse in judgment? You lied about who you were."

"You made assumptions. I just didn't correct you."

"Did you think it would be funny? Something to lord over me all summer? You thought it would be fun to screw with your new brother?"

"First of all, there is no way we're spending the summer together." She speaks in a whisper that's getting louder on every word. "Second, this isn't entirely my fault. I thought my new stepbrother was *Dash Dupree*."

"Oh, I'm sorry, *Morgan*. I should have made sure *you* didn't misunderstand who *I* was."

She throws up her hands, or at least I think that's what she's trying to do when they hit my arms, but the space is dark and I can't see, and we're so crowded in here there's not much room to move. "I didn't think it *mattered*." She grabs my biceps and shoves me away, only there's nowhere for me to go. "We were never supposed to see each other again."

"Which is why you programmed a fake number into my phone under your fake name?" Her hands are still on my arms, and I imagine I could kiss her like this. How am I supposed to have this conversation when she's so damn distracting?

"You called?" She sounds shocked.

"Was I acting like a guy who wasn't interested in seeing you again?"

She drops her hands, and her fingertips skim down my arms in the process. Is she trying to make me lose my mind, or do I just have some faulty wiring in my brain that interprets every move she makes as sexy?

"I texted when I got home," I say, "but I guess the joke was on me. Wrong number." I grit my teeth. I didn't mean to let her know how much the wrong number thing upset me. It's the least of my worries at the moment. "Would you please explain why you lied about who you were if you didn't know we were about to be siblings?"

"Not siblings." She shudders against me. "That's gross. We're *not* related."

"Whatever. Answer the question. Why, Grace?"

"It's been a long time for me, okay? I made bad decisions because I was too . . . too thirsty to make good decisions."

What the fuck? "Thirsty? You're blaming this on the booze?"

"No, not thirsty." She sighs. "*Thirsty.* You know."

This girl makes no sense. "Why didn't you get some water?"

She groans, and I wish I could say the sound doesn't affect me, but it slingshots me back to last night on the couch, and my dick goes even harder. "Not thirsty, you idiot. *Thirsty.* As in, I haven't had my needs met in . . . a while."

"Your needs?"

Oh. Shit. Her *needs.*

"You're so dense. I'm saying I've been relying entirely on my Tumblr account for months. *Many* months."

This girl is trouble. I step back, but my shoulders hit the cold metal of a storage rack. Thinking about her needs fucks with my brain, so I'm about to let her off the hook when I realize she still hasn't answered the damn question. "If you didn't know that I was Becky's son, then why didn't you correct me when I called you Morgan?"

"Because I liked the way you were looking at me."

"That doesn't make any sense."

I can't see her face, but I hear her exasperated sigh loud and clear. "I remembered you from high school, but you obviously didn't remember me. I didn't want to help you remember."

"Why not?"

Another sigh. "Because you were Chris fucking Montgomery, and I'm just..."

I've had enough of the darkness—it's giving me ideas about how I can help her with her *thirst*. And her needs.

I need light to remind me why we're in here. I reach over her shoulder and run my hand along the wall until I find the light switch. The fluorescent bulbs over our heads flicker to life, and I can see her clearly now. Her big green eyes, her full red lips, the swell of her cleavage in that damn distracting dress.

Who am I kidding? Seeing Sexpot Minnie in the light gives my dick more ideas than being with her in the darkness did.

"You're just what?" I ask, trying to snap my brain back to the subject at hand.

Grace squints, and as her eyes adjust she focuses them on her feet. "I'm nobody, Chris." She turns around, pushes the door open, and rushes into the hall, leaving me alone with a bunch of church supplies and dirty thoughts about a *thirsty* Grace.

CHAPTER 7
GRACE

Confession: After my shower this morning, I may have internet-creeped on Chris using Dad's computer. Becky was signed into her Facebook account, so I was able to see pictures of Chris and "his boys" after football games, pictures of him accepting awards, and even a link to a newspaper article with a picture of him in front of a casket with his head bowed.

I told myself it was for research. For self-preservation, I need to know as much as I can about him. And if I spent a little too long staring at the pictures of him on the beach last spring, a little too long admiring that *V* of muscle that dipped into his low-slung swim shorts, so what? I'm a grown woman with working parts. Looking is natural—healthy, even.

The truth is, time has only made Chris hotter. As a junior in high school, he was just a shadow of his current self. But even when his shoulders were half the breadth they are now and the stubble on his jaw was faint, he seemed like this sexy, amazing guy. Fast forward five years, and he's a fucking Adonis, which is just unfair. I wanted him to develop an acne problem or maybe a beer gut from too many frat parties.

The rehearsal dinner is at a steakhouse on the river in downtown Champagne, and the place is filled to the brim with friends of Dad and Becky. It's going to be one of those long, drawn-out evenings where they make you endure an hour of mingling and appetizers with fancy names before they'll feed you dinner.

When I spot Chris watching me across the room, my stomach does a series of flips and double back-tucks. If stomach gymnastics were an Olympic sport, his presence in this room would make me a contender for the gold.

His hair's longer now than he wore it in high school, and it falls over one eye until he pushes it back and tucks it behind his ears. Tonight, he's wearing khakis and a blue polo that stretches across his chest and shoulders.

I'm not the kind of girl who looks at a guy and fantasizes about a romantic night in his arms, but there's something about Chris and his big arms and those dimples that makes me wonder what it's like to be the girl tucked into his side at a candlelit table. All the more reason why I need to put a stop to our previous plans.

I tear my gaze away from Chris and focus on my father, who's sitting at another table. "Daddy?" I force a smile as I sit down at the table across from my father. I was a couple of tiny, insignificant minutes late for the rehearsal, and he's still pissed. Scratch that—he's *disappointed*, which is way worse. He was disappointed in me when I was fourteen and Isaac's mom called him to pick me up from the party. He was disappointed last summer when my drunken choices gave the local girls all the fuel they needed to harass me online. His disappointment is always something I earn, and that eats me up inside. "Sorry I was late tonight." It took me twice as long to get ready as it typically does, and I'd rather not analyze why.

"The best apologies are in actions, Grace."

Oh, goodie. That speech. Today's been a regular stroll down Memory Lane. "I wanted to talk to you about this summer. I'm wondering . . ." I swallow hard. I feel so guilty for bringing this up tonight, but I'm supposed to fly to Indiana on Sunday, so if I want to get out of living with Chris I need to take care of it now.

Dad sets his drink on the table. Scotch on the rocks. "What's wrong?"

"I'm feeling guilty about the whole situation with Chris . . . Dash . . . whatever."

"What situation?"

"Um . . ." *The situation where he had his mouth on me last night? The situation where he has no idea that I'm Gee-Gee from that night in high school? The one where I don't want him remembering? Ever?* "Just staying with him, you know? After getting a chance to talk to him, I'm realizing how busy he is, and I'm not sure it's a good idea for me to intrude. I don't want to disrupt his life."

"Did he say he didn't want you there?"

"No, nothing like that." *That would have been too easy.* "I'm just wondering if we can revisit the idea of me staying in New York. I have a friend who'd let me rent a room in her apartment in the city." I'd be renting a *couch,* not a room, and the apartment's in Harlem, not Manhattan, but now's not the time to get hung up on logistics. "If I work at the coffee shop, I'd only need a little help from you to make it happen."

"We talked about this, didn't we? I don't feel comfortable with you living in New York without some sort of supervision."

I keep my spine straight, imagining it's made of steel so I don't crumple under the force of his lack of faith in me. I just finished my first year of college away from home and managed to do so without failing any classes or picking up any substance-abuse problems. I'm not some kid who needs to ask her father's permission to get an apartment.

And yet I do. Without his money, I can't live in New York. Without his approval, I can't do any-fucking-thing I want, because I need him to pay my tuition when I go back to Carson. And that's not even taking into account the obvious truth that I still hunger for my father's approval.

He swirls his drink, jangling the ice against the sides of the glass. "If you'd gotten a spot in that writers' camp—"

"The summer playwright program," I correct. I'm convinced his inability to get my major right isn't from a faulty memory but part of his great many efforts to get me to major in something more practical.

"Right," he says. "If you'd gotten into a program at the college, this would be a different conversation. But you didn't."

My shoulders drop at the reminder of *that* failure. "I know, but—"

"Being there for a purpose I can get behind, but I'm not going to let you loose on that city. Not yet. I'm sorry, Grace. I'm your father, and I've made up my mind. You're staying with Dash, and unless you have an excellent reason to change our plans this late in the game, I don't want to hear any more about you spending the summer alone in the city."

I could tell Dad about who Chris is, that he was the one to stop everything that night, but it would only reinforce Dad's notion of Chris as the perfect moral compass for my summer.

"I don't feel right about it," I mumble.

"Your mom would love for you to stay with her," he says. He inclines his chin and narrows his eyes slightly, telling me he knows he's thrown his trump card.

I suppress a shudder as I imagine a summer inside the un-air-conditioned church that's Mom's home away from home in Dallas, day in and day out of her making me pray with her, listening to her beg me to promise myself and my "purity" to God long after I'd lost it to the older boy next door. Maybe I could tolerate all that if I had any sort of connection to my mom, but we've never been close. Dad might keep me on a tight leash, but Mom's version of religious expression borders on "zealot," and though I'm not blaming her for my really shitty adolescent decisions, I suspect her unhealthy views on female sexuality had the opposite of their intended effect on her rebellious daughter. "I'm not staying with Mom."

"That's what I thought," Dad says. He stands and presses a kiss to the top of my head in a gesture that makes me feel simultaneously cherished and underestimated. Dad loves me, but sometimes I feel like all he sees when he looks at me are my mistakes. "You know I worry about you. Stay with Dash and consider it a wedding gift to me and Becky."

I nod but don't meet his eyes. "Yes, sir."

CHAPTER 8
CHRIS

I vacillate between being thankful and frustrated that Mom invited half the town to this dinner. On the one hand, having so many people here who want to talk to me makes it easy to hide the awkwardness between me and Grace. If Mom never finds out I felt up her new stepdaughter, it'll be too soon.

On the other hand, I have to talk to a bunch of idiots who wouldn't give two shits about me if I didn't play ball and wasn't Colt Montgomery's son. But I do and I am, so I've been bombarded with questions all night: *Will you go pro next year? Are you excited about the draft? What's BHU going to do about its sudden coaching vacancy? Have you met Peyton Manning?* And my least favorite: *Have you seen your dad recently?*

When we finish eating and we're free to move around again, I'm grateful to step away from all the well-meaning strangers and their endless questions. I scope out the dessert buffet, pretending to consider my options.

Since we arrived, Grace has kept her distance, but again and again, I've caught myself watching her. She ordered a potato and salad when everyone else ordered steak or salmon. She listened much more than she talked, but I noticed she's one of those people who's such a good listener that they feel like she's a bigger part of the conversation than she is.

Passing up the sugar-laden choices, I spoon a pile of fresh strawberries onto a plate and stand in the corner instead of returning to the table. That's where Mom finds me.

She's wringing her hands, and "worried mother" is written all over her face. "Do you want to talk about what's going on between you and Grace?"

Despite the ups and downs Mom and I have been through, I'm always honest with her. This might be the one time I've felt like I can't be. "What do you mean?"

"I want to know about what happened between you two last night."

No, Mom. You don't. You really, really don't.

She takes a deep breath. "I told Eddy I want to cancel our trip."

I tear my gaze away from Grace—because I somehow landed on staring at her yet again—and swing around to look at Mom. "What? No. Why would you do that?"

She tilts her head to the side. "I never should have asked you to do this for us. Taking in Grace is just too much, and you two clearly rub each other the wrong way."

As far as I see it, the problem is more along the lines of us rubbing each other the *right* way, but I don't plan on telling Mom that. "Why would you say that?"

She arches a brow. "I birthed you. I know when someone makes you uncomfortable. And anyway, Eddy told me Grace is trying to talk him out of making her stay with you."

"She is?" Well, fuck. It's not like I'm looking forward to it, but I never intended for the problems between Grace and me to interfere with Mom and Edward's plans.

"She is, and she was fine with the arrangement yesterday. Obviously you two didn't hit it off or it wouldn't be a problem." She holds up a hand before I can object. "I'm not blaming you. I just want to know what's going on. Did something happen between you two in high school?"

I shake my head, thinking of what Grace said in the storage closet about how she didn't want to tell me her name last night because she didn't want me to remember her. She didn't need to bother with a lie because I don't remember a Grace and I can't imagine forgetting a body like that. "I don't remember her."

Mom frowns. "Well, she obviously remembers *you*."

Yeah, *obviously*, but my drama with Grace isn't what matters here. "A summer in Europe has always been your dream. Don't you dare cancel it."

"It would be more of a delay than a cancellation." She rubs her bare arms, worry knitting a crease between her eyebrows as she finds Grace on the other side of the room.

"Mom, could you explain why Edward even needs me to

keep an eye on her? She's going to be a sophomore in college. Why does he think she needs a keeper?"

"I don't know details," Mom says. "Eddy refuses to talk about it. But I know she had a rough time in high school. She got in trouble a lot, and he worries. The only reason he lets her go to school in New York is because she lives in substance-free dorms with strict curfews. He seems to think the RA keeps tabs on her. He's fiercely protective."

Substance-free dorms? "Did she have a drug problem or something?" I really can't have that shit in my apartment this summer. The team is under such fierce scrutiny after what happened last spring when our running back got arrested for having a whole cornucopia of drugs in his locker. Arrow will finish his house arrest and be back at BHU before the season ends, but we have yet to see if those mistakes have cost him his career.

"I don't think so." Mom frowns. "I think she got started drinking young and overindulges from time to time, but I don't know of problems with other drugs."

That's a relief. Then again, it sounds like Mom might be as clueless as I am. "She's an adult. He's going to have to let that go sometime."

"You know that and I know that, but Grace's mother blames Eddy for Grace's troubled past, so Eddy blames himself, too. There's nothing I can say to change that." She turns her attention back to me and gives me a sad smile. "Eddy and I have our whole lives together. We'll travel another time. I don't—"

"Absolutely not. You aren't canceling this trip."

"Dash, I'm not asking you to open your home to a girl you hardly know if you two aren't getting along. I shouldn't have asked you to do it at all."

"I'm *glad* you asked. I love that you get to live your dream this summer. Grace and I are fine. Please don't give canceling your trip another thought." I force a smile and wrap my arm around Mom's shoulders, turning her to face the party. "Now, would you please go talk to all of your friends and stop worrying about me?"

She turns and tilts her head back to meet my gaze. "Are you sure?"

"Positive." *And I'll do whatever it takes to get Grace on the same page.*

Mom takes the hand I have resting on her shoulder and squeezes. "I know I'm being selfish, but I hope you'll believe me when I say I want Grace to stay with you this summer as much for her sake as for mine. She's lonely, Dash. And maybe depressed, too. And I don't expect you to fix that, but I do believe that staying with you will help." Smiling, she presses her palm over the center of her chest. "You bring joy to everyone around you. Maybe you can work some magic on your sister."

My *sister*. I really wish we could nix that word from the get-go, but it's two other words that catch my attention: *lonely* and *depressed*. And last night she was drunk, to top it off. What have I gotten myself into? But one look into my Mom's eyes and I know I have to make this work. "It's only for the summer. I'm happy to do it."

CHAPTER 9
GRACE

When I pull Dad's old sedan into his driveway after the rehearsal dinner, Willow is sitting on his front porch, her feet in bright pink Converse shoes, and crossed at the ankles. After a long day of avoiding everyone but failing to avoid my own thoughts, I'm just so damn happy to see her I could cry.

I park, pull my keys from the ignition, and practically throw myself out of the car to greet her.

"How was the rehearsal?" she asks, standing.

"The part where I closed myself in a tiny closet with the sexy man I can't have, or the part where my dad threatened to send me to live with Mom if I didn't stay the course for his plans for me for the summer?"

Her eyes go wide, and she shakes her head as if to clear it. "Sorry. Back up. What happened?"

"I'm a slut, and my slutty ways fucked everything up. Again. Because Slutty McSlutterson sluts a lot. What is it about this town that brings her front and center, anyway?"

Willow gives me a stern look and sets her jaw. "Grace, cut that shit out."

I sigh but my stomach is in knots. Why do I fuck everything up? "Want to go on a walk?"

She steps back and cocks her head to the side in appraisal. "That serious, huh?"

"So serious I contemplated going for a *run* this morning to sweat it out."

She gasps and throws a hand over her mouth. "You didn't!"

I shake my head. "Don't worry. It didn't come to that after all. I drove into the city and visited Ben & Jerry's."

"Crisis averted," she says solemnly.

We head to the end of the driveway, arm in arm.

When Dad moved back here for his retirement last summer, he bought a house in this country club neighborhood where the streets all have sidewalks and are lined with gorgeous oiled bronze street lamps, so even though the sun set hours ago, our path is well lit. We wander in silence for a while, heading toward the back of the subdivision, where the houses are three times the size of Dad's and overlook the golf course.

"Do you remember me telling you about Chris Montgomery?" I finally ask when I can't hold it in anymore. This new information eats me up inside, and I have no idea what I'd do right now if I didn't have Willow to talk to. I had a plan and it was perfect because it was a plan that made my stubborn father think he was getting his way while really I was getting mine. I'd stay with my stepbrother. Dad would be happy because I wasn't in Champagne alone, and I'd be happy because I wasn't in Champagne at all.

"Chris Montgomery?" she asks. She chews on the corner of her lip like she does when she's thinking hard about something.

I didn't think the name would mean anything to her. "Remember the night in the basement when I was fourteen? With the football players?"

She snaps her fingers. "Chris Montgomery was the quarterback. The good guy."

I love this girl—such a good listener. "That's the one."

"Did you run into him or something? It is a small world, isn't it?"

"I didn't just run into him. He's the one who brought Robbie to your house last night."

"Oh! Chris! Robbie introduced us briefly before we . . ." Her eyes go wide, and I cut mine away from her and study the landscaping around the pond. "Oh my God! The Chris at my house was *that* Chris? What did he say when he saw you?"

"He doesn't remember me. In fact, he thought I was your sister."

She snorts. "You don't look a thing like Morgan."

"I don't think he's met her. He just assumed that's why I was there, and I didn't correct him. And then I made out with him. A little." I tilt my head to look at her, but I can't hold her gaze when her eyes go wide. "Or a lot."

"Holy guacamole. You made out with Chris Montgomery. Was it good? Did it feel like it was five years in the making? He rescues you, and years later you're reunited and sparks fly? Are you going to see him again?"

"Okay, first of all, it wasn't just good. It was so hot, we almost set your parents' couch on fire. Second, I will definitely see him again."

"Yeah?" she squeals.

"Oh yeah. Like, a whole fucking lot. Because as of tomorrow he'll be my stepbrother."

She stops in the middle of the sidewalk. "I thought Dash Dupree was your new stepbrother."

"Dash Dupree is Chris Montgomery. Only he was never *Dupree* at all because his father's name is Montgomery, and his name isn't actually Dash. His mom just calls him that. Dash is Chris and Chris is Dash. They are one and the same. Because the universe hates me or something."

"Well, shit. How did you not know before now?"

That's a fair question. The thing is, Dad and Becky have only been together since September, and during that same period of time I've avoided coming back here at all costs. I talked my way out of Thanksgiving, and the weekend I left college for Christmas, I spent with Mom. I volunteered over spring break, so that was an easy out. Maybe if I had a Facebook profile, I would have seen pictures, but aside from a private and anonymous Tumblr account, I don't do social media anymore. Jewel spitting in my coffee was nothing compared to the hellfire she and her minions brought down on my Facebook wall after my drunken blackout sex with Isaac.

"I just didn't know," I say. "It's lame, and it probably proves how self-centered I've been about everything, but I never really cared about who my stepbrother was. Even when Dad suggested I stay with him, he was irrelevant. A means to an end."

"But then you made out with him and he rocked your world."

Wincing, I start walking again, and Willow follows. "You should have seen the way he was looking at me last night, Willow. I wasn't Easy Gee-Gee. I was a girl he seriously couldn't take his eyes off—a girl he wanted to talk to. I liked it. And maybe I'm to blame for how fast things went last night. I was a little buzzed and said some inappropriate things that may have put ideas in his head."

"You, inappropriate? Never!"

I roll my eyes. "But then this morning, Becky introduced her son to her new stepdaughter and . . . there we were."

"Oh my God, what did he say? Does Becky know? How insane is all of this?" She stops again and squeezes my hand as her eyes go wide. "Holy fuckballs, your dad is going to castrate him."

"He didn't let on to Becky, and I don't think either one of us will make the mistake of telling Dad. Chris is pissed at me for lying about who I was, but I think his primary concern is that our mistake doesn't ruin his mom's wedding."

The clouds shift in the breeze and block the moon.

"So is he as nice as Becky says? Disney princess material?"

I arch a brow. "Right now, he's pissed and not hiding it that well. Even if he gets over it, I don't see how I can stay with him this summer."

"Because you're worried you'll fuck each other's brains out?"

I snort and elbow her in the side. "Because he doesn't remember that night."

"Well, you don't want him to, so that works out, right?"

"He doesn't remember me *yet*. He will sooner or later."

"Maybe," she says. She watches a red Ferrari drive by before turning her attention to me again. "Or maybe not. Maybe a night that was life-altering for you was just another night to him."

"Seriously?"

"I don't mean it like that."

"You think he just rushes in to save the day for idiot girls all the time?"

"Maybe," she says. "I mean, the way you talked about him, it kind of sounds like that's the kind of guy he is, right? Robbie told me he broke up a fight last night—probably saved my man from a cracked skull. Chris *is* the sexy male version of the Disney princess."

Sometimes that memory of hers bites me in the ass. "I thought he was Mary Poppins."

"I think we can agree that he's practically perfect in a Disney princess way."

"I suppose. But what am I supposed to do about this summer? How can I live with him when he . . .?"

Willow waits, watching me, and when I don't finish, she asks,

"When he what? When he was the only decent guy in your entire high school? When he put a stop to something that was—"

"Okay. Enough. I just feel stuck. This isn't what I signed on for."

"Don't tell me you're thinking about staying *here*."

"Even if Dad would let me, you know I wouldn't do that." I shudder. "I ran into Jewel yesterday, and the bitch spit in my coffee. No, three days here is bad enough."

"Good. Glad to hear it." She leads me around the final cul-de-sac, and we head back toward Dad's. "So what's the worst that happens? He remembers that night, and then what?" She dips her head to meet my eyes. "Do you still like him?"

"Don't be ridiculous. He was a childhood crush."

"Hmm. Is that all? Sounds like you were pretty quick to stick your tongue down his throat last night."

"I told you I was *thirsty*."

"Mm-hmm. Is the problem that you two have a history he doesn't remember, or is it that you *like* him and you're afraid he won't like you when he has that history put in front of him?"

I shake my head. "I have a shrink already, hotshot. Stop that shit."

She grins. "I'm just saying that I think he makes you feel vulnerable, and maybe that's good for you."

"And *I'm* just saying that nothing good happens when I find myself confronted with that night."

"Don't confuse him for the other guys around here," Willow says. "We're talking about *Chris*. *The* guy. The hero."

The sound of the cicadas fills the summer night air as I process her response to my mess.

"Do you think I should tell him?" I finally ask.

"I think that would be the easier way to handle it, rather than spending your whole summer waiting for him to find out. Bring the past to light on your terms."

"And spend the summer having my roommate think I'm a dirty, dirty slut."

"Would you stop saying *slut* like it's a bad thing? One, you're not, and two, if you were I would totally support your right to be." She sighs. "I wish you could stay with me."

"You want me to stay with you in London?" I wrinkle my nose. "And, like, change diapers and stuff?"

She chuckles. "Obviously not the job of your dreams. I'm just saying I wish I could help. I don't want you to feel stuck, but since I can't, those are your choices. Tell him and rip off the Band-Aid—let him know that he was once a superstar hero. Or wait until it comes out on its own, and maybe it won't."

We've circled back and find ourselves at the end of Dad's drive as he's pulling in. He stops at the mailbox and rolls down his window.

Becky leans across him from the passenger seat and grins. "Dash was looking for you. He said you left dinner before he had a chance to catch up with you."

"You kind of rushed out of there," Dad says. "Is everything all right?"

From cocktails to dessert, I was there for more than two

hours. I didn't feel like I rushed out at all. "Everything's fine. I'm just tired."

"Are you girls going out tonight?" Becky asks. "Chris was headed to the Bull. He's getting together with some of his friends. I'm sure you're welcome to join him."

I'm sure he'd love that.

Willow and I exchange a look.

"No, I don't think so," Willow says before I can speak. "I only get to see her for a couple of days before I leave for London, so I think we're going to stay in."

God, I love this girl.

CHAPTER 10
GRACE

It's not even eleven p.m., and the house is quiet. Dad's retired, but he's an early riser by nature. He'll never change his schedule.

I've never been much of a morning person. It's all I can do to fall asleep after midnight, and never before. So I'm in the kitchen eating a bowl of cereal when Chris comes in the front door. He's quiet, holding the knob as he closes it so it doesn't pop in the latch. This isn't a kid who's coming in late and trying not to get in trouble. This is a guy who doesn't want to wake his mom up because he doesn't want her to be tired on her special day. That says so much about him—the way he wrapped his mom in a hug this morning spoke volumes, and so does this simple act of consideration.

Grace, you're pathetic. He's no saint.

He slides the deadbolt home before turning into the open-concept living area and spotting me. "Hey," he whispers, lifting a hand. He toes off his shoes and pads through the living room to join me in the dining area just off the kitchen.

I wish I'd gone to bed. Forcing my eyes to close when sleep is still miles away would be better than another conversation with Chris. I don't want to talk to him. I don't want to be reminded how much what we did last night makes me feel like a fuckup in a way that's all too familiar. Then again, maybe he doesn't want to talk to me either. Maybe he's coming this way for a snack or something.

"Can we talk?"

No such luck.

Without waiting for my answer, he pulls out a chair and spins it around. Straddling it to face me, he rests his arms on the back.

"Sure." I attempt my best poker face.

He meets my eyes, and maybe I'm fooling myself, but it seems like some of his anger is gone and replaced by regret. I preferred the anger. I don't want to be something he regrets. I don't want to be the dirty mistake. "Why are you trying to get out of living with me this summer?"

I blink at him. So much for the poker face. "After last night, do you really think we're fit to be roommates?"

He lifts his hands, his palms turning up. "Why not?"

Because just looking into your eyes makes me feel vulnerable. Because seeing you every day will be a constant reminder that I'll never be good enough. "You actually *want* me to live with you?"

He shrugs. "That's the plan, right? We'll be fine. Last night was a speed bump at worst."

I'm staying with Chris. My brief conversation with my father was the perfect reminder that it's really my best option. But Chris isn't stuck like I am, and I can't wrap my brain around why he wouldn't insist I find another arrangement for the summer.

I straighten and let my jaw go slack, pretending to have an epiphany. "Ooooh, I get it." I nod. "You think that since I was easy last night, I'll be down to fuck whenever it suits you."

As I expected, his eyes go wide and he pulls in a sharp breath. "Of course not. Jesus, Grace, I'm not—"

"I know." I roll my eyes. What I just suggested is the opposite of who Chris is, which is exactly why I said it.

He shakes his head. "I want you to stay with me so our parents can spend their summer in Europe. I have no agenda beyond that."

"What about last night?"

"Last night was . . ." He takes a breath and seems to search for the word. I can think of a few. *Hot, sexy, panty-melting, a fantasy come to life,* but I don't think they're the ones he's looking for. He lands on "complicated."

I roll my eyes.

"You don't agree?"

"No, *complicated* pretty much covers it."

"So let's figure it out. We're adults. I believe we can put it behind us and move forward like it never happened." He flashes his dimples, and *fuck me*, those dimples could be my downfall. "I mean, we're about to become brother and sister, right? Come on, let's talk this out. Your dad is gonna notice that you're pissed at me."

Of all the things I once imagined Chris Montgomery saying to me, *"We're about to become brother and sister"* never crossed my mind. Life is so weird. "I'm not pissed at you."

He grunts. "Seriously? If you want me to buy that then maybe you should at least change your tone of voice."

I scoff. "What's wrong with my tone?"

"You sound like you want to chop off my balls."

"I suffer from resting bitch voice."

"I don't think that's a thing."

I arch a brow. "Oh, it's a thing. Trust me." I point to my mouth. "Can't you hear it?"

"You said something tonight about not wanting me to remember you from high school. Is that why you're trying to get out of this? Was it something I did in high school? I know I could be a real jackass back then."

I snort. "Hardly." *Not at all.* Except for those five seconds that broke my heart. I sigh. Memory Lane is not my favorite street in town, so why do I keep hanging out there?

"Ah, so I obviously made some sort of impression." His brow wrinkles in confusion. "Just tell me. If we're going to live together this summer, it's better that you tell me up-front if I've been a jerk. I can handle it."

"I'm not pissed, just surprised you don't remember me." Again, I force a smile. I'm not the kind of girl who regularly forces smiles. I know this is a world that says girls should smile, but I say *fuck them*. It's not my job to make other people comfortable. When I want to smile, I smile. When I don't, I don't. And yet ever since my plane landed in Champagne, I've been forcing smiles right and left.

"I'm sorry," Chris says. "I was really caught up in my own world back then."

I arch a brow. Leave it to Chris to be all cerebral about his adolescent shortcomings. "Don't be hard on yourself. Guys like you usually are, especially in high school."

"Guys like me?"

I skim my eyes over his face and down to his broad shoulders. "Gorgeous, charming, the world handed to them on a silver platter."

Chris grimaces and grips the back of the chair. "Yeah, you clearly got the wrong impression of me. Whatever I did, I'm sorry. If it helps, I'm sure that you were awesome and it's my loss that I didn't pay more attention to you."

His kindness and sincerity make me want to rub every bit of my nastiness in his face. It's unfair because he doesn't deserve it, but I can't have him looking at me with so much compassion—as if he's thinking maybe we can be friends. I can't have that. It's too hard to protect your heart from a friend. "You're used to getting your way, aren't you? You ask a girl to go out, she says yes. You tell her a joke, she laughs. You ask her to drop her panties, and they're on the floor before you can finish the sentence."

His eyes go wide, and he releases the back of the chair. "Wow. That's an awful lot of hostility there for a girl who's supposedly not pissed."

"I'm not being hostile. Just stating facts. Do you deny it?"

"I'm not in the habit of asking girls to take off their panties just because."

"You should try it. I think you'd discover it's like an untapped superpower."

He narrows his eyes at me. "Did we mess around in high school? Is that what this is about?"

I have to stop. I'm antagonizing him, and that's only going to make him more curious about the past. But that's just it. Half of me hopes he never remembers and the other half wants to shake the memory out of him. He's going to be in my life for as long as Becky is, and I want the revelation done and over with. Except at the same time, I don't want there to be any revelation at all.

I'm a hot mess.

"I promise we didn't mess around," I mutter.

"Can we call a truce, then?" He offers me a hand, then adds, "This isn't just about the wedding tomorrow—though to be fair, it would be nice if you weren't shooting daggers at me with your eyes as we walked down the aisle."

"Right," I say. "You get to be my babysitter all summer long."

A wrinkle pops up between his eyebrows as he frowns. "If it's any consolation, I think your father's being ridiculous. Mom said she tried to talk him into letting you stay here. Maybe if she—"

I exhale heavily. "No. It's fine." I'm being a bitch, and that's not fair to him. He doesn't remember our shared history, and even if he did, he wouldn't know that he broke my heart or understand how. And why would he? I was just a girl who needed so desperately to believe that the *good guys* saw her for more than a pair of tits and the things she could do with her mouth, and he was just a guy who saw the long line of guys who hadn't seen her for any more than that. "I'd rather stay with you than stay here," I admit. "Not that Dad would let me have that choice anyway, but there it is."

"You're sure? You'll let your dad know that you're good with the plan? I'm really worried Mom's going to make him cancel."

I'm a little lightheaded as the blood drains from my face. "She wants to cancel?"

"For us." He drags a hand through his hair. "We haven't done a very good job hiding our animosity, and she told me tonight that she wants to cancel the trip so we don't have to live together this summer. I don't want her to miss this chance."

If they cancel, not only am I stuck in Champagne—an idea that makes bile surge into my throat—but Dad and Becky lose their honeymoon. Not even *I* am self-centered enough to want that. "I want them to go to Europe. Please don't let her cancel."

"We agree, then?"

"Yes. If you're okay with me staying with you, I'm okay with staying with you." I nod. It's one summer. I'll keep to myself, and then Chris and I will part ways. I'll go back to Carson, and we'll never have to see each other again. "I'm sure."

He eyes my bowl of Lucky Charms. "Healthy bedtime snack."

Grinning, I slide a heaping spoonful into my mouth. "Mmm," I hum around it. "Magically delicious."

CHAPTER 11
CHRIS

I came into this conversation determined to get her on board with staying in my apartment, and I should feel victorious right now. Instead, I'm feeling royally fucked.

Grace grins at me as she swallows her bite of sugary cereal. In my gut, something unwelcome and unexpected stirs. Lust is never far away where she's concerned. In my brain, warning signals blare.

Mom asks me favors about once every five years, if that. She's done everything for me. She raised me on her own and put every penny of child support into a college fund. When money was tight, she always found a way to pay the expensive uniform fees for my sports, and even when she worked two jobs, she never missed a game. I've never had the opportunity to do anything for her in return, so the second she asked me if I could take Grace in for the summer, I said yes.

Until tonight, I didn't realize Grace's father was more interested in me babysitting Grace than in the roof I could put over her head. She's an adult. By any conventional judgment, she shouldn't need supervision.

Even if we didn't have our unfortunate meet-up last night, meeting her this morning would have been a punch in the gut. Long, silky black hair, striking green eyes, and the kind of curves that, in any other circumstance, would guarantee her a starring role in my fantasies for the next month.

When I agreed to this, I didn't imagine I'd be painfully attracted to the girl who was going to be living with me all summer.

She takes another bite. I never would have thought chewing cereal could be sexy, but I suspect this girl could eat slugs and make it look hot. She chews and meets my eyes as she swallows, darting her tongue out to clean a drop of milk from her bottom lip. My gut goes tight and my dick goes hard.

I don't think this is what Mom had in mind when she said she thought I'd like Grace.

I need to stop thinking of her as the sexpot who pressed her mouth against mine and drew her knees up around my waist. I need to start thinking of her as my sister. "Tell me something about yourself."

She puts down her spoon and narrows her eyes. "Come again?"

I lean forward, pressing into the back of the chair I'm straddling to get closer to her. I smell a hint of lavender again, and I wonder if it's from her laundry detergent or her shampoo. "Let's start over. A clean slate."

"You think you can pretend last night never happened?"

"I've already forgotten it." I extend a hand. "My name's Christopher, and I understand our parents are getting married. It's nice to meet you."

She swallows again, though she hasn't taken another bite since she swallowed the last. She eyes me cautiously before replying. "What are you trying to do?"

"We're going to be spending a lot of time together, right? So I want to get to know you. Tell me something."

She shifts in her seat, and something flashes across her face. Is that fear? But as soon as it's there, it's gone again and she lifts her chin and holds my gaze. "I hate exercise, and the milk on this cereal is the healthiest thing I've eaten all day."

I grunt. She's baiting me—trying to prove we're nothing alike so I won't bother trying to get to know her—and I'm not taking it. Because maybe if I get to know her, this primal attraction will simmer down. Maybe I'll start to think of her as my sister instead of a woman I'd really like to get naked ASAP. "Favorite TV show?"

"You're serious?"

"You're not one of those intellectual artsy types who thinks she's too good to watch TV, are you? Because the TV is on a lot at my apartment."

She narrows her eyes. "*Big Bang Theory.*"

"Mine's *SportsCenter*, thanks for asking."

"Typical," she mumbles.

I ignore her and continue. "What's your major?"

She swallows again before answering, and I think that might be a tell—maybe a sign that I've hit on a subject she actually cares about. "Writing."

God, that suits her. She has that carefree-artist air about her. "You're a writer?"

"I want to be." She shrugs. "Maybe."

"Creative writing or technical?"

She draws back in horror, as if I just asked her if she'd like to smell my shit now or later. "Does anyone *want* to be a technical writer?"

"I'm majoring in communications," I tell her, despite the fact that she's shown zero interest in me since we shut down last night's conversational lane about masturbation and porn preferences. I'm just not sure we should start our new relationship as stepsiblings knowing more about what gets the other off than we do about the stuff you'd tell the old ladies at church. "If the whole football thing doesn't work out, I'd like to go into sports journalism. It's writing too, and I like to think I'm okay at it, though I suck at the creative stuff."

"Good for you."

Okay, so clearly she's not interested in sharing her hopes and dreams with me. That's fine. I shift gears, determined to get us onto the same page. She's stubborn, but I'm undaunted. "Do you have any plans for your time in Blackhawk Valley?"

She pulls her bottom lip between her teeth and cocks her head to the side. "Do all these questions mean you've forgiven me for not telling you my name last night?"

"It didn't happen, remember?" It would be a hell of a lot easier to swallow that lie if she'd quit abusing that bottom lip with her teeth. The nervous habit reminds me of how it felt between *my* teeth and makes me want to taste the sugary cereal from her mouth. Clenching my hands, I glance away from temptation incarnate. "Clean slate."

She takes a breath. "Okay. It never happened."

I exhale, relieved that she seems to be on board. I don't want Mom giving up this trip, and even though I might not understand why, I do know that to make that happen, Grace needs to come to Blackhawk Valley with me. "It'll be fine," I say, more for myself than her. "I'll introduce you to my friends." And she'll be headed back to New York for school in no time.

"You don't need to introduce me to your friends. I'm capable of making my own."

"You're living with me. Whether you like it or not, that means you'll be spending time with my friends."

"And are these friends a bunch of football players?"

"Is that a problem?"

She shrugs. "I don't have the best track record with football players."

"An ex-boyfriend?"

"Not exactly."

Between the terse response and the way she won't meet my eyes, I know she won't say more on the subject, so I tuck it away with the other hints she's given me to think about later.

It's much smarter to focus on her aversion to football players than the way she felt in my arms. She's all smooth, pale skin and soft curves. Honestly, the tattooed, badass kind of girl isn't usually my type. Sweet girls like Olivia are my type. But there's something about Grace. Something about her wicked mouth and her eyes and that big smile that takes up half her face. She doesn't fit any prescribed standard of beauty. She just *is*.

"Why are you looking at me like that, Montgomery?"

I shake my head, as unable as I am unwilling to explain the complicated emotions I've fought since I came down the stairs this morning and found out my walking fantasy was about to become a very big, very permanent part of my life. "Do you think they're happy together?" I ask.

The question that's nagging me is whether or not her dad is good enough for my mom, but that's not a fair question to ask Ed's daughter, so I go about it this way.

Mom has never dated. It seemed important to her to wait until after I was out of the house before she started seeing anyone. But then she met Edward last fall, and everything from there seemed to happen so fast.

"I do," Grace says. She releases a puff of air that's almost a laugh. "Honestly, I don't know what your mom sees in my dad," she adds, and gives what might be the first real smile I've seen from her all day long. "I don't know your mom very well, but she's special."

"I know."

"I'm glad for my dad. Glad they found each other. Selfishly,

I'm glad he has someone to distract him from constantly worrying about me. Before your mom, he worried like it was his full-time job."

"And why does he worry so much?"

She lifts her green eyes to meet mine and holds my gaze before turning away suddenly. "Just overprotective, I guess." She shifts her gaze back to the table. "But maybe I've given him more than enough reason to worry."

"How so?"

She shrugs, and I can tell by her guarded expression that she won't say more about it tonight, but I file it away for later. There's obviously more to Grace Lee than anyone is telling me. Why else would her father want his grown daughter to stay with me while he's out of the country?

I stand up and stretch, yawning. "I need some sleep. I'll see you in the morning."

"The first of many," she says, grimacing.

CHAPTER 12
CHRIS

I've never seen my mother look so happy.

The ceremony was short. Mom and Edward wrote their own vows, and when Mom spoke hers, her voice was so soft I could only make out her words because I was standing so close.

The reception is packed with friends and family. We ate dinner and watched the happy couple cut the cake and dance their first dance, and now it's turned into a veritable party. The alcohol is flowing, and on the dance floor, people are showing their moves—or lack thereof.

"Dash." I look up to see my new stepfather taking the seat across from me.

"Call me Chris," I tell him, not that it's helped before. I'm sure it's hard for him to think of me as anything but Dash, since that's the name Mom uses.

"Chris," he says affectionately. "I just wanted to thank you for talking to Grace last night. I don't know what you said, but she made it clear to your mom this morning that she's looking forward to her time in Blackhawk Valley this summer. Whether it's true or not, your mom's convinced, and I get my honeymoon with my bride."

"I don't think I talked her into anything," I say honestly. "She wants you two to have your trip, and she knows staying with me makes that possible."

He releases a heavy breath and gives me a crooked smile. "I'm relieved, selfishly. I don't think I've ever been as excited to travel as I am for this trip with your mom. She lights up when she talks about Europe."

"Thank you for taking her." I clear my throat. I don't know this guy well enough to feel comfortable getting too sappy, but my mom's happiness is everything to me. "I'm grateful that she found you. You make her happy."

He sighs. "She makes me happy, too." He turns sideways in his chair and scans the party until he finds her, then he smiles. "We're so damn lucky." When he turns back to me, his smile is gone. "Thank you again for taking Grace in this summer. She's a good kid deep down. She just needs some positive influences in her life. It's not just her that I worry about. It's the kids around here who seem to drag her into trouble with them."

"What kind of trouble?" I ask.

He taps his fist on the table as his gaze settles on his daughter, and it's as if he didn't hear my question. "With you, I know she'll be around the right kind of people." When he swings his gaze back to mine, his eyes are weary and intense. "Promise me you'll look out for her as if she were your own sister?"

I'm sure Grace won't give two shits about what I have to say. She's a grown woman and makes her own choices—for better or worse. Just because she's staying in Blackhawk Valley doesn't mean she's going to change her ways. "I'll do my best."

Edward stands. "I'm going to find my bride and make her dance with this old man. Why don't you dance with Grace?" He nods to the bar, where Grace is laughing with a guy who has a face full of piercings. "Someone needs to get her away from that bartender." He shakes his head. "She's drawn to trouble, that one."

I do as I'm asked, and if there's any part of me that's uncomfortable with her dad talking about her like she's a little girl, it's silenced by the part of me that's been unable to take my eyes off her all night. She looks amazing in that dress. It's black and fitted and shows off her curves in a way that makes my hands itch to touch her.

She's laughing about something, but her smile falls away as I approach. "You want a beer?" she asks, already turning to the bartender.

I hold up a hand when he looks at me expectantly. "I'm good." Tucking my hands in my pockets, I rock back on my heels and study Grace. I miss the way she looked at me at Willow's house—like she wanted to devour me whole. Now, she regards me with something that vacillates between irritation and extreme caution. "Actually, I hoped you'd dance with me."

She cocks a brow. "Seriously?"

We're at a wedding. People dance at weddings. Is it that hard to believe I'd want to dance with her? "Seriously."

"I'm sure your decision to ask me has nothing to do with the fact that you just talked to my father."

And now I look like an asshole. "I—"

Grabbing my arm, she tugs me toward the dance floor. "Come on, then. We have to make the groom happy on his big day." She gives a wave to the bartender. "See you around, Tommy."

"How do you know that guy?" I ask.

She shrugs. Once we hit the dance floor, she drops my arm and studies me cautiously.

"Come on, Grace." Stepping forward, I settle my hands on her hips and pull her closer. "I'm not that bad."

Her chest meets mine and her breath leaves her in a rush. Our eyes meet, and I'm nearly paralyzed by the tangle of emotions clouding my brain until she looks away.

"Who's the guy at the bar?" I ask, more to distract myself from the soft curve of her hips under my hands than because I really care.

"My dealer," she deadpans.

Edward might not care for the tattooed, heavily pierced type, but in my experience, the amount of ink on a person's body and the number of holes in their skin is a really shitty indicator for whether or not they're trouble. "You're hilarious," I mutter, and maybe I pull her a little closer. Because I can. Because she's soft and warm and *right here.* It's so hard to focus on learning what I need to know. It's impossible to imagine myself as her protective big brother, but if I'm going to make good on my promise to Edward, I have to try.

I want to know exactly what *kind* of trouble this girl was in. Drunk and disorderly? Drugs? Something else? I guess I could ask Edward directly, but even though I need way more information than I have, I don't feel right getting the information from anyone but Grace. "That's not going to be a problem, is it?"

She frowns. "What?"

"Drugs?" I draw in a breath when her confusion turns into a glare. "Can you blame me for asking? No one's telling me shit about what's going on with you, only that it's my job to keep you out of trouble."

She takes two steps back, and my hands drop to my sides. "That's what he said? He wants you to keep me out of trouble?"

I just fucked this up. Everything I do with her, I fuck up. "Your dad cares about you," I say, trying to pull my foot from my mouth. "He knows you better than anyone, right? So if he thinks you need someone to keep an eye on you . . ."

She laughs, but it's a hard, dry sound. "He thinks I need a babysitter."

"Grace." I take a step toward her but stop when she holds up a hand.

"Listen," she says, still facing me and walking backward off the dance floor. "Don't worry about me. I'll come stay with you because that's what I have to do. But I'll stay out of your hair. I wouldn't *dream* of misbehaving for my babysitter."

CHAPTER 13
GRACE

Me: *Blackhawk Valley is no New York City.*

I text Willow as we drive through town, more to distract myself from looking at Chris than because I think she needs to know.

Willow: *Oh no! Did I almost miss Captain Obvious trivia hour?*

I bite back a laugh and slide my phone back into my purse just as Chris parks in front of a four-story brick building.

I'm not some city snob. I grew up in the suburbs, after all. But the drive from the airport was almost surreal. So many cornfields and then, closer to Blackhawk Valley, rolling green horse pastures that went on for miles. It's not the kind of place you'd expect a twenty-one-year-old guy to live voluntarily.

When I applied for colleges, I looked for the biggest cities. I wanted excitement and lights, true. But I also wanted to fade into the crowd. Everything is so wide open here, if this were my hometown I'd feel like I was living under a magnifying glass.

Chris drops my heaviest suitcase and adjusts his duffel bag on his shoulder as he holds the door for me. I step into his apartment, set down my two other bags, and look around with wide eyes. When you brace yourself to move in with a couple of college boys, you don't expect their apartment to be clean and tidy. Chris is obviously not a partier—not Mr. Perfect's style—but I still wouldn't have been surprised to see a row of empty beer bottles on the counter or empty liquor bottles propped like trophies along the tops of the cabinets. But the apartment doesn't look like it belongs to college guys. It's neat and clean, if sparse.

Ahead of me is the living room with a faded blue couch and matching recliner in front of a TV. On the coffee table there's an empty coffee mug and a couple of console remotes. Behind the couch an island separates the living space from the modest galley kitchen on the wall opposite the TV. Beyond the kitchen is a small four-seater table.

"Mason," Chris calls. "We're home."

In the dark hallway on the other side of this main living space, a door opens, then a black guy steps into the living room. "You must be Grace," he says. "I'm your temporary roommate, Mason."

He's so beautiful that I smile.

I take his offered hand. It's big, and rough, and matches the rest of him. My brain might dislike football players in that whole guilty-by-association sense, but my eyes definitely aren't on the same page. Mason's hair is cut in a short crop, and his eyes are a shade of green that about knocks me on my ass. "And you must be Mr. Tall, Dark, and Handsome."

Mason looks to Chris. "I like her."

Chris groans. "Of course you do."

When Mason releases my hand, I grin and hold his gaze. "Chris didn't tell me his roommate was so hot."

"Grace," Chris says, a warning in his tone.

"What?" I wrinkle my nose and ask Mason, "Does that make you uncomfortable?"

Mason returns my smile and rocks back on his heels. "Not at all. Please, carry on."

"His ego doesn't need to be inflated any more than it already is," Chris says.

"Everything about Mason is big," a feminine voice calls from the dark hallway. A blonde walks into the room wearing a bikini top and cutoffs. She's short, with long hair that hits her ribcage and a build pretty similar to mine. When she sidles up to stand next to Mason, I stiffen, wondering if I just put my foot in my mouth. I don't expect to make friends here this summer, but I don't need my roommate's girlfriend to hate me either, and I'm pretty sure she just came from Mason's room. Then again, she doesn't have the face of a jealous girlfriend. Instead, she's grinning at me as she takes Mason's arm. "His ego is no exception." She slings an arm around his waist, then, as if to answer my unspoken question, she says, "You can stop looking so uncomfortable. I'm not the girlfriend."

Mason cuts his eyes to her and frowns. "Not for my lack of trying, though."

She grins and nudges him with her elbow. "I'm Bailey," she says. "You must be the new stepsister."

"That's me. Are you a roommate?"

She shakes her head. "No, just a friend. But you don't need to worry about me being in your space too much. Honestly, when we all hang out, we tend to go to Arrow's house. He can't come to us, and his house is a veritable resort with the pool and theater and everything else."

"Arrow is . . . ?"

"One of the guys from the team," Mason supplies.

"And why can't he come to you?"

Bailey looks at Chris, who shrugs, and then she looks back to me. "He's on house arrest. Drugs. It's a long story, but I'm sure you'll get all the dirty details before you head back home."

I frown at Chris. I was so offended when he asked me about drugs last night. It never occurred to me that Mr. Perfect might have friends who have issues.

Chris shakes his head. "Don't get the wrong idea. Arrow's a good guy. He just had a rough patch."

"Sounds like a winner," I say, sarcasm making my voice brittle. I don't have a great love for football players, but I'm downright weary of guys who do drugs, rough patch or not. They say "rough patch" and I hear that another entitled rich boy got caught.

Chris lifts one hand and gestures around the room. "So, this is our apartment." His phone buzzes, and he looks at the screen. "It's Mom. They must be in New York on their layover. I'm gonna take this. Mason, want to help her get her bags to her room?"

Mason shrugs. "Sure," he says as Chris swipes his phone's screen to accept the call.

I pick up two of my bags, and Mason grabs the big, heavy one before leading me down the hall. There are three doors, and the one to the left stands open to a small bathroom.

Mason gestures to the door opposite the bathroom. "That's my room." He points to the door at the end of the hall. "And you and Chris are in there."

I stop in my tracks, but he continues on. *Me and Chris?*

I knew I was living with him this summer and that it would probably be cozier than I was comfortable with, but sharing a room with Chris isn't just outside of my comfort zone—it's in a whole new zip code. Hell, it's not even the same planet as my comfort zone.

Mason seems to realize I'm not following, and turns and cocks his head. Numbly, I follow.

"Isn't there *another* bedroom?" I ask, my voice small.

"Other than mine?" Mason asks. "No. I'm sorry."

The room is small and, like the rest of the apartment, neat, clean, and tidy. There's a small desk under a window, and against the far wall is a lofted twin bed with a full bed underneath it sticking out at a perpendicular angle.

Maybe seeing two beds instead of one should help me breathe

a little easier, but it only reinforces that this is really happening and not some nightmare.

Did no one think to pass this by me? Did no one think I'd need to know we'd be sharing a *room*? It's not just about sleeping. It's all the other things you need your own room for—changing, hiding from the world, listening to music. I was counting on having a little space of my own where I could avoid Chris Montgomery of the sexy eyes and big hands all summer. I was planning on taking the awkward and mortifying "when he remembers" moment out of the equation by never spending enough time with him to give him the opportunity.

And then there are the things I'd only assume *he* would want to be able to do in here. I mean, he's a twenty-one-year-old charmer with the body of Adonis. And even if he's not bringing girls home, won't he require a little privacy for other left-handed activities?

My cheeks heat, and warmth rushes low in my belly. I'm *not* going to get turned on thinking about things Chris might need privacy for. I'm immune to those sexy dimples and thick biceps. *I've decided.*

I spin on my heel and march back to the living room. As Chris slides his phone into his pocket, I prop my hands on my hips and announce, "This isn't going to work."

"Is there something wrong with the room?"

I gape. "Seriously?"

Mason's behind me. "I'm guessing you didn't mention that she's sharing a room with you?"

"She's not sharing a room with me," Chris says.

"Then where do you expect her to sleep? On the couch?" Mason asks.

"In your old room," Chris says.

"If by my *old* room, you're referring to my current and only room in this apartment, then fuck no." He turns to me, grimacing. "No offense. I just need my space."

You and me both. "None taken."

Chris shakes his head. "Mase, I specifically asked you if it was okay for her to stay here. You said you were cool with it."

Mason's eyes go wide. "Of course I did. Because *I'm* not a self-centered asshole."

Chris draws back as if Mason struck him. "I'm self-centered now?"

Mason turns to Bailey. "You can head to Arrow's without me. I'll catch up."

She scoffs. "And miss this? As if."

"We had a plan," Chris says. "You'll bunk with me, and Grace will—"

"That was *not* the agreement. You asked if she could stay with us for the summer. You never said anything about me giving up my room."

"You thought I was planning on sharing a room with her?" The horror is so thick in his voice that I'm launched back in time five years, listening to Chris and Isaac talk in the room next to me.

"You want her for yourself or something, Montgomery?"

"As if I'd put my dick near that."

"It's just for the summer," Chris tells Mason.

I feel like a piece of trash, and they're fighting over who has to live with the smell beneath their bed. I want to tell them both they can have their precious rooms and I'll find somewhere else to stay, but I'm feeling so vulnerable I know the words wouldn't come out without a stutter, so I keep my mouth shut.

"The whole point of renting this apartment was for privacy," Mason says. "I'm not giving that up a few weeks after we moved in."

"Stop." Bailey's voice is hard, and the boys stop their glaring match and turn to her. "Stop fighting about this in front of her. Jesus. For nice guys, you're acting like assholes. She's your guest, and you're making her feel like crap."

I'd be grateful that she put a stop to it, but I'm too embarrassed that it was necessary.

I never thought about the roommate part of the equation for this summer. In my mind it wasn't that big of a deal for Chris to take me in. The bigger embarrassment there was that he needed to. That my dad doesn't trust me to be on my own, and that beyond my financial dependence on my father, I rely on his approval so much that I didn't find a way to stay in my own city for the summer, his approval be damned. But now I realize I never really thought about Mason. If Willow and I shared an apartment for the summer and she suddenly brought home a roommate—some relative I'd never met before—I wouldn't like it. And if she thought I'd give up my own bedroom for it to happen? *Hell no.*

I take a breath and measure out my words. "It was n-n-nice—" I wince, but Chris and Mason are too busy glaring at each other to notice my stutter. "I don't want to be in anyone's hair. I'll sleep on the couch until I can find somewhere else to stay."

Chris's face softens. "Grace, you don't need to find somewhere else to—"

I stare at him. Does he have any idea how it feels to hear him scramble for a way to get me out of his room? I feel so dirty. All I want is a good long cry in the shower, and I know that's irrational. My hurt feelings over this whole thing are unreasonable. It's just old Gee-Gee poking her head into my consciousness and reminding me that no matter what sweet things Chris said to me on Thursday night, what happened at Willow's is evidence that you can change your name and your hair and even the way you talk, and everything remains the same. His horror over being too close to me now makes me feel cheap. The fourteen-year-old me is scraping her nails down the chalkboard of my consciousness, screaming, *"I told you so. He doesn't like you. You're not special. He was taking what you were offering. Easy Gee-Gee being easy."*

CHAPTER 14
CHRIS

Grace looks at me as if I've smacked her, and I feel like such a piece of shit for screwing this up. Surely she understands I can't share a room with her. Surely she gets that whether or not her father is out of line in asking me to watch out for her this summer, I take that responsibility seriously, and that means keeping my hands to myself.

"Can I talk to you in private for a minute?" Mason asks.

I tear my eyes off Grace to see Mason already heading to his room. "I'll figure this out," I say to Grace before following him. I step inside the small room and shut the door behind me.

Mason rubs the back of his neck as he studies the ceiling. "I'm feeling like a dickbag here, man."

You and me both. I draw in a deep breath. "It's my fault. I thought we talked about it, and since we've shared in the dorms, I didn't think it would be a big deal."

He looks at me with an arched brow. "And have you forgotten why you switched with Arrow?"

I clear my throat. I haven't forgotten. It seemed like there was an endless line of girls going in and out of Mason's room, and I got sick of coming home to see that damn sock on the door. "That's different now," I say. Then I flinch. It's only different because he's completely hung up on a girl who refuses to be more than his fuck buddy. "I'm sorry. I just didn't think it through."

"When we decided to get this apartment," he says, pacing between the window and door, "the appeal was in having my own room. Some real privacy."

"For Bailey."

Staring at the closed bedroom door, he draws in a deep breath. "She'll come around eventually, but that's not the only reason I need a room of my own."

"It's not?"

"I failed A&P." He points to the fat anatomy and physiology book on his dresser. "Prof agreed to give me an incomplete and let me retake the final this summer because of all the shit that was going down with Arrow. But I get one shot. I need to spend this summer studying my ass off, and I need a quiet space of my own to do that."

I had no idea. "Why didn't you tell me you were having trouble in your classes?"

He shakes his head. "I didn't want to talk about it."

Like me, Mason's going into his senior year at BHU, and like me, he's hoping to be drafted in the spring. But you need some attention to get drafted, and you need to play to get attention. And if you don't have the grades, you don't play. "That's not good."

"I fucking know that, but I'm working on fixing it." He rolls his head from side to side and digs his fingers into the muscles at the back of his neck. "Listen, I'll do it. I don't want to be an asshole. If you need her to have my room, then we'll make it work."

I shake my head. "No. You're right. You need the space to study." I drag a hand through my hair and suppress a shudder as I try to imagine the possibility of a season without Mason Dahl as my number one receiver. With Arrow out for the first half of the season, we're already going to struggle, but without Mason, we'd be fucked. "*I* need you to pass that final. Keep the room."

"Are you sure?"

"I can sleep on the couch. It's not a big deal."

He laughs. "God, you know, I thought it was weird—you sharing a room with your sister all summer. I guess I should have mentioned it, but I didn't want to be that guy who makes everything about sex."

"*Step*sister. We aren't related."

The corner of his mouth quirks up. "Yeah?"

"What?" He looks way too fucking entertained.

"It's interesting that the distinction is so important to you, that's all."

"It's . . ." I take a deep breath. "It's not important. I'm just frazzled."

"And that's interesting too, isn't it?"

I frown. "Why?"

He shrugs. "It's not like you, man. That's all." Mason slaps me on the shoulder. "Bailey and I are supposed to be at Arrow's. I'll catch you later?"

He's right. In fact, I haven't acted like myself at all since I saw Grace in Willow's living room on Thursday night. She does something to me. Something that makes me so crazy for what I know I can't have—what I shouldn't even want—that I'm going to go through a summer of brutal two-a-day workouts while sleeping on a fucking couch.

CHAPTER 15
GRACE

I can't make out anything more than low murmurs coming from Mason's room, but I strain my ears to try anyway. If Bailey weren't standing here, I'd probably sneak closer to the door to eavesdrop. Or not. Maybe I don't want to know what Chris is saying.

"You okay?" Bailey asks. She watches me with her head cocked to one side, as if she's afraid she might miss something if she doesn't focus on my face. I'd rather she forgot I was in the room.

"I'm fine." I walk into the kitchen and start pulling open cabinets for something to do with my hands, but when I find the cabinet with the food, I frown. "Egg-white protein powder is a thing?"

"They drink protein shakes like crazy. They work out too much and don't have time to chew the number of calories it takes to maintain that kind of muscle."

I open the fridge, and my frown turns deeper. Aside from some leftover pizza and a carryout box, the fridge is full of vegetables, fruit, chicken, and steak. "Where's the real food?"

Bailey laughs and walks over to a cabinet beneath the sink. She sinks to her haunches and reaches in, pulling out a family-sized box of frosted strawberry Pop-Tarts. "This what you're looking for?"

My eyes are probably the size of saucers and maybe I drool a little, because she laughs and hands me a foil package before tucking them back under the sink. "You're my savior."

"The guys eat healthy," she says, closing the cabinet as I tear into my package of sugary goodness. "They take their bodies very seriously. They gorge on protein so they won't lose muscle and avoid processed sugar so they don't gain fat. It's enough to give a girl a complex about her own body."

I take a bite and moan around it. "Sugar is my drug of choice. If someone objects to the size of my ass, they can kiss it."

At that moment, Mason steps into the room and laughs, letting his gaze dip to my hips before returning to meet my eyes. "No objections here." Bailey nudges him hard enough to make him sidestep, and he holds up his hands. "What? I thought she might want my opinion." He swings his gaze back to me. "If she doesn't want me looking at other girls, she just has to agree to be my girlfriend. I'm not asking much."

Bailey rolls her eyes. "I never said you couldn't look. Now, what did you and Chris figure out?"

Mason glances toward the dark hallway before shrugging. "I'll let him tell her. You and I are late." Grabbing keys off the island, he heads to the front door.

"Thanks for the Pop-Tarts," I tell Bailey. "You're a lifesaver."

"Any time." She studies me for a beat. "Do you have plans tonight? Mia and I are going out for drinks. You could come."

"I'm not twenty-one."

She snorts. "That doesn't matter. I'll pick you up at eight?"

Chris has yet to emerge from Mason's room, and it feels a little weird to make plans when my fate is up in the air. On the other hand, Bailey's been the best part of my Blackhawk Valley experience thus far, and I'd really like her to be my friend. "That would be awesome. Thanks."

"Sure thing." She smacks Mason's ass and heads out the door.

He flinches and then shakes his head. "See you later, Grace."

"See you."

They close the door behind them, and I take another bite of my Pop-Tart. I'll have to go to the grocery store. From the looks of their refrigerator, Chris and Mason are one leafy green salad away from being complete carnivores. I, on the other hand, don't eat meat and hate vegetables. Unless you count chocolate, of the sacred cocoa tree, which of course I do.

"Oh, good. You found something to eat."

I look up from my sugar-frosted sugar bomb and bite back a whimper. For whatever reason, even a few brief minutes outside of this guy's company, I forgot the magnitude of his hotness. I think it's a real possibility that his shoulders got even broader during his time in Mason's room. His hair's all mussed, which isn't surprising, since it gets in his eyes all the time and he can't keep his hands out of it.

I take another bite of Pop-Tart to muffle another whimper.

"What is that?"

"Food," I say around my double bite.

He steps forward and inspects the contents of the foil package. "That's not food. That's diabetes with sprinkles on top."

"Mmm." I swallow. "My favorite."

"Did Mason and Bailey leave?"

"Yeah. What's up with them, anyway? She said she's not the girlfriend, so what? They just hook up?"

"Not anymore. They're best friends, but Mason decided the friends-with-benefits thing wasn't working for him anymore, so he put a stop to that part of their relationship."

I frown. "What guy ever in the history of guys wouldn't want a friends-with-benefits arrangement with a girl who looks like Bailey?"

Laughing, Chris pulls a premixed protein shake from the fridge, twists off the cap, and chugs half of it in one go. "A guy who wants more than the benefits. Mason's got it bad for Bail. He wants the love story. The planning and the promises."

I'm impressed and more than a little swoony. Who wouldn't cheer hard for Mason knowing all that? "Wow. What's her holdup?"

"No idea." He shrugs and takes another drink from his shake.

I wrinkle my nose. "My food isn't food, but *that* is?"

He inspects the bottle. "It'll do until I have a chance to make us some dinner. Do you want chicken or steak?"

"Neither." *Yuck.* "What do you mean, make *us* dinner? Are you my personal chef as well as my babysitter?"

"I'm not your babysitter, but I'd like to make you dinner. It's the least I could do after the crappy way your visit started. Tell me what you want, and I'll run to the store and get it."

I hate/love the way his kindness makes me feel warm from the tips of my fingers down to my toes. I hate/love the way those dimples make the butterflies in my stomach dance. I hate/love that he can walk in here and turn on the charm and make me completely forget that ten minutes ago, he was making me feel lower than the dirt on his cleats.

"I'd love to go to the store," I say. "I need to buy some of my own groceries, and could we swing by Target or something to get some sheets that would fit on the couch?"

He drains the rest of his protein shake before tossing it into the trashcan. "You're not sleeping on the couch." He tucks his hands into his back pockets and sighs. "I'm really sorry about the room confusion, but we've figured it out."

"Mason's rooming with you?" Why didn't he say so when Bailey asked?

"No. He needs his own space. You can have my room, though. *I'll* sleep on the couch."

"I don't feel right about that." If I were a bigger person, I'd point out that there are two beds in his room, and there's no reason we can't each take one. But I'm not a bigger person. I'm a small person whose inner Slutty McSlutterson would probably crawl into Chris's bed while he was sleeping if she had the opportunity. And anyway, even if it is irrational and a bit hypocritical, his reaction to the possibility of us sharing a room earlier still stings, so if it's going to happen, I want him to suggest it. "Let me take the couch."

"Absolutely not." He shakes his head and sets his jaw in a way that tells me it's not up for debate. "This is my mess. You don't need to suffer because of it. Maybe Mason's right and I assumed. Honestly, I don't actually remember a specific conversation. Things have been so crazy around here." He inhales, slowly. "I'm sorry, Grace. I feel like I really fucked up."

I bite back a smile. It's impossible not to like this guy. "Okay, remedial."

"Did you just call me *remedial?*"

"I did."

"And what's that supposed to mean?"

"If *this* constitutes a fuckup, I don't think you've ever truly screwed up in your life. I mean, other than that time you felt up your stepsister—*that* was kind of twisted. But aside from that, your fuckup skills are remedial at best."

Chris looks offended, his brows scrunched together to match his frowning mouth. He drops his gaze to the trashcan and stares at his discarded shake. "I screw up as much as anybody else."

"Yeah?" God, he's even more adorable frustrated. "Okay, give me some evidence—aside from assuming that your roommate is as selfless as you and was willing to give up his own bedroom for the summer for a girl he doesn't even know. Tell me a time you fucked up. Just one."

A shadow crosses over his face and takes his frown with it. "Just trust me," he says. "I have."

I truly doubt that, but because I can tell he's serious and he thinks he did something terrible, I let it drop and toss my foil wrapper into the trashcan. "So, grocery shopping?"

His shoulders relax marginally. "Sure. Then dinner. Whatever your favorite meal is, I'll make it."

I grab my purse and throw it over my shoulder. "I mean, if you insist, but I've gotten pretty good at pouring my own cereal over the years."

CHAPTER 16
GRACE

Bailey picked me up at Chris's apartment a little after eight, handed me a driver's license for a twenty-two-year-old named "Beatrice"—who could totally be my twin if you only look at her hair and eye color, but who looks nothing like me if you consider little details like facial structure and weight—and drove me to a bar called Tracy's. The guy at the door took one look at Bailey and waved us both in, not even bothering to check my fake ID.

We're already two shots in and sitting in a big booth at the back when a beautiful Latina comes up to our table and slides in next to Bailey. "Is this our new friend?" she asks. She grins at me and offers a hand. "I'm Mia Mendez."

"Mia," Bailey says, "I'd like you to meet Grace, Chris's new stepsister. Grace, this is my best friend in the whole wide world, Mia."

"Sorry if I'm a bit of a spaz," Mia says. "I'm just so excited to meet you!" There's practically a giggle in her voice.

I look at Bailey, who bites back a grin. "I might have told Mia about what went down at the apartment today," she says. "We're both really excited to meet someone who can frazzle Chris like that."

"That was frazzled?" I ask. Really, considering our situation, I thought he did a pretty decent job keeping his cool.

"Did you see his face the moment it sunk in that he's going to be sharing a room with you?" Bailey squeaks and claps her hands as she looks at the ceiling. "It's the best thing ever."

I'm still confused. "It didn't feel like the best thing on my end. That boy is probably two feet longer than the old-ass couch, but he'd rather sleep there than in the same room as me." I frown. I blame the shots for my diarrhea of the mouth. I was in middle school when I discovered that a little buzz made my stutter disappear, and since then the amount I drink is directly proportional to the amount I overshare. I shake my head. "Not that I care. Whatever."

Mia and Bailey exchange another look, and then Bailey leans over the table and says, "It's not that he doesn't want to share a room with you that we like so much. It's why."

Mia nods vigorously. "Exactly."

"I'll bite. Why?"

"So, I suspected as much before I talked to Mason—I mean, *come on,* the sexual tension between you two is off the charts— but then Mason confirmed my suspicions." She waves the waiter over and points to Mia. "She's two shots behind, so we'll need those and another round, of course."

The waiter grins at her. "Sure thing." He winks at her before walking away.

Meanwhile, I'm dying of curiosity. "Mason confirmed your suspicions about what?"

"About how Chris *feels* about you," Bailey says, as if it's obvious.

My slutty stomach butterflies usually reserve their dances for when Chris is in my presence, but they hop to attention now. "What did he say?"

Mia grins. "Mason called you his sister, and Chris corrected him *quickly*."

My shoulders sag, and the butterflies give my new friends the finger. "Oh. That doesn't mean anything."

Bailey slaps the table. "It means he doesn't think of you as his sister, and he wants to make damn sure the guys don't, either. That's not nothing."

"That's not because he's interested or anything." I can't believe I'm still talking. The smart move here would be to say nothing. But there's my mouth, still running as if she has a mind of her own. "It's because we screwed around before we knew who our parents were and he's feeling all *weird* about it."

Bailey's jaw drops, and Mia throws a hand over her mouth.

"The plot thickens," Bailey says, recovering before Mia. "So when you say *screwed around* . . ."

I shake my head. "Nothing too scandalous. We made out at a

friend's house. I'd been drinking and the power went out." I sigh at the memory. "Bad judgment on my part, so now I'm just this thing he regrets."

"Are you buying what she's selling?" Bailey asks Mia, who shakes her head.

"Nope," Mia says, "but I think she might be." She grins. "This summer is going to be *fun*."

I'm only digging myself deeper by trying to explain, so I'm grateful when the server shows up with our shots. He puts three in front of Mia and two others in front of Bailey and me.

"Wait," I say, putting my hand over Bailey's drink. "Who's driving us home?"

Mia smiles. "A girl after my own heart!"

"Mason agreed to DD for us tonight," Bailey says. "He's coming with some of the guys in a bit, and he'll drive us home in my car." Bailey hands her phone to our server, who seems more interested in eye-fucking Bailey than in tending to his other tables. "Would you take a picture of us for me?"

"Sure."

"Say 'cheers,' girls," Bailey says.

We all hold up our shot glasses and smile for the camera.

"What do I owe you for the drinks?" Bailey asks when he hands her back her phone.

The waiter shakes his head. "This round's on me."

"Aww!" She beams at him. "You're the sweetest."

His cheeks turn pink, followed by the tops of his ears. "Let me know if there's anything else you need." He walks away slowly.

"He's cute," Bailey says, loud enough so he can hear. "Damn cute."

I frown, giving our server's retreating form a quick appraisal. "Cute, yes. But Mason is hot. Like, H-A-W-T. What's going on there?"

Bailey shrugs but I can't help but notice—even a little buzzed—that some of the joy that seems so much a part of her personality drains away. "It's complicated."

"It's really not," Mia says. "He's not going to wait around forever. One of these days, you're going to need to admit to yourself that—"

"Not tonight, okay?"

Mia covers Bailey's hand with her own on top of the table and squeezes before she turns to me. "Tell me about your first day in Blackhawk Valley."

"Well, it was pretty uneventful. Chris took me to the grocery store, looked at me like I said I ate small children for breakfast when I told him I was a vegetarian, and then I went around submitting job applications."

"What a drag," Bailey says. "Anything promising on the job front?"

"Plenty of places were happy to let me fill out an application, but no one really indicated they were hiring."

Mia draws in a breath through her teeth. "It's tough finding summer work around here after BHU has let out. All the college kids who want to stick around gobble up all the jobs."

"I guess that means you two don't have any leads?" I ask.

"I work as a nanny," Mia says.

"Oh, my best friend is an au pair. She got a position with this Hollywood couple."

"Mia works for her boyfriend," Bailey says.

I put my shot down untouched. Those first two hit me too hard, and my head feels heavier than the rest of my body and doesn't want to stay upright. "Your boyfriend needs a nanny?"

Mia rolls her eyes. "I work as a nanny to my boyfriend's infant little sister and am employed by my boyfriend's father."

"Oh," I say. "That makes more sense."

"It's a cushy job," Bailey says. "We all hate her."

Mia rolls her eyes. "You love me."

"What about you?" I ask, turning to Bailey.

"Yeah," she says, smirking. "If you want to work with me, you're welcome. We're always looking for new 'talent.'" She uses her fingers to put air quotes around the word "talent."

"Bailey's a stripper," Mia says.

Bailey arches a brow and stares at me, as if waiting for me to make a face.

I shrug. "No judgment here. Is the money as good as they say?"

"Oh, hell yeah," she says. "But I'm about over it. After this summer I'll have enough in savings that I should be able to feed myself and pay for my last two years of college. It'll be tight, but I'm so ready to stop shaking my ass and letting dudes stare at my tits."

"I can imagine." I laugh, imagining what Chris would say

if I started stripping. Hey, maybe he'd come watch. More likely, he'd come and carry me off the stage. That could be interesting. I enjoy the image way more than I should.

"So I want to know more about your night with Chris, episode: 'They Don't Know They're About To Become Related,'" Bailey says, and Mia jabs her in the side with her elbow. "Ow! It's a fair question."

"Stop being so nosy," Mia says. She turns to me. "Sorry. Bailey skipped the days in kindergarten where we learned about personal boundaries."

"No," Bailey says, grinning unapologetically as she messes with her phone. "My favorite soap opera was just canceled, but this has the potential to be even better, so excuse me while I *fill the void*."

"You're going to have to fill it elsewhere," I inform her. "I've got nothing." I take my shot—because why the hell not?—and warmth trails down my throat and swirls in my belly. This will be it. Another, and I'd cruise right past buzzed and land in *toasted* territory.

"You need to come to Arrow's tomorrow," Mia says. "The guys have practice in the morning, and then they get the rest of the day off because they're bringing in some bigwig who might take over the head coach position. Not to mention the baby will be with her mom, so I have the whole day off, too."

I make a face. "You want me to come hang out with a bunch of football players?"

"No," Bailey says, tearing her gaze from her phone to scowl

at me. "We want you to come hang out with a bunch of *shirtless* football players."

Mia sighs. "The distinction *is* important."

"And us," Bailey adds before going back to her phone. "Shirtless buff guys and the coolest girls in town."

I can't help but laugh. "Well, if you put it that way . . ."

Bailey chuckles. "What's your last name, Grace?"

"Lee. Why?"

"Put your phone away," Mia says to Bailey. "What are you doing on there anyway?"

"I'm uploading our pic." Bailey frowns at the screen then looks up at me. "Grace Lee—L-E-E—right?"

"That's my name."

"Why can't I find you on Facebook?" She turns her phone around so I can see her screen. "None of these Grace Lees looks like you."

I shrug. "Because I don't have an account?"

"Oh." She turns her phone back and taps the screen. "What's your Insta handle, then?"

I shake my head. "I'm not on Instagram either."

Her eyes get big, and then she and Mia exchange a look that suggests I'm an alien life form. "Are you Amish or something?" Bailey asks, and Mia says, "Why not?"

"Because people are mean," I answer, and I'm saved from further explanation when a bearded guy approaches our table.

He points to the empty space in the booth next to me. "Is this seat taken?"

"There's a two-shot minimum to sit at this table," Bailey says, and the guy slides in beside me without waiting for me to answer.

"I'm Sebastian Crowe." He offers me a big, work-roughened hand, and I take it. "You're our fearless leader's stepsister?" His voice is the sound of liquid sex, low and scruffy like his beard, and he has tattoos on his biceps peeking out from the tight sleeves of his T-shirt. If men were presented to me in a fancy leather-bound menu, I'd order two of Sebastian Crowe—one for now, and one to enjoy at home later.

"Fearless leader?" I ask, since I figure his question was rhetorical.

"Chris is the quarterback," Mia says. "The quarterback is, like, the one in charge of the offense after the coach."

I swing my gaze around to her and narrow my eyes. "Thanks for the lesson, but I don't have to love football to understand that much." I turn back to Sebastian. "Nice ink."

He grins and nods at the cat eyes tattoo on my bare arm. "You too."

"Careful, Sebastian," Bailey says. "I know someone who might take issue with you hitting on our new friend."

He grins. "Why do you assume I'm hitting on her?"

Bailey scoffs. "Are your eyes working? She's hot."

I grimace. "Because this isn't awkward."

Sebastian grins before dropping his gaze to my face and giving me a look I could only describe as a smolder. "Oh, my eyes work just fine." Not many guys can pull off the smolder, but of those who can, Sebastian's the champ.

I bite my bottom lip, their conversation disappearing into the din of the bar as a group of broad-shouldered guys make their way toward us from across the room. Chris locks eyes with me immediately, and for a second, my heart squeezes and my stomach flip-flops, and I feel damn special because all of his attention is focused on me.

Then I realize he's pissed.

"What's wrong?" Bailey asks, turning in her seat to follow my gaze.

Sighing, I say, "Don't look now, but my babysitter is here, and I don't think he's very happy."

CHAPTER 17
CHRIS

Fucking Bailey. I should have known no good would come of Grace going out with her, but instead of using my brain and trying to change her plans, I was just relieved Grace was already making friends and assumed they'd be hanging at Bailey's or going out for karaoke.

When Mason told me he was headed to the damn *bar* with Keegan so he'd be there when the girls were ready to go home, I realized the flaw in my logic.

Opposite Bailey, Grace is cozied up next to Sebastian Crowe, and the sight makes me want to introduce my new running back to my fist for reasons I'd rather not analyze.

"Oh, look, Grace," Bailey says when I approach the table. "It's your roommate." She turns to Sebastian and gestures to me and Grace. "You know these two are going to share a room this summer?"

Sebastian cocks a brow. "That's . . . interesting."

"It was a misunderstanding," I growl. "I'm sleeping on the couch."

"I was just getting to know your sister," Sebastian says. I'm guessing he can see murder in my eyes.

"They're not actually siblings," Bailey says.

"Yeah," Grace says, "he's more my babysitter than my brother." Her words are slurred. Of course they fucking are. Because she's been drinking. In a bar. Illegally. *Thanks a lot, Bailey.*

"If I'm your babysitter, does that mean I can spank your ass?" *Fuck.* I meant to let her know I was angry and to suggest that maybe she needs the babysitter she accuses me of being. But the second the words are out of my mouth, I hear all of the sexual tension I've been carrying around since Thursday—and I'm pretty sure my friends hear it too.

Bailey bites her lip, and Mia ducks her head as she tries to hide her laugh. Even Sebastian's face says he's fighting like hell to contain his amusement—and I wish I could take it back, but hell, Grace makes me so crazy.

Sebastian slides out of the booth and directs me into his spot, but Grace is already climbing out. "I'm not sure it's my thing, but I'm up for trying anything once."

Bailey isn't as nice as Mia, and she laughs so hard she snorts.

"Bail," I warn. "You don't want to start with me. Seriously." I lower my voice so no one else will hear. "She's not twenty-one."

"Oh my God," Grace says. "Have you ever broken a rule in your whole life?"

"He's not much of a rule breaker," Mia says. She holds her hands a couple of centimeters apart and squints at the space between them. "Straight and narrow."

"Are you all drunk?" I ask, then I spot the miscellany of empty shot glasses on the table. It was hard to see anything else when all I could focus on was how cozy Grace and Sebastian looked next to each other. I sigh. "Fucking fantastic. I'm taking Grace home. Mason's here, and he'll get you two home when you're ready."

"You're embarrassing me," Grace says. She looks at the girls and makes a pouty face. "He doesn't mean to be such a spoilsport, but he takes his job very seriously."

"And that job would be as your nanny?" Sebastian asks, playing right into her hands.

Grace lifts her eyes to the ceiling, as if contemplating the word. "My *manny*?"

The girls burst into fits of laughter, and Mason joins us at the table. "What's so funny over here?"

"Chris," Bailey says. "He's even cuter when he's frazzled."

Closing my eyes, I take a deep breath, hoping to find patience but catching Grace's scent instead. The smell of her does anything but calm me down. In fact, I feel a little crazy, and part of my brain is turning over the possibility of dragging her out of here, getting her home, and smacking her ass just to see what she'd do. "Come on, Grace." I wrap my arm around her waist to steady her. "Let's go." I look to Bailey and Mia, who are still giggling at my expense. "I'll see you guys tomorrow."

As we walk to the back exit, Grace tilts her face up to me and smiles. "I'm not that drunk. I can walk on my own."

"Well, there's an excise officer out front, so I'd rather keep a hold of you and sneak out the back if you don't mind."

"Just don't be trying to cop a feel or something."

"Wouldn't dream of it," I mutter.

"Don't you trust your friends?"

I turn to see her watching me, her eyes narrowed as if she's trying to figure me out. "I trust them."

"Then why did you swoop in there and drag me away like that? We were just having a good time."

Because I didn't like the way you were smiling at Crowe. Because I hate that you're not off-limits to him, but you are to me.

When I went to Tracy's bar, I told myself it was to keep an eye on Grace, to make sure she didn't do anything stupid while in a place she shouldn't have been to begin with. It was only after I saw her with Sebastian that I got a stick up my ass.

"I made a promise to your dad," I say, and even if it's the truth, it feels like a weak excuse next to everything else I'm feeling. "Can we just agree now that you'll refrain from any and all illegal activities?"

She snorts and stumbles a little as we weave around a truck to get to my car. "*All* of them? That doesn't seem likely, considering some of the antiquated laws still in the books. Did you know oral sex is illegal in Indiana? It's also illegal for a man to get a boner in public."

"What?" I rub my forehead. I might not survive this summer. "I'm not even going to ask how you know those things—"

"Weird sex laws are fascinating." She grins. Her eyes float closed, which makes me think of getting her in bed, which makes me think of Grace in *my* bed, which makes me think of Thursday night and weird sex laws in Indiana, which makes me think of how fucking much I want her. Every minute I'm with her, I care less that we're related by marriage. Despite my friends' jabs, we're adults, and our parents' marriage doesn't really impact our relationship aside from pushing us together to begin with.

But what does matter is that she lied to me. I don't have to know what kind of trouble she's gotten into in the past to be cautious of a liar. I've been burned before by someone who had only a causal commitment to the truth and, frankly, it sucked.

I'm not going to make that mistake again, no matter how tempting.

Get her home, get her in bed, and keep her safe.

I help her into the car, checking to make sure she can get her own seatbelt.

"I'm fine," she promises.

I close her door, and as I walk around to my side of the car, I find myself face to face with Sebastian's little sister. "Olivia," I say, lifting my chin. She's leaning against the back of my car in frayed cutoff jean shorts and a dark tank. "What are you doing here?"

"I saw your car. I want to talk."

I exhale heavily. "I told you last week that I don't have anything to say to you. That hasn't changed."

When I make a move to step around her, she closes the distance between us and loops her arms behind my neck. "I've missed you."

"You're full of it," I mutter.

"Come on." Rising onto her toes, she tilts her face up and rubs her nose against my chin. "You've missed me too, haven't you?"

"I caught you with Keegan." I take a big step back, and she can't reach me anymore, so her arms drop to her sides. "I told you it's over."

"Is it really that easy for you?" She wraps her arms around her middle, as if she needs to protect herself from me. "Because it's not for me."

"Is this the girlfriend?" Grace asks.

Fuck. I didn't even hear Grace get out of the car, and now she's leaning against it, watching us like we're free entertainment. How much did she just see and hear?

"No," I say, and at the same time, Olivia says, "Yeah."

I turn to Olivia. "What are you doing?"

Our "relationship," if you want to call it that, was a few months that consisted of us sneaking around so her brother wouldn't know we were dating. The whole arrangement made me feel like an asshole. One, Sebastian's my teammate, and you don't screw around with a teammate's sister. Two, if you must break rule number one, you fucking own up to it. But Olivia was insistent that we keep our relationship a secret, and I liked her enough that I agreed, even though it felt wrong. Then not long after I buried one of my best friends, I caught her kissing Keegan and put a stop to all of it. And now she's going to tell *Grace,* of all fucking people, that we're a couple?

Olivia frowns at Grace, giving her a once-over. "I'm Olivia Crowe. Are you the new stepsister?"

Grace turns her eyes on me. "Is there anyone you didn't prepare for my arrival?"

"We were just leaving," I tell Olivia, sidestepping her to get to the driver's door.

"Nice to meet you, Olivia."

I climb into the car and slam the door shut. I buckle in and wait for Grace to do the same.

Once we're headed home, I breathe a little easier until Grace says, "So does Sebastian know you're fucking his sister?"

CHAPTER 18
GRACE

I wonder if these people have any idea how lucky they are.

We arrived at Arrow Woodison's house (*cough—mansion—cough*) thirty minutes ago, and since then, it's been laughter and smiles and beautiful people without a care in the world. It's unreal. Like an extended beer commercial, only with less alcohol. Despite all the party environments I've been in with Chris in the last five days, I have yet to see Chris drink so much as a beer. Arrow isn't drinking at all. Mason grabbed a beer when we arrived, but he's nursing it, not chugging it. Of the half a dozen other guests at the party, only a couple have a beer in hand, and the rest are drinking tea or water.

Arrow's house is unreal. He lives on this gorgeous property right outside of Blackhawk Valley, and the pool area out back belongs in a vacation brochure.

I came with Chris, but while he's been chatting with his

friends, I've been hanging in the shadows by the back doors. He keeps turning away from his conversation to find me with his eyes, and I keep shaking my head when he waves me over.

Last night was weird, from the part where he stormed into the bar and dragged me out of there like a disapproving father (have one of those already, thanks), to the chick making doe eyes at him in the parking lot, to his insistence on the drive home that there was nothing between him and Sebastian's sister. "I thought once that there might be, but it didn't work out," he told me.

We got home from the bar, and he handed me a glass of water and a couple of ibuprofen, and excused himself to the shower. I climbed into bed, too tired to think about Chris sleeping on the couch, too buzzed to think about what he was or wasn't wearing or if he sleeps with his hands at his sides or over his head.

Then, like clockwork, my insomnia woke me the second my buzz wore off. I padded out to the kitchen to find a snack and there he was, sleeping with one leg off the side of the couch, the other foot dangling off the arm. He was shirtless and gorgeous, a thin sheet tangled around his legs, and when I heard him and Mason up and about before the ass crack of dawn to make it to practice, I felt like a total bitch for not insisting Chris take the bed.

I have a plan for tonight, though. I'm going to claim the couch before he has a chance. Then he'll be forced to get a good night's sleep in his actual bed.

The French doors to the back of the house open and Mia steps onto the patio. She squeals when she sees me. "Grace! You came!" She wraps her arms around my neck, and I let out a little squeak of surprise and pat her shoulder in an awkward attempt to return her hug. I'm not used to this.

It isn't that I'm not an affectionate person, but I've never been the type to hug strangers. But Mia and Bailey seem to have decided that I'm not a stranger—or that I'm not going to be for long.

Willow and I are close, but she's the shining exception to all of my experiences with female friendships. When Dad moved back to Champagne last summer, I got a job at Common Grind to save some money for my first semester at college. She trained me to use the register and somehow knew we were kindred spirits. She befriended me, but it took me a while to trust her.

I've never done very well with other girls. It's not that I don't like being around them or any misogynistic bullshit like that. It's just that sometimes it feels like I don't know how to speak their language.

But Mia and Bailey make it easy because it doesn't feel like they expect anything from me or as if they're waiting for me to embarrass them. They just decided I was part of their group, and therefore I am.

"Are you going to swim?" Mia asks.

Everyone else is in their swimsuits and either on rafts in the pool or on lounge chairs around it. There's a fire pit in the lawn behind the pool, and Chris, Sebastian, and a couple of guys I don't recognize keep feeding wood into the fire as if it isn't ninety degrees out here.

I should probably take off my cover-up and get out of the shadows. It's silly. I've never been uncomfortable about showing my body, but because of where I am and who's around, I'm uncharacteristically self-conscious.

"Come on," Mia says. "Nobody bites. Do you want a drink? Bailey made some sangria."

"Um . . ." I remember Chris telling me he'd like me to avoid anything illegal, and nod. I might joke about him being my babysitter, but I don't intend to let him be the boss of me this summer. "I'd love a drink."

"Coming right up." Mia gives me a big smile. "I'll be right back."

When she disappears into the house again, I peel off my sundress and tuck it into my bag, then make my way to an empty lounge chair under a big red sun umbrella. My skin isn't just pale, it's damn near translucent, and I don't tan—I burn bright red if I lie in the sun.

"Sangria for my new friend," Mia says. She hands me the wine glass and lowers her voice. "Careful with that fruit. It's been soaking in vodka."

I've found my people. "Thanks for the warning."

"Nice suit," a deep voice says.

I turn to see a big guy lowering himself into the lounge chair next to mine. He sits sideways, facing me, and shamelessly skims his gaze from my chest to my bikini bottoms.

As far as bikinis go, this one isn't overly revealing. It's a retro thing with a high waist and white polka dots. I have a thing for polka dots.

"Thanks." I'm gonna need this sangria. I don't like to get drunk in big groups like this, but a little buzz is a social crutch I'm not ashamed to lean on. I slide my sunglasses on to cover my eyes.

He extends a hand. "I'm Keegan."

I shake it briefly. "Grace."

Keegan's broad-shouldered, with muscular arms and a barrel of a chest. He's not anything close to "fat," but he's the biggest guy here. He's got dark hair, a shadow of a beard, and a cute smile, the kind that says he's had a lifetime of using his charm to get away with whatever he wanted. "You're the stepsister?" he asks.

"Yeah," I say. It's weird that all these people knew about me before I knew about them. Knowing Chris, he probably prepared them for my arrival and told them all that they had to be nice. Built-in friends. Damn it. I kind of hate that. Everyone's been so kind, and it would be wonderful to think they liked me and not that they felt obligated. "Did Chris tell everyone about me?"

"Sure," Keegan says, "but he did *not* tell me how hot you are."

I roll my eyes. "Do guys usually talk about how hot their sisters are?"

He chuckles. "Good point. But still, I wish I'd been prepared and brought a respirator."

"Say what?"

"A respirator?" He settles his elbows on his knees and leans toward me. "Because, baby, you steal my breath."

I snort. "God, that's a terrible line."

"Made you laugh," he says, shrugging. "So where do you go to school?"

"Carson College in New York City." It's a small liberal arts college that won my affection because of its writing program—that and the fact that it's located in my favorite city in the world.

"I've never heard of it."

"Probably because they don't have a football team."

"Touché." He chuckles. "So you're a city girl. That's nice."

Someone clears his throat behind us, and I turn to see Chris scowling at Keegan. "What do you think you're doing?"

"Just getting to know your sister. Is that a problem?"

"*Off. Limits,*" Chris says, and I feel an unwelcome and not-so-little flutter low in my belly at his no-nonsense tone.

"Maybe for you," Keegan says.

"For you." Chris's jaw hardens. Is that look in his eyes jealousy, or is he just warning Keegan off because he thinks it's his job as the protective brother? He seems to have taken to that role quite well, which could make for a really boring summer.

Sebastian walks by, wet swim trunks slung low on his hips, and picks up on the conversation. "Leave the stepsister alone." He smacks Keegan's shoulder as he passes. "There's a code, man."

Keegan watches as Sebastian disappears into the house then turns an arched brow on Chris. "I'm thinking you're the last person who should be lecturing me about sisters being off-limits," Keegan says, not budging.

Chris doesn't flinch or swing or call Keegan a jackass—and considering the conversation I heard last night, any and all of those reactions would be appropriate. He simply sets his jaw, closes his eyes, and exhales slowly. I'm beginning to understand what the girls mean when they say he doesn't get frazzled.

"It's fine, Chris," I say. Grinning, I nudge his leg with my elbow, trying to get him to relax. "Keegan's just talking to me. I promise I'll get your approval before we run off to elope."

Chris shifts uncomfortably.

"Stop acting like my guard dog," I say. "We're *talking*."

"Right." He swallows hard and gives Keegan a hard scowl before walking away.

"Well, that's interesting," Keegan says.

"What's that? That he treats me like I'm five?"

He chuckles. "He's not looking at you like you're five."

I try to ignore the flutter in my stomach. There's definitely a tension between me and Chris that's grown over the last two days, but despite Bailey and Mia's suggestions at the bar, I assumed it was one-sided. The truth is that I just *like* Chris so much that I want Keegan and Bailey and everyone who thinks he's into me to be right. I keep reminding myself that my feelings aren't really about who Chris is now. All this slutty, fluttery butterfly business is really about a ninth-grade girl who still needs to prove she's good enough for Chris Montgomery.

"How long are you in town?" Keegan asks. "Are you transferring to BHU?"

I shake my head. "Just for the summer."

"Are you taking any classes?"

"Nope. I'd love to make some money, but I'm having trouble

finding any job openings I'm qualified for."

"I might be able to help with that."

I arch a brow. "Are you hiring?"

He chuckles. "Nah, I have an uncle in town. He's got a fellowship with the college for the summer, and one of his research assistants bailed after her first week with him. I might be able to hook you up if you're into that kind of thing."

"What's his field?" I can research okay, but I don't know how much use I'd be to a chemist or medical researcher.

"He's a writer. Plays, mostly. His name's Drew Gregory."

My eyes go wide. "Your uncle is Drew Gregory? The playwright?"

"*Playwright*," Keegan says. "*That's* the word. I can never think of it. Seems redundant or something. But yeah. That's him."

One, I'm a little impressed that Keegan knows what the word *redundant* means. Two, I never would have guessed this brawny football player could be related to Drew Gregory.

"Are you interested?" he asks.

I can only gape at him. There's no way Drew Gregory is going to want to work with me. Absolutely no way. I mean, I'm not even sure I'm *ready* for an opportunity like this. My hands are shaking just thinking about it. How would I be able to face him or form complete sentences?

"Forget I said anything," Keegan says.

"No!" I bite my lip and force myself to take a deep breath. "I mean, don't forget it. Remember it. I'm a big fan of your uncle. If you could convince him to even consider me, I'd owe you big time."

"Big time like you'll talk to me in public, or big time like you'd let me take you to dinner?"

I laugh. "Do you have to bribe most girls to talk to you in public?"

"Ah, but you're not most girls," he says, flashing that *you know you love me* grin.

"And what about Sebastian's sister?"

The grin falls off his face. "What do you know about Olivia?"

I shrug. "More than I'm supposed to and less than I want to. Chris said she cheated on him with you, but now you're asking me out?"

"He told you that?"

No, it's what I learned from listening to him and Olivia talk last night, but Keegan doesn't need to know that, so I don't answer.

"First, I didn't know they were involved. And second . . ." He drags a hand through his hair. "Not everything is what it seems." This guy has had easygoing all over his features since he came over here, but it evaporated when I mentioned Olivia. Now, his shoulders are tense and his jaw is tight, making him look grim and irritated instead of happy and carefree. "There's nothing between me and Olivia."

"She really messed with your head, didn't she?"

The corner of his mouth hitches up into a lopsided grin. "Yes, and I really need a pretty girl to take my mind off the heartbreak. What do you say?"

"I'm not sure dating one of Chris's friends is a good idea."

"Good thing Chris doesn't really like me then, huh?"

I laugh. I can't help myself. This guy's fun.

"Well, I'll tell my uncle about you either way, but I'm not as bad as they think, you know. I mean, I like girls and I like looking at them and being with them, but I'm good to the ones I'm with. I'd be good to you." His lips curl into a tentative smile, then he turns away from me for the first time and stretches his long legs out in front of him as he looks toward the pool. His chair is just outside of my umbrella's shade, and the sunlight highlights his muscular chest.

It's okay that I'm not interested in Keegan. I'm not going to be here long, and I don't need complications tying me to Blackhawk Valley when I go back to the city in the fall.

My eyes go to Chris. He's standing on the other side of the pool talking to Arrow, but his gaze is on me. Thanks to my sunglasses, I'm guessing he doesn't know I've caught him staring, and he doesn't avert his eyes. His swim trunks are slung low on his hips, and my eyes move over him of their own volition—over his hard chest and across the hard planes of his abdomen and to that sexy *V* of muscle that dips below his waistband.

A slow smile curls my lips without my permission. I like the way he looks at me, and the way my skin heats as if I were in the sun and not in the shade. I don't need complications, but it might be too late for that.

CHAPTER 19
CHRIS

She can't be real. Nothing *that* beautiful exists outside of Photoshop. Grace belongs in one of those calendars of fifties pinup models—the ones with the curves and the big eyes and soft thighs.

Beside me, Arrow chuckles under his breath.

Mia jabs him with an elbow to his ribs. "Stop it."

"It's *funny*," Arrow says. "I've never seen him act like this."

It's all I can do to tear my eyes off Grace. Since she pulled off her sundress and sauntered across the pool deck, I haven't looked away. She's playing the role of Sexpot Minnie Mouse again, this time in a black two-piece with white polka dots and a red bow tying off the bottom of her long braid. The suit covers her body more modestly than any of the other girls here are covered, but somehow that only accentuates her curves. Her ivory skin is pale and perfect all the way to the tops of her thighs. I'm simultaneously grateful that the bikini is so modest and heartbroken that I don't get to see more.

She climbs out of her chair and pulls the bow from her hair before jumping into the pool, shrieking when the cold water touches her skin. Bailey's in the water and laughs before shoving a pool float Grace's way. Grace shakes her head and says something about a sunburn.

"Do you need sunblock?" Mia asks. "We have some in the house."

"That would be awesome," Grace says. "I thought I brought mine, but it must have fallen out of my bag. The higher the SPF, the better."

"Use the baby's," Mia says. "It's the best and I stocked up on it, so there's more than she'll need. It's in the bathroom." She gives me a pointed look. "Chris, will you show her where that is?"

Grace climbs out of the pool, her hair wet, water streaming down her back and over the swell of her breasts.

I swallow hard and avert my eyes, only allowing myself to watch from my peripheral vision as she grabs her towel from her chair and rubs her limbs dry.

"Do you mind?" she asks, squinting at me as she wraps the towel under her arms.

"Not at all."

She wrings out her hair, and I lead her through the back door.

The inside of the house is a quiet contrast to the chatter of everyone outside. It's cool in here, hot out there. Private in here, too many eyes out there. It makes me want to take advantage of the privacy in the best way possible. When it comes to turning off my attraction to Grace, I might be a lost cause.

She follows me into the guest bathroom, and I feel her behind me as I open the cabinet and find the sunscreen. When I turn, she squeaks and hops back, and the backs of her knees bump the toilet.

"Here." I hand the bottle to her, and her fingers brush my hand as she takes it. Something thick clogs my throat. This is probably where I should walk back outside, but I can't get my feet to move.

She shakes the bottle and squirts some out onto her hand as she props a foot onto the lid of the toilet. As she begins applying the lotion to her legs, I'm so entranced, I miss half her sentence before I realize she's talking to me.

"Sorry, what?"

"Keegan said his uncle might be able to give me a job this summer. It's probably a long shot, but would it bother you if I took him up on that?"

"Keegan has an uncle in town?"

"He's a writer and needs a research assistant. Actually, he's not just *a* writer. He's one of my favorite writers."

"Sounds like a great opportunity. Why would that bother me?"

"He's your friend."

I grunt. "Only in the loosest definition of the word. What does that have to do with you taking the job?"

She sighs. "Obviously, you two had some weirdness over

Olivia, and I don't want to contribute to any issues between you."

I shift awkwardly. I can't decide if I don't like her knowing about Olivia or if I'm just uncomfortable with anyone knowing when I never told Sebastian. "Are you planning on doing bad work?"

She grins at me and rubs in the lotion on the top of her thigh, her long fingers sweeping along the edge of her bikini bottoms. "I do *great* work."

It speaks to the serious oxygen deprivation happening in my brain right now that the first time I process her sentence, I think she's making some sexual innuendo. I can hardly think around this girl under the best of circumstances, but watching her long fingers rub sunscreen into her soft skin, I'm surprised any organs north of my waistband are functioning at all.

She sighs and hands me the bottle. "Could you get my back?" Without waiting for my response, she turns around and lifts her wet hair off her neck.

Son of a bitch. My mouth goes dry, and my hands itch to do a hell of a lot more than apply sunblock. I swallow hard, squeeze some lotion onto my good hand, and do the job. Surely I can be more mature than a pubescent boy for the ninety seconds it'll take to get this done.

"I burn easily, so put it on thick."

I lick my lips and start at the back of her neck. She has an ivy tattoo at the base of her neck that dips down along her shoulder blade. It disappears into the top of her bikini and reappears again beneath her arm, where it trails down her side and into her bikini bottoms. I tell myself not to think about where it goes from there, but damn do I want to know.

I move as quickly and clinically as possible as I work in the lotion, but she lets out these little moans as I rub it into her skin. They're barely audible, but somehow that makes them even sexier.

When I drag my thumb across the ivy on her right shoulder blade, she tilts her head to the side and bites her lip. Her eyes are closed, and I take advantage of the opportunity to study her face, her red lips, and inky black lashes.

"You have such great hands."

I jump, as if caught doing something I shouldn't be. And technically, I guess I was.

"Either that or I'm in desperate need of a massage." She opens her eyes and smiles up at me, but it's a dreamy, relaxed smile, the kind that makes me feel like I might just do anything to keep her looking at me like that for as long as possible.

I close my hand around her shoulder and dig my thumbs into the muscle. "You're tense," I say. I was so focused on my own physical response to her before that I didn't even notice.

"Mm-hmm," she says, and then her eyes float closed again and she moans full out. "Such great hands."

"Football," I explain, my voice a little rough. "You have to have strong hands to keep a hold of the ball when you're being thrown to the ground and five different guys are trying to strip it away." I move to her neck and dig at the knots there with my thumbs. I'm rewarded with a moan I'll definitely dream about tonight and every night for all eternity.

"Huh. Maybe I should reconsider my stance on football players."

Only one. I squirt more lotion onto my hand and use it to work on the muscles on either side of her spine. "Are you ever going to tell me what you have against the sport?"

"Oh, I love the sport. I just don't care for the players."

"That's prejudice."

She grunts. "No, it's not. It's wisdom."

"Not liking someone because of the sport they play is prejudice by definition," I say, more to keep my mind off my hands on her skin than because I care. Never mind all the horrible stories on the news; I've met enough asshole football players to understand why some people might hate us as a whole. But I don't care about some people. I want to know why *Grace* has an issue with football players. I want to know a lot of things about her. "How's that?" I ask, squeezing her neck a final time.

"Amazing. Thanks." She points to the strip of skin exposed between the top and bottom of her suit. "Could you put some lotion there, too?"

She might as well ask me if I'd like a critical case of blue balls. "Sure." My voice cracks, but she doesn't seem to notice. I squeeze some more lotion into my hand and cover her skin with it, rubbing it over her spine while being careful not to get it on my bandage. If my hands linger too long at her sides or spend more time than necessary covering the vine of ivy, she doesn't say. I slide my fingers beneath the high waistband before I realize my hand is lower than it needs to go. I pull away quickly. "There you go."

She turns around, and those big green eyes lock on mine. We're standing close, and for a second I think she might be feeling some of the same things I am. But then she says, "So I should apply for the internship, you think?"

I step back into the hall. "Yeah. Definitely."

"Thank you, Christopher." She shimmies past me, and I watch her push through the French doors and go outside to join the group.

When she's gone, I head to the kitchen. I'm in no shape to join the others. I fully intend on standing in front of the open refrigerator until my brain or my balls freeze—whichever comes first.

Instead of finding the main living area of the house empty, I see the guys are gathered around the TV in the living room just off the kitchen.

"What's going on?" I walk into the room and frown when I see the picture on the screen—a still shot of my father walking with his head tucked to his chest. The scroll at the bottom of the screen reads, *Coach Colt Montgomery reported to have met with Blackhawk Hills University board today.*

A hot, needy tightness coiled in my gut during my time in the bathroom with Grace, and now it goes cold and hard.

Arrow looks over his shoulder and meets my eyes. "We don't know what it means."

BHU has been completely tight-lipped about who they're considering in their search for a new head coach, and that's pretty much par for the course in filling a position like this one—maybe even more so after our previous coach's high-profile exit from his position.

Keegan rubs his hands together, his eyes bright when he turns them on me. "Has he said anything to you?"

What a joke. My dad hasn't talked to me since I turned eighteen and petitioned the court to change my name. In the end, Mom talked me out of it, arguing that I'd built a reputation for myself as Montgomery, but my father took the attempt for the insult it was intended to be and hasn't forgiven me. But Keegan's still waiting for an answer, and to give him some credit, at least he's attempting to keep a lid on his glee at the possibility of playing for Coach Montgomery.

"He hasn't mentioned it to me," I say.

Mason rubs the back of his neck, his eyes glued to the screen. "They might have hired him as a consultant. Who better than Colt Montgomery to help them pick between some potential candidates?"

I sink into a chair. The guys are all standing and blocking my view of the screen, but I don't want to look at that asshole's face anyway.

Arrow turns his back on the screen to face me. "Are you okay?"

I meet his eyes and can only pray he knows me well enough to understand how much this is going to fuck with my head. This year is arguably the most important of my career. Last year, we made it to a bowl game for the first time in BHU history, and everyone's watching to see if I can take my team there again—this time without Arrow there to help me lead the charge. Added to that, it's my last year at BHU, and my last year before entering the draft. It doesn't matter how well I played in every season leading up to this. If I have a shitty season now—like, say I'm benched because my coach hates my guts—all the other shit was for nothing.

Mason turns his back to the screen, too. "Chris?"

Sebastian follows their lead, giving the TV his back and facing me. "We're *your* boys first." Maybe it means the most coming from him because I'm not as close to Sebastian as I am to Arrow and Mason, and since he sat out last year because of his transfer, he needs a great season this year more than I do. I want to believe his allegiance is symbolic of the team.

Keegan turns, too. "What can we do for you, man?"

I draw in a deep breath and exhale slowly. There's no point in freaking out about something so completely out of my control. "I need a beer."

CHAPTER 20
GRACE

I make a little nest of blankets on the couch, open a bottle of cheap red wine, turn on *The Very Best of Prince*, and settle in for an exhilarating evening of filling out job applications for local fast-food restaurants. I'm hoping the job with Keegan's uncle pans out, but I don't want to put all my eggs in the Opportunity of a Lifetime basket, so I'm looking for other, less thrilling possibilities just in case.

Under the stack of apps is my journal, a place where I sketch out scenes and ideas for plays and short stories, and if I get through these applications, journaling time will be my reward.

The afternoon turned weird after my interlude with Chris in the bathroom. When Bailey offered to put lotion on my back and I told her I had Chris do it, she declared I was her soul mate, and then I swear she giggle-snorted for half an hour.

But it wasn't the sexy, entirely-*too*-enjoyable sunscreen

application process that was weird. The weird part was when the guys all went inside and never came back out.

Bailey and Mia told me they were in the middle of some "team drama" and to let them be, but the whole thing was bizarre. When I did venture inside to pee, the guys were gathered around the TV, and the mood in the room was definitely somber.

Is there such a thing as a football emergency? I vaguely remember drama over the New England Patriots' partially deflated balls—a news story that was only interesting to me in its comedic potential—but I really don't know enough about the sport to speculate what could have been going on.

Eventually, there was laughter coming from the house, Bailey offered me a ride home, and I accepted. I don't have to understand the sport to understand when a guy needs his friends, and Chris gave me a key to the apartment yesterday. Bailey stopped at a liquor store for cheap wine and then brought me here, promising to call tomorrow. Because apparently we're best friends now. I'm not sure what to make of that.

When my phone buzzes just after ten, I expect it to be her. Instead, it's a text from Willow.

> **Willow:** *How's the bustling metropolis of Blackhawk Valley, Indiana treating you?*

Reading the text is the next best thing to hearing her voice, and I smile as I type out my reply.

> *Me:* Way better than expected. How's the new job?
> *Willow:* Oh, no big. I'm just working for Maverick Christianson and Eva Connelly.

I gape at my phone. Maverick Christianson is by far the sexiest villain in Hollywood.

> *Me:* Are you shitting me?
> *Willow:* I wouldn't lie about Maverick.
> *Me:* Well, holy shit. Meet any sexy Brits to distract you from the sexy American you're living with?
> *Willow:* Everywhere I look. Which is good, since Robbie fucking broke up with me via TEXT MESSAGE today!

I draw in a breath. I knew that asshole didn't deserve her. Okay, actually, I didn't know that. I thought he was an all right guy who was head over heels for Willow, and the breakup comes as a shock. His lame-ass way of doing it I find less shocking.

> *Me:* He didn't! OMG. Are you okay?
> *Willow:* Feeling a bit shallow and bitchy because I was relieved, but otherwise fine.
> *Me:* You are neither shallow nor bitchy. In fact, you're excused from the generally required post-breakup abstinence because he did it by text.
> *Willow:* Thanks for that. How's Mary Poppins?

Me: Who?
Willow: Mr. Practically Perfect in Every Way?

There's a scrape in the lock and the door swings open.

"Speak of the devil," I say as Chris strides in the front door.

After such a long bro session at Arrow's, I expect him to stumble in the door half-drunk, if not three sheets to the wind. Instead, he gives me a completely sober, dimpled smile, and drops his keys on the island.

Mason follows him in, equally sober, but less bright-eyed. "Nice music," he tells me.

"Thanks." I type a quick response to Willow.

Me: Mary Poppins is good. Sweet. Thoughtful. Fucking gorgeous.
Willow: And what about you? How are you doing?
Me: I AM THIRSTY.

"Who are you texting?" Chris asks from behind the couch.

I jump and tuck my phone under my leg so he can't see it. "Willow."

"Willow?" He arches a brow. "Have her tell her sister I said hi." He winks, and the slutty butterflies do the wave like they're in the stands at a baseball game.

"I need to get some sleep before tomorrow," Mason announces. "Night, you two."

I grab my portable speaker off the coffee table and turn down the volume.

Chris turns a questioning eye on me. "Is that Prince?"

I lift my chin. "Yes. And before you ask, I was a fan long before he died and made everyone else remember how awesome he was."

He folds his arms across his chest and cocks a brow. "Of course. And you got your tattoos before they were trendy too, right?"

Laughing, I throw a pillow at him. "Shut up."

He grabs it out of the air, puts it back on the couch, and takes the spot next to me. "What is all this?"

"My idea of an exciting evening in?" I lift my stack of papers. "Job applications." I point to my brimming wine glass. "And alcohol to make me forget that I don't actually *want* to work the Taco Bell drive-thru."

He grimaces. "Can't blame you there, but I mean all the blankets. Are you cold? Want me to turn down the AC?"

"Don't you dare touch that thermostat!" Mason calls from the bathroom over the running water. Judging by his muffled words, I'm guessing he's mid-tooth-brushing.

"Wouldn't dream of it!" I call before turning back to Chris. "I'm not cold. The blankets are for bedtime. I'm sleeping out here."

Chris reaches across me with his big arm and grabs my wine off the end table. He takes a drink and makes a face. "You and Bailey like the same sweet shit, don't you?"

I shrug. I like about anything that doesn't make my tongue feel like sandpaper, so I was happy to let Bailey choose. Way more interesting than my choice in wine is that Chris just grabbed my glass and drank after me. Is he this familiar with everyone? Not that I'm going to overanalyze it. Definitely not.

Which is why my brain is already examining twenty-five possible explanations for his actions.

He takes another sip, makes a face again, and sighs. "We've been over this. You're not sleeping on the couch."

I take my glass back from him and drain it. Because if he's going to sit this close and drink after me and then carry on as if this doesn't affect him at all, I *need* it. "I've *decided*. It's no use talking me out of it now."

"You've *decided*?" He cocks a brow. "Do I get a say in this decision?"

"No, but your long legs do, and when I came out here in the middle of the night, they were all over the place." I wriggle my butt, burrowing into my blankets, and pull a pillow to my chest. "You're too big for this couch, but I can sleep here quite comfortably."

"Sure. You'll sleep just fine until Mason and I are clanging around getting ready for morning practice and wake you up."

"If you want me off this couch"—my empty glass *tinks* as I set it down on the end table—"you're going to have to pick me up and move me."

Sighing, he stands.

"Ha! And my dad told me being stubborn wouldn't get me anywhere!"

"You should listen to him." Chris squats in front of me, slides his arms under my thighs and my blankets, and lifts me and my comfy nest into his arms.

I shriek, instinctively clinging to him by grabbing fistfuls of his shirt. "What are you doing?"

He shakes his head and walks toward his bedroom. "End of discussion." He plops me onto the full-sized bed. "My mother didn't raise me to put my guests on the couch."

"Don't *do* that." I grab a pillow off the bed and hurl it at him. "Oh my God, my ovaries will never be the same."

He frowns and sinks to his knees as he studies my stomach. "Did I hurt you? Are you okay?"

"No, I'm not *okay*." I smack at his hand as it comes toward my shirt. "You just *carried* me, Christopher. You picked me up and *carried me*, and now all the weakling men out there who try to impress me with their brains are going to make my girly parts *yawn*. I am *ruined* for normal men, and it's all your fault!"

His face splits into a grin. "I lift more than you in my warmups, Grace."

"Fine. I'll sleep in the bed, but for the love of God, *stop it*," I growl. "That information is not helping." I throw myself back onto the bed and stare at the ceiling fan overhead. When I roll my head to look at him, that shit-eating grin is still covering his face. I need to put a stop to *that*. "What about Sebastian? Can *he* lift me?"

That does the trick. His grin falls away in a blink. "Do you need anything from the living room before I crash?"

I want to tell him I was joking about Sebastian, but I bite back the apology and point to the top bunk. My pride be damned—we need to be mature about this. "Why are you sleeping on the couch when there's a perfectly good bed up there?"

He lifts his eyes to the lofted bed and then back to me. "I wanted you to have your own space."

Every minute with this guy only confirms everything I already thought about him. He's such a capital N, capital G, Nice Guy. And I don't know if it's despite or because of the one exception five years ago that every additional piece of evidence makes my heart ache.

"You want her for yourself or something, Montgomery?"

"As if I'd put my dick near that."

The memory is like a hot poker to the heart every fucking time.

"I *will* have my own space," I say, subdued now. "You're about to start two-a-days, right? You'll be taking up residence on the football field. That'll give me all the time I need. Never mind the fact that I'm an insomniac, and I want access to the kitchen for midnight munchies. In fact, I need some now."

"You're sure? It won't be weird for you?"

I hop out of bed and head to the door. "Not weird at all." Then, because I feel like he can see the vulnerability on my face, I add, "I mean, assuming you're not going to spank the monkey while I'm sleeping beneath you."

"Spank the . . ." He drags a hand over his face. "You know normal women don't talk about masturbation like the weather, right?"

"I'm not normal."

"And *I'm* not a total creep. You don't have to worry about me doing *that* when you're in the room."

I shrug, only mildly disappointed. "Then we don't have a problem. Goodnight, Chris." I shut the door before he can respond.

CHAPTER 21
GRACE

*I*t's *just a job interview*, I tell myself, smoothing my skirt for the hundredth time because I'm about to be interviewed for a research assistant position with none other than *Drew Gregory*.

I'm no good at lying to myself, and this is *just* a job interview in the same way that ice cream is *just* food.

It happened so fast. Yesterday, I was at Arrow's pool talking to Keegan about his uncle, and then this morning, the shrill ring of my phone pulled me from a deep sleep. It was the drama department at BHU, and they wanted to know if I could be there at two for an interview with Mr. Gregory. I said yes—*of course I did!*—and a series of panicked texts later, I found out that they got my number from Keegan, who got it from Chris. Meaning, not only am I about to have the most important interview of my life to date, *everyone* knows about it.

I enter the stairwell and head up to the BHU drama department to meet Keegan's uncle. I've spent most of the morning training myself to think of Drew Gregory as *Keegan's uncle* and not as a playwright I adore or a possible mentor. And definitely not as the best opportunity I've ever been handed and one I'll hate myself forever for fucking up.

The guest lecturer's office is just past the secretary's office, and I freeze at the door. I was hoping for a walk through the halls before I reached my destination—anything to put this off. Instead, I'm here, standing in front of his office long before I'm ready.

I tuck my hair behind my ears and smooth my skirt again.

"Well, don't just stand out there, come on in!"

Shit. I paste on a smile and enter the office. It's larger than I would have expected. There's a couch and an oversized leather chair in front of the double windows that overlook the rolling hills at the center of campus. The other half of the space is filled with a big walnut desk, piled with books and haphazard stacks of paper. A tiny laptop is perched crooked on top of an open book.

Then there's the man himself, standing at the large bookcase and running his index finger along the spines. Mr. Gregory is bigger than I imagined—in height and breadth. He has the same broad-shouldered build as his nephew and the same dark brown hair.

"Library of shit is what they have here," he says, shaking his head. "*Salinger*—as if anybody ever got a good word from that man."

Personally, I love J.D. Salinger and everything he ever wrote, but I decide to keep that piece of personal trivia to myself.

Mr. Gregory turns to me and arches a brow as he runs his gaze from my black flats to my fitted black skirt that hits below my knees and my black-and-white polka-dot blouse. He stops when he reaches my eyes and gives a satisfied nod. "Keegan told me you were pretty."

Well, shit. I'm sure he's not looking for a *pretty girl* to do his research this summer. He needs someone talented, and I'm not sure I fit that bill, frankly.

Girls everywhere want to be pretty. I've been told I'm pretty all my life—with tattoos, without, with red hair and blond hair and black hair. Pretty is easy. It's literally as simple as my DNA, and while beauty has its perks, my biggest, most secret fear is that being beautiful is and will forever be the most remarkable thing about me.

"Why do you want the job?" he asks.

I'm a little taken aback. No introductions or how-do-you-dos, but maybe that's my fault for waiting outside the office so awkwardly. "Um . . . uh . . ."

"*Um* doesn't pay the bills, sweetheart. Keegan told me you were smart, so I assume you *can* string a few words together to create what we call a *sentence*?"

My cheeks heat, and I want to turn around and run out the door and never come back. Maybe there's a reason his first research assistant "bailed" on him so quickly.

This is the opportunity of a lifetime, I tell myself, rooting my feet in place. Sure, this isn't the best first impression, but I'm the one who's supposed to be trying to impress him, not the other way around. And aren't all the greatest artists a little odd?

I swallow hard and remind myself to take deep breaths and to speak slowly and in short sentences. Even though stuttering is a well-known problem, people still associate stuttering with stupidity and a lack of self-confidence. I don't want to stutter ever, but especially not right now with a man I respect so much. "I'm studying playwriting at Carson College in New York."

"You fancy yourself a writer, then?"

I swallow hard. "Yes, sir."

"Ever done any stage managing?"

"I thought this was a research assistant position?"

"It's an assistant position, and I'm tasked with putting on a new play before I leave this Podunk town. Anyone can call themselves a writer, but can you be part of making that writing come to life?" He makes a fist and taps his chest. "The heart of theater. I need somebody who can help me create something entirely original and put it on the stage."

"Are you writing and producing or just producing?"

"I can't write for shit anymore," he says, and I try to hide my shock, because it's kind of like hearing Santa say he doesn't give presents anymore. "They don't care what we put on that stage as long as the summer ends with some sort of production that will give this college some press. It's all about the press, you know." He releases a grunt and shakes his head. "So, you and me, we have to find something worth producing. Something that's already great, and we can add the signature *Drew Gregory* twist to make it better."

Well, fuck. I was hoping I'd get to work for him and mostly hide in the library. "I've never done anything like that before, but I'd be willing to learn."

He gives a sharp nod and gives me another shoes-to-eyes once-over. "Well, my nephew seems to respect you a great deal, so we'll do this. You're hired. On a trial basis, of course. If after two weeks, you're not happy or I'm not happy, we're off the hook, no questions asked."

This is officially the strangest job interview I've ever had. "That sounds fair."

"Good." He grabs a stack of papers off his desk, shoves them into a manila folder, and crosses the office to push the folder into my hands. "This is what we're working with. Read my notes tonight and come back tomorrow with your ideas on different projects. Remember, I need something original."

I'm afraid to look. I don't want to dissolve into a puddle of fangirl mush and rave about how excited I am for the opportunity he's offering me. So I just nod and clutch the papers to my chest.

"You're out of here, then," he says. "Go fill out the paperwork with the secretary. I'll see you tomorrow at eight a.m. Don't be late. I can't stand waiting on people."

"Yes, sir. Thank you," I say, and I rush out of the room and to the secretary's office. I stare at her for a solid thirty seconds before I can find the words to ask for what I need.

I'm going to spend my summer working for a famous

playwright.

Holy shit.

Chris is waiting for me when I walk in the door. He's sitting on the couch in basketball shorts and a T-shirt and tying on a pair of running shoes. "How was the interview?" Standing, he props his hands on his hips.

I grin—and I know it's one of those giant grins that takes up half my face and makes me look more like a caricature than a real person, but I'm so excited that I don't even care. "It was fine. I . . . I got it." It feels weird to say it. I don't think I expected that to happen. "It was the weirdest interview ever, honestly. It's not even for research. He needs an assistant to help him produce a play."

He returns my smile and my insides turn to warm, gooey heat. "Well, Keegan put in a good word for you. That's gotta help. And I bet you're talented."

But I'm not, and I feel like a phony for not correcting him, but to tell him the truth would make it sound like I'm fishing for compliments from a guy who's never even read my writing. I trust the professors at my school, and though they're complimentary to my work, it's never been good enough to be chosen as one of the student plays they produce each semester. *Good* doesn't matter if it's not *good enough*.

"When do you start?" Chris asks.

"I guess right away. He gave me some stuff to work on tonight, and we're meeting to talk about it tomorrow." My stomach shimmies with nerves at the thought.

"That's awesome," Chris says. He nods to the door. "I'm about to head out on a run, but I wanted to hear about the interview before I left."

"I thought you were doing two-a-days with the team."

He nods and sighs. "Yeah, I'm a little antsy." He shrugs as if it's nothing, but I can tell something's bothering him. "I need to blow off some of this energy. I'll feel better after a few miles."

I nod stupidly, as if I know anything about training for football or even basic working out.

"If you ever want to come with me," he says, "you'd be welcome."

I blink at him. "Like, running?"

He cocks his head to the side. "Yeah. The apartment complex doesn't have a gym, and since you're not a student you can't use the university one, and I figure you don't want to waste money on a membership to a gym. I just wanted you to know you could run with me if you wanted."

I drop my gaze to my feet and then back up to him. "These legs don't run. I don't understand why anyone would inflict such torture on themselves."

"It's not torture once you get used to it."

"You can keep lying to yourself, but I'm fine knowing the truth."

"You're a trip," he mutters, rubbing his palm and turning toward the bedroom.

"Hey, wait a minute," I say, stopping him. "Let me have a look at that hand."

He turns back to me and extends his hand. The wound isn't bandaged anymore and it's scabbed over into a thin red line. "It's fine," he says, his voice rough.

"I think you'll live." I lift my eyes to meet his and find him studying my mouth. I want him to dip his head and kiss me so badly, I can hardly breathe.

Pulling his gaze from my lips, he meets my eyes. "I need to grab my headphones," he says, but he doesn't pull away.

"Chris?"

His lips part. "Yeah?"

I have no idea what I want to say. *Kiss me? Don't look at me like that? Do you feel this thing between us?* I release his hand. "Thanks for letting me stay here this summer."

He blinks at me. "No problem."

The moment gone, he goes to the bedroom, and I open up the cabinet and find the box of Lucky Charms, pouring myself a bowl and adding milk before I take a seat at the counter with my cereal and the stack of papers from Mr. Gregory. I need to think about something other than Chris and his eyes on my mouth. And anyway, I want to impress Mr. Gregory when I see him tomorrow. I want to learn everything I can from this man.

When I open up the folder and start leafing through the hundreds of papers, my stomach sinks. I want to impress Drew Gregory, and I've already fucked up.

CHAPTER 22
CHRIS

I grab my earbuds out of my top drawer and fist them in my hand, forcing myself to take a deep breath before heading back out to the kitchen. I've used running and exercise as a tool for clearing my head since I was a kid. Judging by past experience, I should be able to shake off this day if I just run roughly four hundred miles.

Because *fuck*. I've never felt less control of my life than I do right now.

I had less than sixteen hours where I got to lie to myself and pretend that maybe, just maybe, my father wasn't in town to interview for the head coach job. That optimism was shot to hell the minute I walked into the locker room this morning and everyone was buzzing with the news that Colt Montgomery is considering leaving Texas Bright University to take the position at BHU.

I pushed hard through morning practice and made Mason stay for an hour of his break to run routes. I threw and threw and threw until my arm felt like lead and Mason was cussing at me.

Then Grace. *Grace.*

I planned on a good run to get this ugliness out of my system, but then she took my hand in hers. Her simple touch sent a shock wave through my body and I imagined something else that would be a hell of a lot more effective in taking my mind off how fucked my season is about to get.

I feel frenzied and chaotic inside, but the second she walked in those doors and grinned, everything dropped away, and for a few seconds, football didn't matter.

Last night, I fell asleep before she came into the room, but it didn't stop me from thinking about her while I drifted off. About how it felt to have her soft hair slide through my fingers and how much I like having that wide smile aimed in my direction.

The thing is, I fucking know she's trouble. I know it from the way we ended up kissing at Willow's, and I know it from the questions that come out of that wicked mouth of hers. I've always avoided trouble and have never been attracted to it, but trouble in the form of Grace Lee seems to be my exception. All I want is to be close to her. Right now, I want to break every promise I made to her father and myself and be closer than I should.

She'd quiet the chaos in my brain. She'd make everything feel *right* again.

Instead, I'm going to run fast and hard until my lungs burn.

When I return to the kitchen, she's sitting at the bar flipping frantically through papers, stress all over her face.

"Grace?" I put my hand on her arm.

She jumps then shakes her head when she sees it's just me.

"What's wrong?"

"I'm supposed to go through his notes and get ideas for a production. But there are no notes here. I don't know if I lost them, or if they're in invisible ink, or if he gave me the wrong file, but there are blank dog-eared pages, and I feel like I'm losing my mind. Surely he wouldn't have given me a file full of blank pages, right?" Her hands shake, and I take them in mine and squeeze them tight.

"It's gonna be okay. We'll figure it out, all right?"

She shakes her head. "I'm so out of my league, and I don't want to fuck it up. I feel like I failed my first job, and it's my fault because he gave me the file and I didn't want to look at what was inside. I didn't even ask what play he had in mind. I w-w-was so afraid I'd s-s-say something s-s-s-stupid." She stops, squeezes her eyes shut, and takes a long, slow breath. "I just wanted to leave."

"Hey, look at me." I dip my head and force her to meet my gaze. She bites her lip as her big green eyes meet mine. "It's gonna be okay. We'll figure it out." Her shoulders fall a little as she relaxes. "They're all blank?"

She nods. "Every single page. Do you think it's some kind of a joke? Maybe he doesn't mean for me to work for him. Maybe he knows that I'm . . ." She bites her lip again.

"Have you called him?"

"What?"

"Keegan's uncle. What's his name?"

"Drew Gregory."

"Have you called Drew at his office to tell him what's in the file?"

She shakes her head. "He's going to think I'm an idiot."

"Grace." I look down at the pile of white paper and flip through them. "You're not an idiot, and this was probably an honest mistake. Just call him and let him know you'll come by to pick up the right file so you can get started for tomorrow."

She nods and takes a deep breath. "I don't normally flip out like this," she says quietly, her eyes fixed on the blank pages. "I just really don't want to fuck this up."

"This job means a lot to you, doesn't it?"

She nods, and my chest aches for her. I can see all over her face the anxiety I feel every time someone wants to talk to me about the draft.

Having someone hand you your wish on a silver platter seems like reason to celebrate, like endless happiness, but the reality of it is that it's terrifying. Someone gift-wraps an opportunity for you—your dream—and hands it over, and even though you're grateful to have it, you can't stop thinking about how it's in your hands now, and if it drops to the ground and shatters, it's your fault.

Last semester, I watched Arrow nearly throw away his football career. He almost lost his dream. Now I'm the one with the ball on the five-yard line and the defense lining up to cover the pass, and I need the courage to rush it in.

I don't know anything about writing or plays, but I can see it in her face. Working for Drew Gregory is her NFL draft.

I realize I'm still holding one of her hands, and I force myself to let it go.

I grab her purse off the end table and bring it to the counter, and she pulls her phone from inside and shoots me a grateful smile as she dials.

A minute later, she's frowning as she ends the call. "He's not answering. I guess I'll send him an email?"

"Great idea. It's going to be fine. You'll see." I barely resist the urge to lean forward and press a kiss to the wrinkle in her brow. "You good?"

She nods slowly. "I'll email him. You go run."

"Good. I have my phone. Call me if you need to, okay?"

"Sure," she says, and I make myself leave the apartment. Because all I want to do is stand by her side and convince her it's going to be okay, and somehow that seems far more dangerous than how much I want to touch her again.

CHAPTER 23
GRACE

After Chris leaves, I type a quick email to Drew Gregory—*oh my God, my first email to Drew Gregory and it's to admit that I'm an idiot. Awesome!*—and then my phone buzzes with a text.

A quick look tells me it's from an unknown number, and I tap my screen to open it.

> ***Unknown:*** *Talk is that Chris's dad might be his new coach. I'm wondering if Coach knows what a whore Chris's new "roommate" is. I doubt he'd approve.*

I know without asking that the text is from Jewel or one of her cronies. I wish she didn't know anything about my life or living situation, but in Champagne, gossip spreads faster than syphilis at a sex club.

I read the text three times, and with each pass something different stabs me in the gut. The word *whore*. The quotes around *roommate*. The implicit threat. The fact that if what she says is true, it's big news for Chris and he hasn't said a word about it to me.

I won't reply. You don't bait the trolls. I'll let her think I didn't see it, let her wonder if I changed my number, anything but give her the pleasure of knowing she's gotten through to me.

But doing nothing makes me want to pull my hair out, so I do the next most obvious thing. I pull out a bottle of Bailey-recommended cheap red, and I start drinking.

Half a bottle of wine and a disproportionately sized pity party later, I decide there's no reason to be in my interview clothes when I can be in pajamas. I find a pair of cotton sleep shorts and a fitted polka-dot tank top and brush my hair into a ponytail.

When I get back to the living room, I stop in my tracks. Chris is lying in the middle of the floor, shirtless and sweaty, and doing sit-ups. He's so focused on the movement that he doesn't notice me at first. I just stand there for a minute, admiring the way the muscles in his abdomen bunch and flex, and concocting inappropriate fantasies in which I put the look of sheer concentration on his face into another context.

When he spots me, he stops and pushes himself off the floor. "Hey!" He grabs his shirt from the back of the couch and uses it to dry the sweat off his face.

I swallow hard just to keep the drool from dripping down my

chin. "Were you exposed to radioactive slime as a child?" I swear, his chest has gotten even broader since I last saw him.

Frowning, he looks down at his sweaty skin, confused. "What?"

"You know, like the Teenage Mutant Ninja Turtles? Were you exposed to the slime that turned them from adorable little creatures into mammoth-sized heroes?"

He laughs and heads to the kitchen, where he fills up a glass of water. "No slime and no rat dojo."

He lifts it to his lips and drains it in one go, his neck working as he swallows gulp after gulp. A bead of sweat rolls down the side of his face and along his neck, and I practically have to bite back a whimper as it hits his pecs. His shirt is still in his fist and not covering his body. I'm going to need him to not do that. I don't think I can stand a whole summer of him walking around shirtless and sweaty.

"We're going to have to set some rules," I say, scanning his chest.

He sets the empty glass down. "Yeah? Rules about what?"

"Maybe you should wear a shirt." I nod. The wine left me feeling fuzzy. "I think shirts should be required. If we're going to live together this summer, we should both keep our shirts on."

He coughs and wipes the back of his mouth with his hand. "Wow. Um . . . does this bother you?" He drops his gaze to his bare chest, and when he lifts it back up to meet mine, there's a shit-eating grin on his face. *Bastard.* "I don't even think about it. I didn't mean to make you uncomfortable."

I'm not uncomfortable. I'm *thirsty*. For Chris. "It's good that you're comfortable in your own skin, but since your mom probably doesn't want me hatching dirty fantasies about her baby boy, covering it up would be a good idea."

He squeezes his eyes shut and drags a hand over his face, muttering something I can't make out. He cracks one eye open to peek at me. "How dirty? Do I want to know?"

"Seriously dirty. Tumblr-porn dirty. NC-17 dirty. It's not personal. I'm just genetically programmed to drool over excess muscle. So, rule number one: Wear a shirt. I will return the favor in kind."

His gaze drifts down to skim over my polka-dot tank. "You got it, boss. Anything else? Any other *rules* I should be aware of?"

I've given away too much. I was going for bold and unapologetic, but I feel like he can see that my attraction is about more than his muscles, and Jewel's text has left me raw. "If I bring a date home, we need some sort of system so that, you know, I can have privacy." His eyes go wide, and I say, "I'd do the same for you, of course. I mean, at some point this summer you're going to want to have that room to yourself, right?"

He freezes, and it's as if he's not even breathing. Then he exhales slowly. "Is this about Sebastian?"

"Doesn't matter who it is, does it?"

His jaw goes hard. "Do you think it's a good idea to date this summer?"

"Were you expecting me to be abstinent under your watch?"

"I wasn't . . . I . . . It's not like . . ."

"You were." I exhale heavily. "Newsflash, Mr. Perfect: Girls like sex, too."

"I know that." He's all adorable when he's defensive. He frowns and those dimples disappear, as if they never existed.

"Not just *making love*. Girls like fucking. Doing the nasty."

"Is the distinction important?"

"Sometimes." I grin. "Come on, Chris. I'm not a nun, and it's not like I'm looking for a husband. Summer's a long time, and I imagine I might go on a date or two." He just stares at me, so I add, "If my *babysitter* is okay with that? I mean, I assume *you* weren't planning on going without all summer?"

"Jesus, Grace." He turns around and runs a hand through his hair. "I don't think working out a system to hang a sock on the doorknob was what your dad had in mind when he—"

"Let me guess. He probably used the words 'misguided' and 'attention-seeking.' My poor judgment was probably mentioned once or twice?"

"He's just worried about you."

I prop my hands on my hips. "You really are my babysitter, aren't you?"

"Stop calling me that."

"If the shoe fits."

"He wants me to keep an eye on you. But listen to you, Grace. Can you blame him? You haven't even been on a date and you're planning—"

I'm going to tear my hair out. "Don't be so sexist."

"How am I being sexist?"

"If a guy planned on *eventually* having sex even when he hadn't had a date, you wouldn't label him as trouble or needing a keeper. You'd think he was a healthy, normal guy." I shake my head. "I thought you were above all that double-standard bullshit, Chris."

He throws up his hands. "Fine. You want the room, give me notice. I'll plan on sleeping on the couch."

"And if you plan on bringing a girl home," I say, "you can tell *me* in advance."

"That's not likely."

I don't know why that annoys me. It's not like I *want* him to be with other girls. "Why not?"

"I don't—" He shakes his head.

"You don't date? Don't screw? Don't like to get off every once in a while?" I saunter up to him so we're inches apart. I lift my chin and meet his eyes. I want to rub who I am in his face. I might not be brave enough to tell him, but he'll find out soon enough anyway. Jewel will make sure of it. I'm the slut. Easy Gee-Gee. And his father certainly *wouldn't* approve. "You never bring a girl home and push her to her knees? You never slide your hand into her hair and show her just how fast you need her to move while she sucks you off?"

"Grace . . ." His voice is low and he takes a step back. "You're trouble."

And don't forget it. "You didn't answer my question." I shake my head. "But no, you only date *good girls*, right? Not the kind who come home with you just to fuck? Not the kind who get off on pleasing you? You wouldn't be caught dead with the kind of girl who cares more about getting off than whether or not you call the next day. You wouldn't want *that* kind of girl, would you?"

His eyes drop to my mouth, and his Adam's apple bobs as he swallows hard. "And what kind of girl are you, Grace?"

"I'm the easy lay." And *fuck me,* because the words come out sad. I want to say it without apology, to throw who I am in his face and not back down. But there it is—sadness in my voice. Because Christopher Montgomery was my hero once, and then he turned around and became the reminder of what I'd accidentally become, a reminder of who I couldn't be and what I couldn't have.

"I don't want to see you get hurt, Grace. This might be a small town, but that doesn't mean the guys are all good." He shakes his head and his shoulders drop. Then he turns on his heel and disappears down the hall, and I hear the bathroom door slam and the shower turn on.

I rub my palms against my eyes. I'm not the girl I just made myself out to be. I'm not the girl I just rubbed in his face. I don't need a shrink or another five years of therapy to know that I just said all that as a defense mechanism, a knee-jerk reaction to the burn of Jewel's text message. I want him to think I'm the kind of girl he avoids. Because then him not wanting me is under my control. My mind is a clusterfuck of emotions, and I drive my hands into my hair and tug.

I shouldn't care what Chris thinks of me. It shouldn't matter whether or not I'm the kind of girl he'd want to be with.

But it does. Fuck, but it does.

First crushes die hard, I guess.

CHAPTER 24
CHRIS

My shower is filled with more visions of Grace on her knees and opening her mouth than I'd like to admit. It's a tormented kind of fantasy. Images soured by the horrifying possibility of her bringing Sebastian or Keegan back to my apartment and asking me to sleep on the couch so they can have the room to themselves.

She's an adult and capable of making her own decisions. I know that—despite what her father may think—I can't keep her from doing whatever or whomever she wants this summer. And I know that my reasons for not wanting her to fuck my teammates or anyone else have more to do with the number of hours I've spent thinking about that mouth and that body and the way she felt in my arms than they do the promises I made Edward.

Fifteen tormented minutes later, I climb out of the shower, dry off, get dressed, and go to find her in the kitchen. I tell myself

I need to make sure she's not chugging wine and that she drinks some water before bed, but I know I also want to reassure myself she's still here, that she's not with Keegan or some other asshole who's entirely unworthy of her attention.

I pull on a pair of cotton shorts and head to the living room.

Grace is on the couch with her legs curled under her, and she's scribbling in a notebook in her lap. I don't realize I'm staring until Mason clears his throat.

I turn around. I didn't even realize he'd gotten home, but he's standing in the kitchen. He arches a brow and then turns around and scrapes chicken off the cutting board and into a skillet on the stove. It sizzles when it hits the hot oil.

"Are you gonna have chicken stir-fry with us, Grace?" he asks.

She lifts her head and blinks at Mason and then me. I get the impression she was so lost in whatever she was writing, she had no idea she wasn't alone in the room. "No thanks. I don't eat meat."

Mason looks to me, and I nod in confirmation. He turns his head back to Grace. "What do you eat, then?"

"The hearts of lovesick men, mostly."

Mason grunts. "No wonder you and Bailey get along so well."

Grace climbs off the couch and stretches, lifting her arms above her head and exposing a strip of skin between her shorts and that polka-dot tank top. "I'm going to work in the room for a while," she says to me. "Do you need the desk for anything?"

"It's all yours."

"Thanks." She clutches her notebook to her chest and heads to the bedroom, closing the door behind her, and when she's gone I realize how much I wanted her to sit and have dinner with us.

"How's the room-sharing thing going?" Mason asks, stirring the chicken.

I grab a glass from the cabinet, fill it with water, and stare into it like a psychic reading tea leaves. "You ever meet a girl who gets under your skin so much you can't see straight?"

"Once," he says. He puts down the spatula and turns to study me. His scrutiny gives me the sensation of being a bug under a microscope. "Then she slipped away, and ever since my skin feels like it doesn't fit right. My advice to you? Hold on tight."

GRACE

My stomach is a tangle of nerves when I get to Mr. Gregory's office. The door is closed, and when I knock, he doesn't answer.

He said he couldn't tolerate tardiness, so I arrived five minutes early.

I knock again, in case he didn't hear me the first time, but no one comes to the door.

After a few minutes, I check with the secretary, who says she hasn't seen him yet this morning.

I take a seat by the door, my legs extended in front of me, my feet crossed at the ankle, the big stupid folder of blank pages in my lap. And I wait.

It is 9:07 a.m. when Drew Gregory approaches his office door. His eyes are bleary, his button-up shirt wrinkled and untucked. He stares at me hard as he unlocks his door, and I scramble to my feet.

"Are you okay?" I ask.

He grunts and mumbles something unintelligible, but I find this situation far too awkward for me to ask him to repeat himself. I put my head down and follow him into the office.

"About this file you gave me last night—"

He scowls at me over one shoulder. "Let me stop you there."

"Oh. I'm sorry." I put the file down on the chair that sits just inside the office. "Do you want me to wait out there until you're settled?"

"Coffee, girl. Don't I look like a man who needs a cup of coffee?"

My stomach sinks, but I'm not too proud to fetch a cup of coffee. "I'll be right back."

I find some disposable cups in the department kitchen and a half-full pot on the coffee maker. I pour a cup and bite my lip as I stare at the sugar and cream. He would have told me if he wanted something in it, right?

I grab a couple of packets of sugar and powdered cream and return to his office. He's sitting at his desk and has rolled his shirtsleeves to his elbows.

I set the coffee on the desk before him. "Here you go, sir."

He stares at the cup as if I've just presented him with a dead rodent. "You first."

"Excuse me?"

"You heard me. Take a drink."

Does he think I'm trying to poison him or something? I can't decide if I'm the worst intern ever or if this man has a few screws loose. Seeing no reason to argue, I lift the cup to my lips and take a quick sip. Then I grimace. This is why I grind my own beans and brew my own joe. How can coffee taste so weak and so burned all at the same time?

"I asked for *coffee*," he says. He pulls out his wallet and throws a hundred-dollar bill on the desk. "There's a Starbucks in the commons."

I nod to the hundred. "Exactly how much coffee were you wanting me to buy?"

"Venti bold coffee. Black. I'll need coffee every morning, but don't get it until I arrive. I hate cold coffee."

"Okay."

He gives a curt nod. "And hurry back. We need to talk."

"Yeah, about those papers—"

"Not before coffee."

Right.

By the time I make the coffee run and return to his office, I've relaxed a little about the file folder of blank pages and my inability to properly fulfill his request for coffee on the first try. I still don't know what exactly he expects from me this summer, but whatever it is, I can handle it. I'm not going to let him scare me off. Even if he plans to treat me like an errand girl.

I hand him the coffee and think twice before I open my mouth again. I take a seat and stare at the folder, giving him a chance to caffeinate before I admit that I'm not prepared.

Finally, he says, "What'd you come up with?"

I swallow hard. "Sir, I think maybe you gave me the wrong file? I tried to call and email but wasn't able to get a hold of you."

"What's wrong with it?"

"It's . . ." I clear my throat. "It's just a bunch of blank pages?"

"And what? You thought the fairies were going to come fill them for you?" He narrows his eyes. "What's the problem?"

"I thought these were your notes. That I was supposed to get some ideas for the production? Putting your special twist on someone else's play?"

"You're a writer, aren't you?"

Normally, answering that question in the affirmative wouldn't be a problem, but this is *Drew Gregory*. I lift my chin. "I try."

"Try?" He grunts. "You're a writer. So write something."

I'm beyond confused. "You want me to gather notes for you? Ideas for a new play, maybe?"

He drags a hand through his light brown hair. "Lotta good that would do you. No, I want *you* to write a play. I thought that's what you wanted."

"But I thought—"

"You get my coffee and look shit up whenever this old brain of mine comes up with anything it gives enough fucks to care about, but with all your other time, you write a play, and I'll make sure it doesn't suck before we put it on the stage. Does that sound like an okay way to spend your summer?"

Well, fuck me standing. "Yes sir. That's . . . amazing, really. Thank you."

CHAPTER 25
CHRIS

I've discovered something Grace will eat that doesn't come out of a cereal or Pop-Tart box. This feels like a not-so-minor victory, and when she avoids contracting scurvy before the age of twenty-five, she'll have me to thank. She grabs a box of vegetarian fried rice off the coffee table and stirs it with her chopsticks.

Over the last week and a half, we've fallen into a routine. Mason and I get up early for practice, and sometime after we leave, she goes in to BHU, where she fetches Drew Gregory's coffee and does the occasional Google search on a topic if inspiration strikes him. Mostly, though, as far as I can tell, she spends her day with her laptop working on a play. At the end of the day, we eat dinner here together, and some nights we go over to Arrow's to hang out, and sometimes she retreats to the bedroom to type at the desk.

After finding her at the bar with Bailey her first night in town,

I was worried about what kind of trouble I'd have to keep Grace out of—and whether or not I could—but since Drew Gregory told her to write him a play, she's been content keeping her nose to the grindstone instead of making my life hell by getting drunk or talking about fucking my friends.

She puts her rice down and goes to the kitchen. "I feel like we're getting this brother–sister routine down."

When she pushes onto her toes to reach into the cabinet and my gaze settles on her ass, I bite my knuckles. Yeah, we're really getting the hang of this brother–sister thing, except I can't keep my eyes off her.

"You're totally into football, right?" She grabs a glass and fills it with water before turning to face me.

I arch a brow. "That's kind of like asking the Hulk if he's green."

"Right. It's what you hope to do for a career and what you've loved most since you were a kid."

"Yeah." I put my plate on the coffee table and lean forward, my elbows on my knees, to study her face. I'm not sure where she's going with this, but the wrinkle in her brow tells me it's important.

"Why did you leave Texas? Your mom told me you could have gone anywhere for college, that all sorts of schools were trying to recruit you. Isn't Texas *the place* to be for college football?"

"I thought you didn't know anything about football."

She returns to the living room with a full glass of water and sits by my side on the couch, one knee drawn in to her chest so she's turned to face me. "I said I didn't like it, not that I didn't know anything. Dad is a football freak. It would be hard to grow up in his house and know nothing about the sport that consumes so much of his attention. I know some, and I know that Texas is where it's at, and I know that BHU has a great program, but the Blackhawks are no Longhorns."

I grab my water and take a long drink from it before wiping my mouth with the back of my hand. "I didn't want to end up playing for my dad. I *do* love the sport. I love being part of a team and pushing my body through training. I love both the physical and mental aspects of the game." I take a breath, pondering the question that no one else since my high school football coach has bothered to ask. "Dad's been pulled around different Texas football programs since I was a kid, and staying in Texas meant there was a chance he'd be my coach someday. He's the one thing that could kill my love of football."

Grace swallows a bite of her dinner then settles her box next to mine on the coffee table. "But now he's going to be your coach in Indiana."

I shrug. "Maybe."

"You two don't get along?"

"We haven't had the chance to get along or not get along. He's never been part of my life—not in any way that counted. After I started playing ball in high school and getting some media attention, he'd call every so often and give me tips based on the footage he saw." My stomach turns with the memory of those phone calls—how excited I'd get for them at first, how thrilled at even the scraps of attention he threw my way. "Once the season ended, he'd get too busy to call—ironic, since his busiest time of the year is the football season."

"That's so shitty."

I shrug. When it comes to my dad, I don't let the facts hurt me anymore. "It is what it is. Fathers who don't bother to be dads are more common than people realize. Sometimes it feels like half the guys on any given football team were raised by single moms. Maybe that's not accurate, but it starts to feel that way when you hear the stories year after year. My dad didn't beat my mom—didn't even break her heart, as far as I can tell. I know it could have been worse."

She pulls her bottom lip through her teeth. "Just because he wasn't worse doesn't mean you forfeit your right to be angry. He failed you. And now he might be taking a job at BHU for the prestige of coaching a team *you* made great."

"It wasn't me. We have so many amazing players right now. Arrow's probably going to be the first running back picked in the draft next year, and I bet Mason will go in the first round too. I have a badass O-line, and—"

She puts two fingers against my lips, silencing me. "And they're all led by the most skilled and charismatic quarterback in the game. He's got a great arm and can chuck it down the field when the time is right. He can run, too, and can break through a hole like an old-school NFL running back."

She drops her hand as if suddenly realizing she was touching me, and scoots back on the couch. But it's not even her soft fingers against my lips that fucks with my head. It's everything else she said. Everything else I needed to hear. It's the fact that she—a self-professed football hater—cares enough to pay attention to the way I play.

I want to kiss her so badly that I don't even trust myself to speak.

"Sorry." Grace clears her throat. "I need to go get dressed. Bailey's going to be here to pick me up any minute."

I watch her clear her dishes and don't stop her until she reaches the hallway. "Grace?"

She turns and her eyes meet mine.

"Thank you for saying all that." I swallow hard. "It means a lot."

She smiles. "It's true."

"What are you doing this weekend?"

She shrugs. "Bailey and I talked about hanging out with Mia at Arrow's tonight, but I don't have any other plans."

"Don't make any for tomorrow, okay?"

She frowns. "I guess. Is everything all right?"

"Yeah." Standing, I grab my plate and pile it with my empty carryout boxes. "I just want to spend the day with you."

CHAPTER 26
GRACE

"So Keegan's uncle is a bit of an asshole," Bailey says, recapping our conversation. "But he's an asshole you admire, meaning you're willing to be his punching bag for the summer. What about Chris?"

I take a sip of my wine before setting it back on the coffee table. We're gathered in Arrow's living room while Arrow's in the basement, training. Mia has some pop music playing in the background, and we're just relaxing like girls who have been friends forever. It feels good, but I'm determined to be good tonight and not drink too much. I don't want to be hungover for whatever Chris has planned for us tomorrow. "What about Chris?"

"You're sleeping in the same room now," Bailey says from the other side of the coffee table. "I can practically smell lust in the air when you're anywhere within one hundred yards of each other."

"What does lust smell like?" I ask, dodging.

Mia shrugs. "She's not lying. There's definitely chemistry."

"I asked Mason," Bailey says, "and he insisted there aren't any sexy times happening."

"I can confirm. Absolutely no sexy times." And after my drunken conversation with him about wanting to be able to fuck guys in his room, I've been on my best behavior. As much as I didn't want to be affected by Jewel's text, I was, and I made an ass of myself in front of Chris because of it.

"It just seems like a waste to me. Ever read *Stepbrother Dearest*?"

"Can't say that I have."

She groans and smacks her forehead. "Oh my God. I'm gonna get you a copy. It's so hot. And maybe it'll help you get over any reservations you have."

I roll my eyes. "I promise that our parents being married has nothing to do with us not hooking up."

She narrows her eyes and leans back in the booth. "If it's not that, then what's the holdup?"

"Do you think people have to have a *reason* not to hook up when they're alone in a room together?"

Bailey lifts her palms. "Um, yeah."

Mia sighs. "She really does."

"I think people who look at each other like you two do should have a reason, yeah." Bailey grins. "Come on, tell me what it is."

I shake my head. "He's not interested."

"It's cute that you think that," Mia says. "But you definitely shake him up."

"Chris might have the hots for me, but he doesn't want me." Not the *real* me, at least, and damn, that sucks, because just looking at him makes me ache all over. "I'm not his type."

"And how do you know what his type is?"

I instantly think of Olivia and her dark hair and soulful eyes. Somehow, everything about her screams sweet and innocent—and that was *before* I found out the girl was majoring in early childhood education. Of course, once Chris mentioned her cheating on him, it was hard for me to hold on to the idea of her as this sweet thing who could do no wrong. If it weren't for that piece of information, I could absolutely see Chris with a girl like her. I don't know why she messed around with Keegan, but I do know the one time she tagged along with Sebastian and hung out at Arrow's with the rest of us, she looked devastated every time she looked in Chris's direction. I'm surprised no one else sees it. Then again, maybe it's so clear to me because I know exactly what it's like to want Chris and know he's dismissed you.

Bailey mistakes my silence for discomfort and holds up her hands. "I'm not pushing. Just curious."

"I heard Keegan asked you out again," Mia says. "Are you interested?"

"No." I laugh. "But, God, he's kind of adorable, isn't he?"

Bailey snorts. "Keegan? Adorable? He's kind of a manwhore."

Mia shrugs. "Adorable manwhores are a thing." She turns to me. "But I'm glad you're not interested. I think he has a thing for Sebastian's sister, and I was worried he was just trying to use you to distract himself."

"Olivia?" Bailey says. "Seriously? She doesn't seem like his type."

"The manwhore and the sweet virgin," Mia says. "It happens."

"In romance novels," Bailey says.

I bite my lip, but my laughter comes out in a snort. I'm pretty sure Olivia isn't a virgin, but I can't mention that without explaining what little I know about the Chris-Keegan-Olivia love triangle, so I don't say anything at all.

"Who is *Easy Gee-Gee*?" Mia asks, frowning at her phone. "And for that matter, who is Jewel Feldman?"

I freeze, my glass halfway to my lips, my skin going cold. "What?" My voice is small, but I swallow my fear and lift my eyes to meet Mia's. "What are you looking at?" It takes everything in me to ask the question. All I want to do is stand up and run out of here. I feel like someone stole my clothes, but instead of Bailey and Mia looking over and seeing me naked, they're about to see my past.

"This morning I posted a picture on Facebook from the pool party at Arrow's last weekend." Mia's nose wrinkles as she makes a face at her phone. "This Jewel girl just commented." She taps on the screen. "Oh, it looks like she's Facebook friends with Chris."

Bailey grabs the phone from Mia's grasp. "What kind of bitch makes a comment like this on someone else's picture?"

No, no, no. "What does it say?"

She hands me her phone, and my insides busily twist themselves into a complex origami pattern. The picture is from

Arrow's backyard, and Mia caught the moment when I was talking to Keegan, and both Chris and Sebastian were standing by our lounge chairs. Mia captioned the picture: *Friends. New and Old*, and she tagged the guys, but couldn't tag me since I don't have an account anymore.

Jewel's comment threatens to tug me down into darkness I don't want to see again, and I take a deep breath and push against that old self-loathing as I read the words the girls at Champagne Towers liked to whisper.

Easy Gee-Gee, being easy.

A nasty insult from someone whose opinion shouldn't even matter to me, but she might as well have come to Blackhawk Valley and knocked me on my ass. The nastiness is worse here somehow. In Champagne it hurts and it sucks, but I've been wrapped in this cocoon of friendship since I arrived in Blackhawk Valley. I'm *not* Gee-Gee here because no one treats me like I am. It's the difference between facing someone as they throw a punch and being kicked in the back while enjoying the sunset.

"Is she talking about you?" Bailey asks.

I lift my chin. Chris was tagged in this post. Did he see the comment? If he did, would it make him remember? Does he even know who Easy Gee-Gee is?

"Grace?" Mia says, worry softening her voice.

"When I was a kid, I went by Gee-Gee. It was a n-n-n-nickname." I shake my head but my vision turns blurry with tears. Even away from Champagne, I can't escape that ugliness. Hot tears roll down my cheeks, and I wipe them away with the heels of my hands. "So stupid."

Bailey's eyes blaze with anger. "And, let me guess, Easy Gee-Gee is what this bitch called you?"

"Not just her. A lot of people." It felt like half the high school called me that, though in truth, I doubt that many people even knew who I was. I was only at Champagne Towers for a couple of months. "I had a reputation."

Bailey snags Mia's phone back and taps on the screen. "I deleted it," she says. She continues to mess with the phone, then scowls and mutters, "Bitch." When she hands the phone back to Mia, she lifts her eyes to mine, and there's a Hallmark greeting card of emotion written on her face. "I blocked her so she can't post on Mia's stuff anymore. I'll block her from my page, too."

Mia frowns. "But this girl saw the post because she knows Chris. How does she know you? I thought you were from Maine?"

"I grew up in Champagne, but Chris and I went to high school together briefly. I had a crush on him." I'm surprised to hear myself say it out loud, but there it is.

"Oooh!" Bailey presses her hand against her chest. "I knew there was something between you two."

"You have a history," Mia says.

"No history." I draw a heart in the condensation on my glass and then wipe it away. "Back then, I overheard him tell someone I wasn't his type." That's a) an understatement along the lines of "the *Titanic* might have been somewhat sinkable," and b) only a small part of the story. Nevertheless, I'm still surprised to hear myself share even that.

Willow, who knows everything else about that night in the basement, doesn't even know what Chris said while I waited for my dad to get there.

"That was a long time ago, though," Mia says. "I don't think you should assume he feels the same now."

I can't explain how Chris's casual rejection of me is something I've carried around with me for years, something that shaped my definition of myself all through high school.

"He doesn't look at you like he's not your type," Bailey says. "He looks at you like he wants to devour you whole."

I shake my head. Chris might be attracted to me, but it's not as intense as Bailey makes it out to be. She's imagining things—seeing the drama she wants to see. I graze my fingers over the carpet again and again, focusing on the colors of the individual strands. "The thing is, Chris doesn't remember me. He's forgotten all about Easy Gee-Gee. My hair was different, and no one but my mom called me Grace." I swallow hard. "He doesn't remember me because I wasn't that important to his life, but if he saw that post, he will." I hate myself for hoping he didn't see it.

"You don't want him to remember," Bailey says.

Without looking up, I know they're both watching me. Bailey always seemed to understand me. I feel like she can see right through me, and because this whole new awesome world of mine might just fall apart at any minute, I want to talk. I want these girls who were so inexplicably kind to me from the first to understand who I am before someone else can poison their idea of me.

"No," I admit. "I don't want him to remember. I don't want him to remember Easy Gee-Gee or Juh-Juh-Gee-Gee." I lift my eyes to Bailey's and force a smile as I shift my gaze to Mia's. "Juh-Juh-Gee-Gee," I repeat. "Clever nickname for a girl who stutters, isn't it?"

"Shit," Bailey breathes.

"That's horrible," Mia says. She clicks off the music, and I let the silence stretch between us again and again, and it softens my bristly edges.

"I lost my virginity when I was thirteen." If the girls have any reaction to this, I don't see it. I keep my eyes on the carpet, examining the strands like we'd examine the clover in the fields growing up. Except there's no four-leaf clover hiding in this rug. No luck to be found. "I had a stutter and everyone made fun of me for it, including this high school kid who lived next door. His name was Isaac. He was four years older than me, a football player, and so damn cute." I take a breath. "When I got boobs, he was the first one to make me realize I could use my body to distract him from the stutter. I preferred it that way. If he was touching me, he couldn't make me feel stupid for not being able to control my speech."

"Grace," Mia whispers, but Bailey stays silent.

I feel the story jumbling inside my mouth, and I cut my eyes away and count out the syllables. When they still don't want to come out, I count carpet strands. I hit twenty before I take a breath and start again. "It didn't take long to realize it wasn't just him. All the boys at school who teased me, the ones who called me Juh-Juh-Gee-Gee, I could make them stop. If they were thinking about sex, about what they wanted from me, they would be sweet to me."

"Oh my God," Mia says. "You were just a kid."

"I made a choice. I wanted them to focus on my body instead of the words coming out of my mouth. I couldn't control my stutter, despite my mother's attempts to pray it away." Bitterness hardens those words. I needed speech therapy, not prayer, but my mother's idea of faith precludes medical interventions. *Give it to God* has always been her reason and excuse not to help herself.

"But you could control the boys," Bailey says, and when I risk a look at her, I can see she understands me better than even Willow ever did. Maybe it's her experience as a stripper that allows her to understand me on a level none of my other female friends have. After all, in one way or another, both Bailey and I have used our bodies and our sexuality to get what we needed from men. For her it was money, and for me it was a different kind of attention.

I nod. "I was in eighth grade. I stopped talking in school except when it was absolutely necessary, and I used my body to make friends. At least, I told myself they were friends. I made out with so many boys—during school, after school, under bleachers, behind garages. Sometimes we did more than make out. I loved the attention. I loved that everyone had forgotten that horrible nickname—*Juh-Juh-Gee-Gee*. It wasn't until the next year when I started high school that I realized they'd given me a new nickname. One they only spoke when I couldn't hear. *Juh-*

Juh-Gee-Gee had become *Easy Gee-Gee*. They'd never stopped making fun of me. I wasn't in control at all. Just an idiot girl."

Mia's quiet, but her lips are twisted and her brow is furrowed. I can tell this whole story surprises her. I rarely stutter anymore, and Easy Gee-Gee is a reputation I discarded like an old pair of jeans when I left Texas. I went through high school liking sex and boys, but I learned to be discriminating about whom I shared that with.

"I got a reputation in Champagne," I continue. "I earned that reputation. And it got ugly. When it got out of hand, Dad took me out of there. We moved to Maine, where I introduced myself to everyone as Grace and learned to control my stutter. High school went from a nightmare to bearable up there, and we stayed until I graduated."

They're both quiet for a few breaths, and when I can't stand it anymore, I look up to see Bailey staring at me. "They called a high school *freshman* Easy Gee-Gee? That's fucking cruel."

"I earned it." I drop my gaze to my hands.

"Fuck that. You were a child."

"I wasn't a child last summer." I lift my chin. Determined to look them in the eye while I confess this. "We went back after I graduated from high school. Dad was retiring, and that's where he wanted to buy his retirement home. I think he thought it'd be fine. I'd be going to college in the fall, and even though I'd had more boyfriends than he approved of, nothing had gotten as horrible as it had been in Champagne." In fact, my life in Maine had been so close to normal that I'd almost forgotten what it was like to be the butt of the joke. "Most of the summer was okay. People's memories are longer than Dad anticipated, but I managed okay until the end."

"What happened last summer?" Mia asks.

"Right before I left for college, I went to a party and drank too much, and good old Easy Gee-Gee came back in full force."

Bailey shakes her head. "Grace, don't do that to yourself. Don't talk about yourself like that."

"It's the only time I've ever blacked out from alcohol." My spine stiffens. "But I set out to get drunk and get laid, and that's exactly what happened. Or so they told me. I went to the party, and the next morning everyone was whispering about me. I remember enough to know I slept with Isaac."

"The boy from next door," Mia says.

I blow out a stream of air. "Yeah. And maybe that would have been fine, but Jewel was my friend, and I knew she had a thing for him. I screwed it up."

"Shit." Bailey shakes her head. "And she blames you."

"Can you blame her?"

She lifts her palms. "Of course I can. If you were drunk enough that you can't remember, this guy had no business fucking you."

"She's right," Mia says.

"You guys, if Chris saw her comment, if he sees that name, I'm sure he'll remember."

Mia draws in a sharp breath. "Back in high school, Chris wasn't one of the guys who . . ."

I shake my head. "No. He was one of the good ones."

"Well, that explains it," Bailey says.

"Explains what?"

"You started high school with a bunch of assholes who took advantage of you and called you terrible things behind your back, but Chris never did either." She cocks her head to the side, and a long lock of blond hair falls from her sloppy bun and over her shoulder. "And that explains why your heart is in your eyes when you look at him."

CHAPTER 27
CHRIS

"Where are we going?" Grace asks.

She looks so damn cute today. She's wearing this white dress with black polka dots and a pair of red Converse Chuck Taylors. The dress is strapless, exposing the top of her ivy tattoo. I've never been much of a tattoo guy, but Grace's ink is beautiful, thoughtful, and seeing a small piece of the ivy when I know there's more makes me want to unzip her dress and peel it off her so I can start at the tiny leaves on her right shoulder blade and follow it down. The way it trails around her side is emblazoned on my brain, but it disappeared into her high-waist bikini bottoms and I'm dying to see the rest. I want to trace it with my fingers. Taste it with my tongue.

"Chris," she says. "Why are you looking at me like that?"

Fuck. Because I'm the worst.

I force a smile and swallow hard. I thought I could keep my

fantasies about Grace in check, but it's getting harder every day. "I hope you don't mind doing something a little different. You're okay with being outside, right?"

"If I wasn't, I would have mentioned it when you suggested I put on sunblock." She grins at me, reminding me of the way she stood in front of me in the living room, rubbing lotion into her creamy skin. "If we're going to build a Habitat for Humanity house or something, I wish you would have told me so I could have dressed more appropriately."

I suddenly envision Grace on a ladder and I'm holding it beneath her, getting to peek up that dress. It's a pretty juvenile fantasy, but it's not a bad one. "We're not building a house," I tell her, clearing my throat. "I think you're going to like this."

The truth is, I have no idea what she'll think of my plans for our day. Her dad asked me to keep an eye on her and keep her out of trouble, and since I couldn't handle another day of Keegan eye-fucking her at Arrow's pool, I decided we should try something else.

And, yeah, maybe I want her all to myself for a day. I want her attention to be on me and her words to be for me. There are always too many people around, at Arrow's, at the apartment, at Tracy's. I want her for myself this afternoon.

We drive in silence. She fiddles with the radio, and I grip the wheel to keep myself from reaching across the console and sliding my fingers over the smooth ivory skin of her thigh below the hem of her dress. She's such a contradiction to me. Sometimes it seems like all she does is spout sarcasm, and other times it's like

I can hardly get her to speak two words to me. Maybe she's no contradiction. Maybe *I'm* the problem.

Last night after Bailey dropped her off, I couldn't get a word out of her. I tried hanging out with her in the living room, but she kept her head buried in her laptop, her fingers busily tapping on the keys. I felt like a jerk for wanting her attention when she was trying to work, so I went to bed, but I lay there awake until I heard water running in the bathroom and the soft click of the bedroom door. When she came into the room, she slid under the cover, and I actually envied the fucking sheets for getting to touch her bare legs. She tossed and turned for a while, sighing occasionally. I wanted to tell her I was still awake, but I thought she might be embarrassed to discover just how well I've come to know her insomniac sleep patterns in the last couple of weeks.

When I pull up to the gate at the state park just outside of Blackhawk Valley, Grace gives me the side-eye. "Camping?"

I hand my season pass to the attendant. "I thought we'd start with a picnic, but if you do well, maybe we can graduate to camping next time."

"I'd like that." She turns to look out her window, and I can't see her face. "I love camping."

The attendant hands back my card, and my smile falls away because now that's what I want. Camping with Grace. A fire, a few beers, our bodies keeping each other warm inside the sleeping bag, the patter of nighttime rain on the tent.

I shove the fantasy aside and focus on the road as I pull past the gate and follow the road to find the picnic area. I park the car, and Grace gives me a shy smile before unbuckling and climbing out. I grab the cooler from the backseat and follow her, damn proud of myself for keeping my eyes off the swish of her hips in that dress.

GRACE

It's as if Chris was given the role of "big brother" and he took it and ran with it. He didn't just accept that I'm going to be part of his life; he set out to do what Christopher Montgomery does with every role he's been given: be the best.

If I wanted a brother, I'd be elated. But I never wanted a brother. I did, however, want Chris.

If he saw Jewel's comment on Mia's picture, he hasn't mentioned it, and he's not treating me any differently, so I can only assume he hasn't remembered me since yesterday.

He sets the cooler on the table, and I watch as he pulls out container after container of food. One holds sandwiches, another strawberries and blueberries, another a salad that looks like it might have quinoa and black beans. The last item he takes from the cooler is a container with chocolate-chip cookies, and my heart melts. He rarely eats sugar. He packed those for me.

I take the seat across from where he stands, prop my elbows on the table, and rest my chin on my hands.

When he looks up and catches me staring, he stops working.

"What?"

I sigh dramatically. "Just thinking about how romantic this is. A picnic in the park with a cute boy."

He blinks, and I expect him to object to my choice of words and tell me this isn't about romance, that he's just trying to hang out with me like a big brother should. Instead, the corner of his mouth quirks up in a grin and that dimple appears. "You think I'm cute?"

I roll my eyes. "You know you're cute. Quit fishing for compliments."

"I might know that there are women who find me attractive, but I don't know how *you* feel about the way I look." He pulls two plates from the cooler and sets them on either side of the table before pulling the lids off the various containers.

I grab a bottle of water from the cooler and twist off the top. "You gonna pretend you need me to stroke your ego?"

"I wouldn't turn down a good . . . *stroking*."

I cough on my water. "Holy shit."

"What?" He grins. "Something wrong with the water?"

"I can't believe you just said that." I bite back a laugh and start filling my plate. "Dad called this morning. He wanted to make sure I wasn't giving you too much trouble." I'm busy avoiding his eyes by studying my food, so it's not until I look up to see why he's being quiet that I realize he's gone tense. I want to kick myself for bringing up our parents. He doesn't need a reminder of what he's supposed to be to me, and I don't want him to have one.

"I talked to Mom this morning, too," he says, his shoulders

relaxing a bit as he fills his plate. "It sounds like they're having a great time. She said she hopes we can go with them next time."

I take a bite of the quinoa and moan. "This is so good," I say, pointing with my fork.

He grins. "Careful. I think that almost qualifies as health food."

"Shh!" I shake my head and shovel another bite onto my fork. "I'm going to pretend I didn't hear that."

"You were awfully quiet after you came home last night," he says, and when I lift my eyes from my plate, he's studying me. "Did everything go okay? You didn't get into a fight with the girls, did you?"

I swallow and lick my lips. "With Bailey and Mia? No. They're great. I just wanted to work."

"You were working on the play you're writing for Gregory?" he asks between bites of his sandwich.

He's so sincerely interested, and in light of Jewel's comment last night, his sweetness makes my chest ache. "I was—" I shake my head. I always feel a little stupid talking about my projects. When I see them on paper, they seem important and so *big*, but when I try to boil it down to a few sentences, I inevitably feel like an idiot. "I was working on something else." I take a bite of my chocolate-chip cookie because this conversation requires sugar-fueled bravery.

"So you're writing two plays right now?" He props his elbows on the table and leans forward. "That's so amazing to me. All the details and characters—how do you keep them straight?"

I shrug as my cheeks heat. "It's just the way my brain works." I wave my hand by my head. "There are always too many stories running around in there, but these two projects are easy to keep straight. One is a more traditional three-act play, and the other one is a bunch of monologues tied together by a common theme." I bite my lip. The second play is one I've been dabbling with for years and have been compelled to work on since getting here this summer. I'm writing it entirely for myself, and although I sent part of it to Willow this morning, I doubt I'll ever let anyone else read it. I trust her to see the brash, unpolished, angry me that comes out in there, but it's too personal for anyone else to see.

"Tell me about the one you're working on for Mr. Gregory."

"It's called *Pinkerton and Polly,* and it's about a brother and sister who run a PI agency and end up investigating each other."

He grins. "Is it a comedy?"

I bite my lip. "I think so. I hope." Laughing, I shake my head. "Writing is hard. Just because I think something is funny doesn't mean someone else will." And then there's the fact that I keep putting it aside to work on my monologue project. If I can't keep *myself* interested in *Pinkerton and Polly*, how am I going to keep an audience engaged?

"I don't think you have anything to worry about. You make me laugh all the time."

I look up at him and feel an all-over warmth that has nothing to do with the sun beating down on us. His soft blue eyes are so kind and sweet, and I can almost imagine what it would be like to be someone else and be here on an actual date with him.

"Why plays?" he asks. "I think it's awesome, but most writers our age want to be poets or novelists, and you want to be a playwright. Do you want to act, too?"

My eyes go wide. "Absolutely not." I shudder. "No. I have no desire to be on stage. The opposite, in fact."

He folds his arms on the table and leans forward.

I take a breath and try to figure out how to explain a passion I take for granted. "When I was younger, I spent a lot of years not wanting to talk in front of people." I shrug. "I still don't like to, honestly. Public speaking is terrifying to me. But then one day, my dad took me to a play, and the characters on stage were bold and funny and unapologetic. I loved the idea that someone behind the scenes got to write those characters and give them the perfect lines and watch them deliver them flawlessly. It was brilliant. The author gets to have her say without ever speaking."

"I bet you have a lot to say."

I grin. "You have *no* idea."

His gaze dips to my lips, and my stomach flutters. "You have . . ." He points to the corner of his mouth and the slutty butterflies simmer down, ducking their heads in mortification. I bring my fingers to my lips, and he reaches across the table. Cupping my chin in his big hand, he grazes his thumb over my bottom lip. "Chocolate," he says. "Got it."

The butterflies swoon and demand mouth-to-mouth resuscitation.

"What's next?" I ask. Because the moment is awkward and charged with something I'm sure is more one-sided than those slutty butterflies want to admit.

"I thought we could walk out to the overlook," he says. He points to a break in the trees. "It's just a short walk back there. All easy and paved."

"Paved?"

He laughs. "You sound disappointed."

"I don't know." Standing, I start putting lids on containers and repacking the cooler. "I was looking at the pamphlet, and they have some cool trails. The real, unpaved kind."

He arches a brow and skims his gaze over my body—*correction,* my *dress* and Chucks. "You're gonna go hiking in *that*?"

I shrug. "It's not like it's full-length and gonna get tangled around my legs or anything."

His gaze drifts down my body again, this time landing on the thigh visible beneath the hem of my dress. "It's certainly not," he mumbles, and the way he says it has my cheeks burning and me reaching for my water.

So damn thirsty.

We finish packing up our lunch together, and after we put the cooler back in the car, I grab the park pamphlet out of the front seat. "Come on," I say, nodding in the direction of the outlook. "It's my turn to be in charge."

The park is beautiful, but as soon as we enter the woods and I see the overlook, my breath catches. From here, we have a view of the ravine below and the creek rushing through the bottom. Mossy rock faces make up the ravine walls, and trees protrude from them. It's possibly the most beautiful thing I've ever seen.

I head past the overlook and take the stairs down into the ravine. It's shady back here and feels ten degrees cooler than our picnic table in the sun.

At the bottom of the stairs, the trail splits in three directions, and when I follow the sign with the three, Chris puts his hand on my arm. "Hey, this one has ladders."

I arch a brow and drop my gaze to my shoes. "I can handle it."

Something passes over his face I don't understand, and then he sighs and nods. "Okay, but I'm climbing the ladders behind you. If any creep is going to be looking up your dress today, it's gonna be me."

My cheeks heat, and my brain instantly diagrams his words and starts analyzing the nuance of each. Just comedy or more? *Stupid brain.* "Fair enough."

He mutters something that sounds like "Dreams really do come true," but I can't be sure.

The trail leads down into the ravine and along the creek bed. It's so much cooler down here, and I love the sound of the creek rock crunching under my feet as we walk along.

There's a family up ahead—Mom, Dad, a Golden Retriever, and a little girl with a long ponytail riding on her father's back. When I turn to Chris, I see he's watching them. "Do you know them?"

He gives a bashful smile and shakes his head. "No. I just like seeing families together. You know what it's like."

"What does that mean?"

"When did your parents get divorced?"

"Oh. I was ten." I cock my head, studying him for a beat. "I'm not one of those people who thinks my parents' divorce was this terrible tragedy I had to endure. It was a good thing. My parents were miserable together, and I was grateful Mom didn't stay in some misguided idea of what was best for me."

He grimaces. "I guess you have a different perspective. Maybe I idealize the traditional family more than I should. I never had both parents around. My dad couldn't be bothered. Mom more than made up for his absence—as best she could, at least. I always had everything I needed, but it seemed like she got the short end. I'm glad she found your dad."

"Me too." I swallow hard because I feel like there's a lot he's not saying, but I don't want to push unless he wants me to.

By the time we come upon the first ladder, the family with the dog has circled back to the beginning of the trail and there's no one else around.

"Ladies first," he says, gesturing toward the ladder.

"Pervert," I mutter, but I move forward and begin my climb. The rungs are coated in mud, and when I'm halfway up, one foot slips and suddenly Chris's hands are there, holding me steady, his hands strong and warm against the backs of my legs.

My breath catches, and I force myself to breathe and find my footing. The feel of his hands against my skin causes something to swirl hot and tight low in my belly.

"Are you okay?" he asks, his voice as thick as the forest beyond the trail.

I'm not okay. I'm afraid to move. Afraid not to move. Trapped by a fear that has nothing to do with a slippery ladder and everything to do with falling.

Then, slowly, his thumbs begin to slide over my skin. His hands inch up my thighs until his fingertips skim the bottom edge of my underwear and slip under to trace the bottom curve of my ass.

I cannot breathe.

I force myself to turn my head and look down at him. His jaw is set tight, a picture of self-control, but when his eyes meet mine, his face relaxes and he shoots me a boyish grin. I attempt my best poker face. "Are you copping a feel, Christopher Montgomery?"

His grin goes wide, putting his dimples on full display. "I don't know what you're talking about," he says, his Southern accent drawing out his words. "I'm just trying to perform a necessary rescue mission."

"Do I look like I need rescuing?" I ask. Under the lace edge of my panties, his thumb strokes again, a long, slow motion that makes me want to close my eyes and moan. I resist and hold his gaze.

"Who said you're the one I'm rescuing? Maybe I'm trying to save myself." He drops his hands and grabs a hold of the sides of the ladder, then he climbs up behind me so his body is pressed against mine, my back to his front. His mouth hovers above my ear, his breath hot and uneven. "Because I swear if I have to go much longer without touching you, I'm going to implode."

His lips skim my earlobe, and my eyes float closed. My brain has no room for sight when it's overloaded with sensations. His lips on my ear. His hard chest against my back. His breath against my neck. "I need to know, Grace."

I open my eyes and swallow hard. I don't want to talk. Not right now. I'm too afraid I'll ruin this moment with my choppy stutter. "What?"

"I need to know . . ." He leans his forehead against my shoulder, and I watch his knuckles turn white as he tightens his grip on the side of the ladder.

On the ground beneath us, someone clears his throat. "You two heading up or down?"

Chris mutters a curse and takes a step down so I have the freedom to move. I scramble up the ladder with him behind me. When we reach the top, I can't look at him.

"Sorry about that," he calls to the people below, then he grabs my wrist and pulls me off to the right toward a rocky alcove just off the trail. A wooden sign tells me this is "The Devil's Ice Box," and beyond the sign, a thin waterfall drizzles into a pool of crystal-clear water. Chris leads the way, following the rocky edge around to the backside of this semi-secluded space and stopping by the waterfall. I pass him, feigning interest in the rocks and water so I don't have to meet his eyes. There's a cavern behind the waterfall, a haven from the falling water.

"I have to know," Chris says, his words nearly drowned out by the falling water. "Is it just me? Everything I feel when you're close to me? Tell me you feel it too."

Without looking back, I escape through the falling water

and shriek. I'm soaked before I land safely in the solitude of the cavern.

I'm not alone for long. Chris comes through the waterfall after me.

I'm dripping with water. It rushes down my face and my dress is plastered to me, and under here with the spray of the waterfall against our skin and the rock shading us from the sun, a chill runs through me that causes me to shiver.

Chris takes a step toward me and runs a hand over his now-wet hair. His shirt is soaked and clings to his chest.

"I don't know what you want from me," I say, but I practically have to shout so he can hear.

He stalks toward me, and his nostrils flare with his exhale. "Isn't it obvious?"

I'm not sure if time actually slows as he lowers his mouth to mine, or if he's just moving that slowly and giving me a chance to shut this down before it goes any further, giving me a chance to tell him I don't want his kiss.

After I moved to Maine, I indulged in fantasies of this moment. I imagined how good it would feel if, one day, the perfect and indelible Christopher Montgomery would want to kiss *me*. I would look him in the eye and tell him he wasn't my type, that I wouldn't want his dick anywhere near me. But that was Gee-Gee's fantasy, and today, I don't feel like that brokenhearted little girl is anything more than a character from a sad movie I watched once.

Chris wants *Grace,* not Morgan, not Gee-Gee. And I want his kiss.

I don't stop him. I don't tell him that he's not my type or even remind him that I'm not his. I wait, suspended in time, as his mouth finishes its too-slow journey. And when his lips brush mine, soft and sweet, it's like releasing a pressure valve, and all of the tension rushes out and away.

He smells so good, like soap and his aftershave, and when his lips brush over mine a second time, I let out a moan that feels like it comes straight from my chest.

"Is this okay?"

Why'd he have to ask? Why couldn't he be like every other guy and just *take*?

"Grace," he says against my lips. When I'm quiet too long, not giving the permission he seeks with my words or body, he pulls back. "I'm sorry. I shouldn't have— I didn't—"

For once, I'm not the one fighting my mouth to form the right words, and that realization tugs at me so hard I close the distance between us, loop my arms behind his neck, and press my mouth to his. He stiffens for a split second as he draws in a breath, then his hands are in my hair and his body presses against mine, and he's kissing me.

The sound of the rushing water fills my ears, blocks out the world and then disappears completely, as my senses have no room for anything but Chris—his tongue sliding against mine, his hands fisting in my hair, his strong arms cradling me and pulling me closer all at once.

I could kiss him forever—stay here, cut off from the world, away from everything else. I want the kiss to fill me so completely

I forget who I am, so that I lose myself and all I've known. I want it to erase the things I've done and wash away the girl I once was. And right now, suspended in this magical moment, it feels like it could.

He breaks the kiss before I'm ready, moving it from my mouth to the side of my neck. His hot mouth opens against that tender skin, and my disappointment dissolves under the spell of soft lips and searching tongue. He finds the sweet spot behind my ear, and when I moan, he groans and sucks lightly.

One hand drops from my hair, runs down my side, and comes back up to cup my breast. I gasp.

"Chris." I tense, surprising myself. "I can't—"

He nods as he drops his hands to his sides. "Okay."

"No." I swallow hard, not even sure what I'm trying to say or why but knowing I need to figure it out and tell him. "I don't . . . I c-c-c—" *Fuck. Slow down, Grace.* "No sex. Kissing is fine, but no sex."

His grin is slow and satisfied, and he nods before stepping close again, his mouth hovering over mine. "That's not a problem, Grace. Not a problem at all."

We stay longer than we should—kissing, touching, his hands exploring over my dress but never under, his mouth sliding down my neck but never lower. At some point, we make our way to the ground, and his body is over mine, his delicious weight on top of me.

We're both out of breath. We're both clinging and wanting more.

He pulls back, props himself on his elbows, and studies my face. "Your lips are blue." He shakes his head. "I'm one shitty date. Let me take you home and get you warm."

I open my mouth to ask a sarcastic question about whether he makes a habit of getting girls wet on the first date, but I press my lips together before the question can escape. I don't want to do that. Not to this. A girl like me doesn't get many perfect romantic moments in her life. This one's worth protecting, so I don't let myself fuck it up.

CHAPTER 28
CHRIS

The whole drive home I can taste Grace on my lips. My mind is too tangled up in the memory of her body under mine to focus on the road. I fucking *ache* for more. No girl's ever done this to me before. I was so anxious to get her home and warm and *alone* again, my hands practically trembled when I put my keys in the ignition.

She said no sex and looked at me like she expected me to argue—as if I'd walk away if kissing her wasn't going to lead to getting off. I don't know what kind of assholes have fucked with her head. All I know is that I'm willing to be whatever it is she needs, give her however much she needs, and not ask for any more than she's able to give.

When I pull into the lot at the apartment complex and park the car, she grabs my hand before I can open my door.

"Chris..." She sinks her teeth into her bottom lip, and again

I'm struck by these conflicting versions of Grace. The big mouth and the girl who's afraid to speak. The raunchy jokester who calls herself "easy" and the girl who went tense when my hand found her breast.

"What's wrong?"

She releases her lip from her teeth, and it's red and swollen, and I'm struck by the urge to lick it. "Can we keep this between us?"

Something in my gut goes cold. "What do you mean?"

"Can we not talk about this to . . . everyone else?"

It's not like we just had some one-night stand, an accident we plan to never repeat. We kissed. Exchanged touches that were damn near innocent. And she's telling me not to tell our friends. It's déjà vu, and it doesn't sit well.

"I'm not ready for them to know about whatever this is."

"And what is this, Grace?"

She shifts in her seat and looks out her window, avoiding my gaze.

I understand what she wants. I just don't understand why. "Listen, I'm not trying to push you," I say, but I feel very much like the pushy-ass man I know she doesn't need right now. "I know that you and I are complicated before we even get started, and I don't think we need to make it any more complicated by being on different pages. So, I'm asking you, what is this?"

She stares outside and twists her hands in her lap. "Do we have to put a label on it?"

"I think that would be wise, yeah," I say, and she flinches.

I rub the back of my neck. I'm royally fucking this up. "I never would have touched you today if I hadn't thought long and hard on how I feel about you. I wouldn't have kissed you if I didn't have feelings for you. This wasn't like the night at Willow's house."

"I know. It's different, and . . . I have feelings for you, too." She doesn't sound *happy* about it, but at least she turns back to me and looks at me again. I cup her jaw and stroke her bottom lip with my thumb. "It's so complicated."

"Sure, but I wouldn't have kissed you if I didn't think you were worth a little complication."

"I don't want your friends making more of this than it is." Her eyes search mine.

"Maybe I'm the one making more of it than it is." I swallow hard, choking down all of my vulnerability so I can give her the honesty she deserves. "So what is it to you? Is this the start of something that we're willing to give a chance? Or is it a summer fling?"

Is it a mistake? I don't say the last. Maybe because I'm afraid that, for her, it is.

"You don't have to answer now," I hear myself say. I don't like to let fear keep me from going after what I want, but that's what I just did. I want an answer. I want to know what I am to her and what she's willing to let this be. But I'm afraid that if I rush her, she'll shut it down before we have the chance to start.

I hold my breath and count to ten as I mentally shift gears. Because if I'm honest, I was ready to walk into the apartment with my arm around Grace and make it clear to everyone that she's mine now. "We won't tell them until you have a chance to decide what you want."

She scans my face. I don't know what she's looking for, but I hope she sees that she can trust me. "Thank you."

Maybe this is a mistake. Maybe we're just asking for trouble and drama. *Fuck.* She's here because her dad wanted me to look out for her, and I don't think this is what he had in mind. But she's had my heart in her fist since she bandaged my hand in Willow's living room. I'm willing to take a risk if it means she might give this a chance.

GRACE

Mason and Bailey are both studying in the living room when we get inside. I'm a coward, so instead of facing our friends, I go straight to the bathroom before they even have a chance to look up from their books. I strip off my wet dress and climb into the shower, letting Chris deal with the explanations of why we both came home soaked through. I know that's unfair because I'm the one who doesn't want them to know the truth.

I'm shaken by the whole day—from the way he planned something so special just for me to the gentle way he first brushed his lips over mine. If Bailey finds out that Chris and I are involved, she'll want to know if I've told him who I am. I don't think I have the courage to do that yet, but just because I'm scared to do something doesn't mean it isn't the right thing.

I run the shower long and hot, and when I climb out, I take my time moisturizing, and even swipe on a quick layer of mascara before tucking my towel under my arms to go off in search of pajamas.

I don't make it to the bedroom when I realize our friends are gone. Chris is sitting in front of the TV. His brow is wrinkled as he stares at a couple of talking heads on ESPN.

"To be honest, the Blackhawks are a big question mark for me," a bald guy on the left of the screen says.

"You can't deny they have talent," the man on the right says. "Even without Woodison, that team is stockpiled with skills. Mason Dahl at wide receiver and Sebastian Crowe stepping in for Woodison—Christopher Montgomery has plenty of targets."

"My question," the bald guy says, holding up a finger, "is can they get through the first part of the season without self-imploding before Woodison's return? With an unexpected coaching change, the Blackhawks don't need Montgomery to be their quarterback—they need him to be their *leader*."

"He's certainly capable," the guy on the right says, and I tuck my towel tighter under my arms and give a little victory fist pump. These lazy idiots sit there and make a living talking about kids who have more pressure on them than they could imagine. It's good to hear one of them stand up for Chris.

"There's no doubt that Chris Montgomery has the technical skills required of any D1 QB," the bald guy says. The camera clicks to a highlight reel of Chris throwing touchdowns and making runs into the end zone as the guy talks through Chris's stats. "But let's look at his stats in clutch situations," he says. "In the last two seasons, there have been eight games that have come down to two-minute drills where they had possession and were down by a touchdown or more. They won five of those games, which is a respectable number. In all five instances, Arrow Woodison was responsible for the play that won the game. The three times it was left to Montgomery's arm or legs, when he needed to do something phenomenal to lead his team to victory—I'm talking a Hail Mary pass or a crazy trick play—he played it safe, and as a result, the game was lost. I'm not saying they would have won if he'd gone for the impossible, but I'd like to see him *try*."

The other analyst nods. "This is a kid who has ability down to his DNA, but I agree that the film supports your assertion."

"He's so controlled and mechanical that he doesn't take the risks necessary to win those tough games. If the Blackhawks want another bowl season without Woodison in those early games, their QB is going to need to find a fire in his belly that I, personally, have yet to see."

"Who knows?" the other guy says. "Maybe if the rumors are true and Colt Montgomery is considering the job as the Blackhawks' new head coach, he'll be able to light that fire in his son."

They move on to speculations about Ohio State, and I tear my eyes off the screen to look at Chris. He hasn't moved, but his eyes are closed.

I walk around the couch and sit on his lap, wrapping my

arms around his neck.

He opens those gorgeous baby blues and scans my face. "Did you have a nice shower?"

I touch my forehead to his. "Don't let them in your head. Don't let them decide who you are. Only you get to decide that."

CHRIS

Watching sports analysts pick apart your team is always a game of Russian roulette for the pride, but knowing Grace heard what they had to say about me makes the words hurt like a punch in the junk. "Can't argue with stats."

She arches her back and presses her chest against mine. "Those so-called stats were based on three games over two years. That's bullshit, and you know it. The idea that you don't play with passion just because you don't lose your temper or your cool on the field? That's bullshit, too. You hold that team together. They don't need a hothead right now; they need you."

This girl claims to dislike football, and yet every time my football career is the topic of conversation, she seems to have the words I need to hear. "How do you know exactly what to say?"

"I only know what's true."

And just like that, the assholes on the screen don't matter. I have a gorgeous woman on my lap who isn't covered with anything more than a thin towel.

I slide my hands up her bare thighs and under the plush material, keeping my eyes locked on hers. Her tongue darts out to her lips, and I slide my hand into her wet hair and bring her mouth down to meet mine. I squeeze her hips under the towel but force them to stay put and remind myself I'm supposed to take it slow with her. I can give her slow. I can give her gentle.

I can give her anything.

Shaking my head, I slide my hand behind her neck and skim my thumb down the side of her jaw. "I didn't think you could be any sexier, but I like it when you talk football."

"Mmm, maybe I should tell you how I feel about the way these guys look in their football tights."

I grunt and lead her closer to me. "One, they're *pants*, not tights. And two, I don't need to hear how you feel about my friends' asses."

"Even if it's all good?" She smiles innocently.

"Especially if it's good," I growl.

"I should probably tell you that Keegan's asked me out a few times."

"Say what?"

"He asked during my first visit to Arrow's. But he's brought it up again a time or two."

I was teasing before, but now the jealousy in my gut is real and I'm reminded just how much I hate the idea of keeping this thing between us from my friends. "What did you say?"

"I said yes, obviously." She grabs the front of my shirt and pulls me forward. "I'm with him right now, pretending to listen to him talk while I fantasize about how sexy his quarterback looks in his football tights. He wants to invite me to his place, but I'm going to make an excuse so I can get home to this boy I like."

"Fuck yeah you are."

She giggles, but I press my mouth to hers and swallow the sound with my kiss. I've never been jealous before. Even when I walked in on Olivia with Keegan, I wouldn't describe what I felt as jealousy. I felt angry and betrayed, but not jealous.

I can't say the difference is in Grace's insistence on keeping this a secret, because Olivia had the same requirement. But it is different. I want everyone to know Grace is mine. I want to kiss her in front of my friends any time I want, and stop sneaking around as if we're doing something we should be ashamed of.

When she breaks the kiss, she's breathing hard. She leans her forehead against mine and licks her lips. "I should put some clothes on."

"Whatever you need to do." I squeeze her hips and let one rebellious hand trail up to her belly, letting my thumb circle her navel. "I like you like this, but maybe it makes touching you too easy."

She draws in a ragged breath. "You make me not want to go slow, and that's . . ." She pulls back and searches my eyes. "That's exactly why I need to."

"Anything you need is yours. Don't apologize."

But instead of climbing off me and heading to dress, she shifts to the side, leans back, and settles her head against the arm of the couch, shocking me when she pulls me with her.

As I settle on top of her, she moans. I trail my mouth down the side of her neck, finding the sweet spot behind her ear. I snake my hand between our bodies, and her towel falls open, giving me access to the soft curve of her breast. Grace is naked underneath me, making sexy little sounds every time my lips skim over her skin, arching into my touch with every brush of my thumb.

"I've wanted this from that first night," I say.

"Me too," she whispers.

"I couldn't forget about how you felt under me, or the taste of your mouth."

Just as my thumb grazes her nipple again, she yelps and pushes on my shoulders with her palms. I withdraw quickly, sitting up. And then I hear it.

The scrape of a key in the lock and the voices on the other side of the door.

CHAPTER 29
GRACE

I roll off the couch and to my feet and dash to the bedroom just as the door swings open, leaving a dazed Chris on the couch. I hear Bailey and Mason's voices as they enter the apartment, the sound of keys being dropped on the island, and cabinets opening and closing.

"I'm stealing a Pop-Tart, Grace," Bailey calls as I lean against the other side of the bedroom door.

"Go for it!" My voice is steady but my hands shake as I discard the towel and walk to the closet to find some clothes.

"Get dressed," she calls again. "Mia wants to go to the Cavern and do karaoke."

I hear the deep rumble of the guys talking, but I can't make out their words. I grab my phone to send a quick text to Willow and see I have one waiting from her.

> **Willow:** OMG. This ANGRY SLUT play is the best fucking thing ever. Send me more!

I bite back a smile. I've been working on the play for Mr. Gregory, but every time I sit down to write that, I end up wanting to spend time on the silly project I'll only let Willow read.

> **Me:** *I need to focus on PINKERTON AND POLLY for Mr. Gregory, but when I'm done, I will finish ANGRY SLUT just for you.*
> **Willow:** *I don't want to wait. (Imagine that in the whiniest voice possible.) How's Chris? Are you still dying of thirst?*

I stare at the screen and take a deep breath.

> **Me:** *He kissed me today. I kissed him back. So complicated. Don't think we'd be making out if he knew about Gee-Gee. What do I do?*

I pull on some underwear and a tank top, and I'm digging through a basket of clean, unfolded laundry, when someone knocks on the door. I figure it's Bailey, so I call, "Come in!"

Chris steps into the room and rakes his eyes down my bare legs and back up to my polka-dot panties. My cheeks heat in a flush that radiates through my whole body when he pushes the door closed with a flat palm.

"Why are you looking at me like that?"

"You've screwed up my brain," he says quietly. He stalks toward me, his eyes hot. "Do you have any idea what it's like to get turned on every time I see *polka dots*?"

I bite back a laugh, and he grins.

"It's really fucking awkward, Grace." He steps forward and hooks two fingers under the thin cotton above my hipbone, and I instinctively sway toward him. The ache I've been carrying around in my belly sinks lower and begs for attention. "But they make me think of you. And knowing even your underwear has polka dots is not going to help my problem."

"Erection via polka dots," I whisper, tilting my face up to his. "Sounds like a serious affliction."

"You have no idea." He drops his mouth to mine and presses a hard kiss there before releasing my underwear. He breaks the kiss and groans. "I have to go. Mason and Sebastian and I are going to go to Arrow's and watch game film from last year. Are you gonna go to karaoke with the girls?"

I shrug, craning my neck to look up at him. "If it's okay with my babysitter." He gives my ass a sharp, unexpected smack, and I gape at him. "What was that, Mr. Nice Guy?"

Grinning, he rubs his hand over the stinging skin and arches a brow. "I'll keep smacking your ass if you keep calling me your babysitter."

"What if I like it?"

He groans and grips my hip with one hand, taking a fistful of my wet hair in the other as he kisses me. The kiss is long and hungry, and by the time he pulls away, I'm ready to tell the world we're together just so I have an excuse to keep him in this room with me tonight.

"I want to find out everything you like," he whispers. "And I want to know what scares you so I can prove that you don't need to fear that from me. Do you understand?"

I nod.

He steps back and licks his lips, raking his gaze over me one more time before he leaves the bedroom and shuts the door behind him with a click.

It's another five minutes before I manage to get my jeans on, and then I notice the text from Willow.

Willow: *TELL HIM.*

CHRIS

The guys keep me out too damn late, and though it feels good to run plays with Arrow, I'm anxious to get back to Grace. To have her alone.

When I get home, her bed is empty. I reach for my phone instinctively, then force myself to put it on the desk without texting her. She's already giving me a hard time about acting like her babysitter, and I don't want to give her any more fodder.

But it's hard. At the very least, I want to text Bailey and find out if they're still at the Cavern, but I don't let myself. I trust Bailey not to let Grace drive if she's been drinking, and I know Bailey and Mia would never get in the car if they'd had anything to drink.

I strip down to my boxer briefs and eye Grace's empty bed one last time before climbing up to my lofted one. The minute I climb onto the mattress, I know there's someone in it.

I reach for the curtain and pull it aside. From the light of the streetlamps slanting through my window, I see her. Grace isn't still out with our friends. She's sleeping in my bed, her hair spread out on my pillow, her curves draped under my sheets. There's just enough light for me to make out the sleepy flush of her cheeks and the angle of her jawbone, the slight part of her lips. God, how I'd love to wake her up by tasting those lips. Her eyelashes don't have their usual coating of mascara, and they look almost blond.

Between the way she tensed when I first touched her today and her insistence that I understand she's not ready for sex, I'm surprised to find her in my bed. I swallow hard, trying not to think about what kind of invitation this might be. Failing.

"Grace?" I reach out to touch her bare shoulder, and her eyes flutter open. I don't want to move my fingers off that soft, pale skin. Does she have clothes on, or is she covered by nothing more than my sheets and the vine tattoo that runs along her back? "Are you okay?"

She smiles at me, her eyes half-mast. "Good," she murmurs before letting her eyes float closed.

"Is there something wrong with your bed?" I ask. "Did you

want to switch?"

She rolls to her side and murmurs something I can't make out, so I take a breath, push the curtain closed, and scoot back to the ladder. "I wanted to sleep in your arms," she says. "Stay?"

GRACE

I had planned on waiting up for him, but between the long day and the smell of him on the pillow, I felt so relaxed that it was like I melted into sleep. Now he's sliding under the sheets behind me, and I'm wide awake.

I roll over, turning to face him. "You have a good night?"

He cups my jaw in his hand and slides his fingers into my hair. "Yeah, but I couldn't stop thinking about you."

That makes my breath catch. He's so damn sweet.

"How was your night? Karaoke go okay?"

"Yeah. Mia's crazy good."

"Mmm, yeah. She really is."

I slide my hand over his chest. He sleeps shirtless, and I've fantasized countless times about curling into this broad, strong chest as I slept. Only now that I can, I don't want to sleep. "Are you sure you're okay with my no-sex rule?"

His breath catches, and he shifts to move infinitesimally closer. He sweeps my hair back before running his thumb down the column of my neck. "Why wouldn't I be? This isn't about me wanting to get laid. This is about me wanting you."

The sweetness in those words makes my heart stutter.

"I just need you to tell me what's allowed and what's not."

"I . . ." I don't know. I haven't really thought it through. I know that it's a bad idea to have sex before I find the courage to tell him the truth.

He lowers his head and presses his lips to the sweet spot behind my ear. "Can I kiss you here?" he whispers.

The ache in my chest blooms into heat, and I nod. "Yes."

His mouth opens against that tender skin and works its way down. I tilt my head to give him better access to that sensitive juncture of my neck and shoulder. He finds the hem of my shirt and toys with it. "Can I take this off?"

"Yes."

We shift awkwardly in bed, trying to maneuver enough for him to pull my shirt off in the small space. He leans back and tucks the curtain behind the footboard to hold it in place. Light from the streetlamps streams over me, and when he turns back, his nostrils flare. I'm laid out before him in his bed, wearing nothing but a pair of polka-dot cotton panties, and his eyes are all over me—taking in every inch of me as if he might not have another chance.

"Can I touch you here?" His knuckles skim over the tops of my breasts, and I shudder in his arms.

"Yes." I want to scream *yes, yes, yes*. I want him to touch me everywhere. To stop asking and start doing. I want . . .

I want exactly what he's doing. Because he seems to know

this is what I need. I don't know how or why, but he gets it. He understands this deep, secret, terrified part of me better than even I did.

"Can I put my mouth here?" he asks, scraping my bare nipple with his thumb. My nipples are so tight, they ache. "I'm dying to taste you here again."

I swallow hard. "Yes."

He sits sideways on the bed so his back is against the wall, and leads me to straddle his lap. I straddle him. His eyes darken. "Jesus, Grace, you're a dream."

And that's what scares me. I know he believes the words, but I don't want him falling for someone I'm not. "I'm no one's dream."

He laughs. "Yeah? Tell that to my subconscious. You've consumed my fantasies since you walked in the door." He kisses me, his hands tangled in my hair, our bodies pressed together. I feel the ridge of him between my legs, his length and heat through the cotton, and it's hard not to take this farther. It's hard not to fall back into old habits and fuck him just because I don't feel like I have anything else to offer.

But this isn't just any guy. This is Chris, and his kisses turn me into a wind-up toy clicking tight. Each touch makes me want to believe new beginnings are possible.

I don't know how long we kiss before he slides us down into the bed and pulls the blanket up to cover us.

"Sleep well," he whispers.

"Are you okay, though?"

He laughs. "Are you kidding? Do you have any idea how

many times I've imagined you like this? Bare? In my arms?" He swallows before adding, "Mine."

My heart aches at that word. I want to be his. I want to give him my body and beg him to never let go. But I can't do that until I give him the truth.

Tell him.

CHAPTER 30
CHRIS

A man stands at my door, staring at me like I should know why he's here. He's tall, has a head of thick, curly blond hair, and broad shoulders, and I can hardly meet his eyes without scowling.

"Can I help you?" I ask, looking into blue eyes that match the ones I see in the mirror every day.

My father tucks his hands into his pockets and runs his gaze over me. "Can we talk?"

I nod, not trusting myself to speak. "Come on in." My voice breaks on the words, like a rusty hinge that's never been used. This guy walked away from me when I was a baby. He never bothered to send me birthday cards or Christmas presents. And he certainly wasn't the one who taught me how to throw a fucking football.

I step back and pull the door open wide.

He walks through, looking around the small apartment. I don't know if he's curious about who I am, or how I live, or if this is as awkward for him as it is for me.

"You're taking the position?" I ask. I know there's no other reason he'd be here.

"We're entering negotiations, so it's all but done." He tucks his hands into his pockets and turns to face me. "I thought you should hear it from me first."

"If you're worried that I'm going to expect special treatment because you're my dad—"

"It's probably better that you don't call me that." His eyes seek out mine, something that looks like regret in the wrinkle of his brow. "Chris . . ." He sighs and hangs his head. "I came here to talk to you because I wanted to make it clear now—in private— that I think it's better that we leave things as they've been. I don't want you getting the wrong idea about why I'm entertaining the offer. This job doesn't change anything."

Everyone loves Colt Montgomery. I've read interviews with his players talking about how he wasn't just a coach—he was a father figure. For me, he's nothing but an old wound that refuses to heal, and by coming to my door to lay it out for me like this, he's ripping it open again with his bare hands. "I'm not asking you for anything."

He nods, chews on the inside of his cheek, and cuts his gaze to the couch, as if some invisible third member of this conversation is sitting there and he's waiting for them to chime in. "I have a family. I have a wife and a daughter."

"You have a *son*," I say. And I hate myself for saying it, but *fuck*, how much of an asshole can he be?

"What do you want from me? What is it that you need in your life that you think I can offer? Your mom did fine."

"You're right. She did." We stare at each other, the silence between us growing taut, like a string about to snap. "You can go."

I watch him leave—this man who isn't anything like I imagined he was, this man who didn't have any good reason to abandon me and my mom. "Selfish prick," I mutter as he closes the door behind himself.

I walk to the counter, wrap my hands around the back of a barstool, and squeeze. Grace is at Bailey's, and I suddenly wish she were here. I need her.

When I hear the door open again, I'm looking into the open refrigerator, staring at the contents and struggling to remember what I opened it for.

"Did I just see your dad leave?" Mason asks.

I shut the fridge and turn to Mason. "He's not my dad. He's nothing more than a sperm donor."

***

A day at Arrow's pool is just what I need to get my mind off my father's visit. Scratch that. What I *need* is a day hanging with my friends with Grace tucked into my side, reminding me what really matters. But since she's not ready for that, I'll settle for a day with our friends.

Sebastian's in the kitchen when I go in for a bottle of water. I grab it from the fridge.

"Montgomery," he says, stopping me before I can go back outside.

The hair on my arms stands up. When it comes to Sebastian, I'm stuck between a rock and a hard place. On the one hand, it's not like me to keep secrets from friends or teammates, and I would like nothing more than to come clean to Sebastian about what happened between me and his sister. On the other hand, I owe it to Olivia to keep the secret, even if I never understood why it was important to her. It would be one thing if we were still together, but since that ended and she still doesn't want her brother knowing, I'm not sure what good would come of me telling him. In fact, it seems like more bad would come of it than good.

Not only would he be pissed at me, but that would lead to trouble on the field. He'd want to know why we broke up, and that would cause grief between him and Keegan, too. I don't want my team torn apart because of my bad judgment. It's going to be hard enough to keep everyone's morale up with my dad's attempt to "rebuild" a team that already stands strong.

Sebastian scratches his beard and drops his gaze to the floor. "I feel awkward as hell bringing this up," he says.

Shit. "What?"

"You need to watch Keegan with Grace. I know he's interested, but I'd tell her to tread carefully."

My stomach knots at the idea of Keegan pursuing something with Grace. If she would just let me tell everyone we're together, it would put an end to that shit. I could tell him he needs to back off. But she's just as insistent on secrecy as Olivia was. What the fuck is it about me?

As much as I don't want to compare Grace's request for secrecy to Olivia's, it feels too fucking familiar. With Olivia, I never could shake the feeling she was playing me, and that it was less about her not wanting Sebastian to know about us and more about her not wanting the other guys to know. Then I walked in on her kissing Keegan, and all my suspicions were solidified. And while I don't think Grace is playing me, her reluctance to share our relationship with our friends cuts at an old scar.

"I'm not trying to start anything between you and K," Sebastian says, seeming to mistake my silence for anger. He sets his jaw. "You and I both understand that there are rules. You don't fuck with a guy's sister." He looks over his shoulder to the windows that overlook the pool area. Grace is out there, standing around in that polka-dot bikini and looking like something out of a pinup calendar. "Keegan doesn't care about that, though."

"Thanks for the heads-up." I'm not sure what else to say. Sebastian looks way too on edge, and even though I'm glad he's looking out for Grace, I'm not sure why he cares so much.

"Someone broke Olivia's heart," he says, "and I think it was Keegan. I don't want Grace to be next."

Well, fuck. "I don't think there was anything between Olivia and Keegan." It's all I can offer him, and I feel like a dick for hiding the truth that matters. If Olivia has a broken heart and it's my fault, I should stand here and own up to it.

"He was always flirting with her and leading her on, and then it stopped all of a sudden, and now she walks around the house like she's been beaten down. She won't tell me why or what's going on, but I saw the change in the way they act around each other. I just wanted to give you a heads-up." Sidestepping me, he leaves the kitchen and pushes through the French doors to the back patio.

Grace laughs at something Keegan says to her. They're side by side, stepping into the pool, and he has his smile on full voltage. I drag a hand through my hair. When it comes to Grace, I feel so fucking crazy I could pull it out.

"Are you okay?"

I turn away from the window to see Olivia stepping into the kitchen. "I'm fine."

She steps close, those sweet eyes on me. "You look upset." Her voice cracks, as if she's afraid to talk to me. Was I that big of an asshole when I broke it off? Sebastian makes it sound as if she's miserable, but I honestly didn't think she cared enough to be heartbroken.

"What is it about me?" I hear myself ask. "You didn't want anyone knowing we were together, and then you kissed Keegan like . . ." I draw in a deep breath. "Like I was inconsequential."

"It wasn't you. He'd been trying to get my attention for weeks, and that day he just walked up to me and kissed me." She puts her fingers against her lips, then drops her hand and shakes her head as if she's shaking away the memory. "But I'm glad you brought it up. I was hoping we could talk. About us."

I let out a long breath. "I don't want to go through this again. I don't have the patience or energy to rehash why you did what you did or why I couldn't let it go." Her big brown eyes fill with tears. *I'm an asshole.* "I'm sorry." *Fuck.* "Listen, maybe things could have been different, but I have feelings for someone else."

Her lips part, and a tear rolls down her cheek. "Grace?" she asks. "You're falling for her?"

"Yeah." I won't lie about how I feel. "Pretty much from the moment I met her in Texas this summer."

"Are you two together?"

I shake my head. "I don't know what we are."

A second tear joins the first, and she drops her gaze to the ground. "I see."

I drag a hand through my hair. "Listen, if you and I were supposed to be together, you wouldn't have kissed Keegan."

"He kissed me," she says, her voice creaking. "I didn't even know he was going to do it."

I smile. "Yeah, but when I walked in you were definitely kissing him back."

"I was confused. I wanted *you* to want me the way *he* wanted me."

"What does that mean?"

"I never felt like you wanted to be with me. When I said that about you never being impulsive, I meant with *me.* I wanted you to be so into me that you'd do whatever it took for us to be together." Wiping at her cheeks again, she shrugs, and I'm confused as hell.

"I'm sorry if I hurt you."

She nods. "Yeah. Back at ya. Or maybe I'm sorry you didn't care enough to be hurt."

GRACE

I smile at my reflection in the mirror above the sink in Arrow's guest bathroom. I thought my pale skin could only be white or sunburn red, but in the three weeks since I arrived in Indiana and have started spending days at Arrow's pool, I've developed a light golden tan.

I wash my hands and leave the bathroom to join my friends out back, but as soon as I step into the hallway, Chris is there. He grabs my wrist and pulls me into the dark, far corner of the hallway, pressing me against the wall before bringing his mouth down to mine.

I melt beneath him, sliding my hand into his hair, and his kiss goes from hard to sweet, demanding to tender. I've been watching him all day. I both love and hate pretending we're nothing more than friends. On the one hand, I love having the secret and enjoying the relationship without the opinions of anyone else. On the other hand, it means I have to settle for glances when I want touches.

He breaks the kiss with a gasp. "I'm losing my mind."

"I think I like it," I whisper against his mouth.

He slides one hand under my jaw, and the other over my side

and down to cup my ass. "I want you to be mine."

"I am. All yours."

"No, you're not." His grip tightens. "Not until you're willing to let them know we're together. Until then, I only get part of you part of the time."

My racing heart stutters. It's not just my past that's holding me back. Whether or not I tell him, the truth is, Chris is too good for me. I'm so scared that once we tell everyone, it's going to make it real, and once it's real, it will fall apart. Like when you dream you can fly and wake up feeling like you fell onto your mattress. I'm not ready to wake up yet. "Why isn't that enough?"

"Because it's not." He pushes his body closer and nestles his knee between my thighs. All I would have to do is rotate my hips the slightest bit and I'd be rubbing against him. "Because I want all of you."

Is it the position of his body against mine or the words themselves that makes something flare low in my belly, like the hot embers of a campfire that burned all night long?

The hand on my jaw slips into my hair. "You make me fucking crazy, Grace."

I smile, determined to keep my cool, determined not to let him see how much I want what he's asking. "I didn't think anyone could make you crazy. I thought that was what you were known for—being a quarterback nobody can rattle. Right?"

His thumb traces my bottom lip in a touch that is so faint, so light, that it sends butterflies skittering through my belly. "Why are you so set on tormenting me?" he asks. "Why don't you want this to be real? Is it because of our parents? If you're worried about your dad, I promise you I'll be the one to—"

"It's not about my dad."

"Then what is it? I want to be with you, and I want it to be real. And it's like you already have one foot out the door."

That's so far from the truth, but I can't explain without saying more than I'm ready to. "I'm here. With you."

"Yeah? Because you could've fooled me." He steps away and shakes his head, his jaw hard. "I know I said I'd play by your rules, but I'm running out of patience." He turns on his heel and leaves me. The back door clicks closed as he joins the others outside.

I close my eyes and take a deep breath to find my balance, but there's not enough oxygen in the air to make the world right itself. I can't be with Chris for real until he knows the truth about who I am, and telling him now feels like emotional suicide.

CHAPTER 31
CHRIS

I roll over in bed, and there she is. It's still dark in the room, and the clock tells me it's just after one a.m., but the realization of Grace being in my bed wakes me like sun pouring in the window. I fell asleep before she came home.

Wrapping an arm around her waist, I pull her close to me, press my nose into her hair, and draw in a deep breath. She moans in her sleep, and I kiss her forehead, running my hands down her back. I love the way her body feels, her curves and softness such a contrast to that wicked mouth.

"Hey, you," she whispers in the dark. She rolls to her side and slides a hand behind my neck and presses her mouth to mine. I'm so glad to have her here. In my arms. In my bed. Suddenly, I don't care. Right now, in this moment, I don't care about all her rules. It doesn't matter that she wants to keep this a secret. I just need her.

She slides her tongue against my lips and our mouths open

and our tongues tangle, slow and searching. I roll her onto her back, and she draws her knees up on either side of my waist, bringing my cock to nestle between her thighs. I love the sounds she makes—something north of a moan, south of a gasp, and just left of a whimper.

Her hands tighten in my hair, and if I weren't already hard, I would be now. She rocks against me. Our bodies are so close, with nothing but the fabric of her shorts and my boxer briefs between us. I kiss the corner of her mouth and work my way along her jaw, down her neck, and back up, sucking her earlobe between my teeth.

She lifts her hips again, circles, lifts, and circles, rubbing against me until I have to squeeze my eyes shut because it would be so easy to get off like this. She turns me on so much, makes me so hard, I could come in my shorts without ever getting inside her. I could get off on the simple friction of her writhing under me.

I slide my hand up her shirt, and her skin is so soft, her response to my touch so electric that I gasp right along with her as I cup her breast, as I squeeze her nipple. Everything's slower in the darkness, like we have all the time in the world. I take my time, exploring each inch of her neck, her collarbone, using my tongue and my teeth to study her skin and memorize her taste.

I can't lose her.

The thought invades my mind, and the fear that comes with it nearly makes me gasp. I'm not ready to think about that yet. I'm not ready to contemplate what happens when summer's over and she goes back to New York. I'm not ready to imagine nights without her sleeping in my bed. But it keeps coming up in my mind.

I won't ask her to stay when her dream is in New York, but I do want this to be real, and that means holding on until I can convince her to try. It means holding on until she's ready.

"Chris," she whispers.

I lower my head and kiss my way down her body, latching on to her breast over her tank and sucking on her nipple through the fabric. She cries out and rubs her hips harder against me. She arches, and I keep my mouth on her breast because I recognize the hitch in her breath, the desperate pull of her hand in my hair. Her knees tighten at my sides, and it's so easy to imagine what it'd be like to slide into her like this. How good it would be.

Then she's coming, arching, gasping. She cries out, and I cover her mouth with mine, kissing her to silence only because I know that's what she'd want. But the truth is, I want to hear it. Cutting her off is painful when I want to know every sound she makes when she climaxes. She grinds her hips and rides the wave down, breathless, her body soft under mine. All those tense muscles seem to melt beneath me, and she relaxes into her pillow.

"What was that?" she asks.

"I think it's called an orgasm," I say with a grin I know she can't see.

She laughs and swats my arm. "I know what an orgasm is."

"You sure?" I kiss her bare shoulder. "Because I'd be happy to spend some time getting you intimately acquainted with the concept if you need me to."

"I can honestly say I've never done that before."

"No one's ever gotten you off with your clothes still on?"

She shakes her head and licks her lips. "What about you?"

I shrug. "I *was* a teenage boy once. I definitely had a couple of hand jobs that ended in an unfortunately messy way."

She giggles. "No. I mean, what can I *do* for you?" She pushes against my chest with her palms, and I take the hint and roll to my back.

"Grace." She's already kissing her way down my chest, and my throat is clogged with this tangle of want and need and fucking adoration.

She curls her fingers into the waistband of my briefs and tugs them down. Then her lips are on me, and I can't fucking breathe because it's so good. The heat of her mouth, the swirl of her tongue, the vibration of her soft moan. I can't breathe because it's Grace, and this feels fucking huge, a big step I didn't expect and wouldn't have thought she was ready for.

I reach down and find her hair. I slide my fingers into the silky strands just to give myself that connection to her, to root this pleasure in our connection to each other. She takes her time, moving over me and licking and sucking and moaning until my back arches and pleasure shoots down my spine.

"Grace." A whispered warning in the dark. "Jesus. I can't . . ."

She doesn't stop, and I let go, my hips bucking, and pleasure coiling and releasing in a hot rush.

When she climbs back up my body, I draw her against me

and hold her tight. "You're so fucking amazing," I whisper into her hair.

I feel her shrug. "I give a good blowjob."

Something about the way she says it makes me uncomfortable, and I pull back, wishing I could see her better in the darkness. "Don't do that."

"Do what?"

"Don't pretend that this thing between us is just about getting off. It's not like that. At least it's not for me." I gather her into my arms and take a deep breath. "If you don't know that, then I'm not doing this right."

"I didn't . . ." Her voice cracks, and she takes a deep breath before sliding a hand behind my neck and resting her forehead on my chest. All I can do is wait in the darkness, paralyzed in that space between wanting more from her than she's offered and being terrified I'll scare her away. She presses her lips on my chest, right above my heart. "It's not just sex for me, either."

GRACE

My phone buzzes with a text alert, and I see it's from Jewel. I should delete it without looking. I shouldn't torture myself by seeing what she has to say. But ignoring it feels too much like choosing not to look at what weapons you're about to be attacked with.

I open the text and see that she's sent me a link to a video on Instagram. I watch it without sound, but I know what the girl on the screen is saying. I watch her lips as she says, "I'm gonna get *laid* tonight." I watch her sultry smile and the flip of her hair, remember Dad making me watch Jewel's Instagram post from right before I left for the party last summer. She took the video of me as we dressed for the party and posted it on Instagram as a joke.

It didn't feel like a joke the next morning. It was embarrassing.

And now Jewel's rubbing it in my face again. After I shut down all my social media accounts and left for New York, she stopped with her incessant bullying. Why is she at it again?

I close out of the video and put my phone down. "If you could start over with Mason, would you do anything differently?" I ask Bailey.

We're sitting on the floor in her living room, the soft bass of her music rolling in the background. She called this morning and asked if I'd keep her company while she studied. *"And what I mean by 'keep me company' is force me to fucking do it, because I would literally rather watch paint dry."*

I wanted to get some writing done today anyway, so I met her at her apartment at lunchtime. We shared a nutritious meal of leftover cheese pizza, and we've been working in silence since.

She studies me, her Mason-specific poker face faltering. "Everything, maybe." She drops her pencil and takes a deep breath. "Is this about Chris?"

I shrug. "My friend Willow thinks I should remind him of

Gee-Gee so he really knows who I am."

"But is that who you are?" She pushes her textbook to the side.

"I don't know. I don't think so, but then . . ." I shrug. "I can't run from my past."

She sighs heavily. "But you can't move on if you keep clinging to it."

CHAPTER 32
CHRIS

I've looked forward to tonight since we made plans a week ago.

I want Grace alone. In my arms by the fire, by the lake, under the stars.

There's a chance of rain, but when I asked her if she wanted to reschedule for a weekend with a dry forecast, she just laughed at me and told me she's not a prissy little girl. To be honest, I like that about her. I liked that when we went hiking she wasn't afraid to get her shoes muddy or walk under the waterfall. And I like that she's as excited about tonight as I am, and that she won't let a little rain scare her off. But mostly, I like that I finally get to be alone with her.

When I agreed not to tell our friends, I don't think I thought through how much sneaking around would be involved, but it's definitely getting old fast. It seems as if there's always someone around—Mason, Bailey, Mia. Even Keegan has been over more than he ever has in the past. And since I'm going to be working with Sebastian so closely in the fall, he's been spending more time at the apartment, too.

But there's always somebody around, keeping me from touching her when and where and how I want. To have one night where I can lean over and kiss her? One night where I can slide my hand into her hair and look into her eyes, or touch her arm so I can remember the feel of her skin against mine? I'm more than ready. Tonight is long overdue.

Arrow's dad has a bunch of property and agreed to let me camp out at the back of it tonight. July is popular for camping, and we were too late to snag a campsite at any of the decent spots within driving distance. And anyway, the Woodisons' property is perfect. It's more than a mile from the house, it's secluded, and there's even a lake.

"Is that everything?" Grace asks, throwing her backpack over her shoulder and looking at the packed trunk. I've set us up with a two-man tent, a cooler with the necessities for dinner and breakfast, and a couple of bottles of wine.

"You're sure you don't need an air mattress?" I ask. "We could swing by Target and pick one up."

"I can manage a night on the ground. I'm not an old woman just yet."

"Clearly." I skim my gaze over her approvingly. She's wearing a red tank top and cutoffs that show her long, pale legs and hug the curve of her ass. "No polka dots today?"

She shrugs. "Contrary to what you seem to think, not everything I own is polka-dotted."

"I like them on you." I step forward to pull her into my arms, and she tenses and looks up at the window to our apartment above.

I truly doubt that Mason is standing there watching us, but I sense her discomfort and back away. I hate that she doesn't want them to know, but I said I was willing to do this on her terms, so it is what it is. "Are you ready?"

She nods and climbs into the car. Since my aborted embrace, the air between us has gone tense with everything we didn't say. She knows how I feel. I know how she feels. Why rehash it?

As we get closer to Arrow's property, she turns to me. "Should I duck down so they don't see me as we drive by?"

"I really doubt anyone's going to be looking that closely," I say, trying and failing to keep the grumpiness out of my voice. "But if you want to, I won't stop you."

"Hey." She cocks her head and frowns. "Are you sure you're okay with this?"

I assume by *this* she means continuing our relationship in secret. "You know how I feel."

"But isn't it a little fun? Having a secret? Sneaking around? This way what's happening here is just *ours*."

I swallow hard. I want to see it her way. I do. "I don't want you to be my secret, Grace. I want them to see that you're mine."

"How caveman possessive of you."

"It's not about claiming you like a piece of property. You're not something I'm ashamed of. You're one of the most important parts of my life. Why would I want to hide that?" I cut my eyes to her before returning them to the road and see that her cheeks have blossomed red.

"You're unreal. You know that? An honest-to-God nice guy."

It seems like when Grace uses the words "nice guy," she usually says them with derision, but this time she sounds impressed.

I turn onto the property, and she squeaks and drops her head down into my lap. Her face is against my crotch, and I go hard in an instant. I swear she nuzzles my hard-on, and I growl a sound that might be her name but that sounds far more desperate.

"See?" she says. "Secrets can be fun."

I grip the steering wheel tighter and focus on the road. It's not like there's traffic back here, but I still wouldn't want to be distracted to the point of not seeing a kid wandering along.

She grins up at me as we pass the house, and I follow the lane back to a spot by the lake where we should have all the privacy we need.

When I park the car, she doesn't move her head. She lies there and looks up at me, her head in my lap, her silky black hair spread out around her face, her lips curved into a soft smile of contentment. My throat goes thick, and my heart feels as if it's caught in a fist.

"Grace?"

"Yeah?"

The words are right there, but I swallow them back before they can come out. I can't think of anything that would scare her off faster than *I love you*. So I'll keep it to myself. Even if it's true. Even if she needs to hear it more than anyone I know. I want to keep her for as long as she'll let me. Instead, I say, "Thank you for coming with me tonight."

She snakes a hand up my shirt and scrapes her nails over my chest. "Maybe I just wanted to get you alone."

"Damn straight."

She lifts her head, and I tilt down, and we meet in the middle for a soft, sweet kiss. It feels so good to kiss her out here in the light. I wouldn't give up our nights together, but I wish every significant moment of our relationship didn't have to happen in secret in the dark. Tonight, sitting around a campfire and sleeping with her in my arms, I can pretend for a minute that we're a normal couple and that this is just another night.

It's one of those kisses that feels like it could go on forever—until it's torn apart by the sound of honking behind us.

She jerks upright in her seat.

I barely have time to process that Bailey's car is coming up the drive before she's pulling in to park beside us. She looks over and waves merrily, oblivious to what she just interrupted.

A few seconds later, another truck pulls up behind her. It's Sebastian, with Mason in the passenger seat.

"You invited your friends?" Grace asks.

"Fuck no. Why would I do that? God, I love them all, but lately they're like a parasite I can't get rid of."

She takes a deep breath before pasting on a smile and climbing out of the car.

Bailey steps onto the gravel. On the other side of her car, Mia is climbing out. "Surprise!" they call.

"Sure is," I mutter. I pull the keys from the ignition and try to think up a good excuse for Grace's presence.

"Arrow told us Chris was camping out here this weekend. We thought he might want some company." Bailey's eyes swing to Grace, and then something seems to click in her mind because her eyes go wide as her mouth opens and then closes again. "Grace, I thought you were visiting a friend this weekend."

Grace leans against the side of my car and throws a glance over her shoulder. "No, Bail. That's just what I said so I could have the weekend alone with Chris."

"What?" Bailey says. Her expression morphs from suspicious to delighted, and she grins. "You two are screwing around? Seriously?"

I hate the assumption that this isn't anything meaningful, but before I can say anything, Grace says, "Actually, we're kind of dating." She turns and locks her eyes on mine. "Chris is an important part of my life."

And I'm speechless.

But Bailey's not. She's clapping and dancing in place. "I knew you two would be so good together. But oh my God, look at us! Interrupting your romantic night. Do you want us to leave? We should leave, shouldn't we?"

Grace walks around the car and wraps her arm around my waist. She bites her lip as she looks up at me. "I've never had a campout with friends."

She's so gorgeous and sweet and perfect, and right now she could tell me that she wanted our tent floating in the middle of the lake and I'd find a way to make it work.

"Stay," I say. "It'll be fun."

GRACE

Camping with friends means laughter and beer and s'mores around the fire. Camping with Chris means snuggling against his chest while he plays with my hair, and listening to Mason and Sebastian talk shit about freshman recruits.

I didn't come here expecting to share our relationship with our friends, but when I saw his face after they pulled up, I knew what I needed to do. Suddenly it clicked that I was cheapening what he was giving me by refusing to share it. I did it for him—because he deserves more than a secret fling. I took the leap and I landed in his arms.

It's late and the moon is high in the sky when Bailey pops up from her spot by the fire and stretches. It's impossible not to swoon a little over the way Mason watches her move, the way his eyes drink her in every time he thinks she isn't looking.

Mia stands, too. "Do you guys mind if I skip on the camping part and head back to the house?"

"Go sleep with your boyfriend," Bailey says, grinning. "Tell him we're counting down the days until he can join us out here."

Mia smiles. "I will."

"Are you ready to turn in?" Chris asks me after we've watched her pull away.

The night has been so perfect I'm reluctant to let it end. The stars reflect off the lake and the fire crackles. I gave my play to Mr. Gregory today, and on Monday morning he's supposed to give me feedback. *That* terrifies me. But this moment is warm and peaceful. I feel safe and more myself than I ever have in my life. Somehow, someway, I've found myself in this short summer with these strangers.

"Go to bed," Bailey says, as if reading my mind. "Grace, if I have to watch him make eyes at you for another minute, I'm going to fuck him myself just to put the poor boy out of his misery."

Laughing, I climb off Chris's lap and out of the camp chair. I use a bottle of water to brush my teeth and settle for a wet washcloth for my face. When I return to the tent, Chris is propped up on pillows, his chest bare and his legs stretched out over a pile of blankets, a battery-operated lantern next to him.

Straddling him, I trace my fingers down his chest. I'm addicted to the sight of his muscles under my hands. Too often we're in the dark, and I don't get to see it enough. I love the heat of his skin under mine and the way he watches my eyes as if he's waiting for my secrets. I love that I'm beginning to believe that my secrets might not matter.

I want to be with him in every way. I want to give him everything I can.

I dip my head to kiss him, and he takes my shirt in his hands and slides it up my sides. I lift my arms over my head as he pulls it off, and then we kiss again, his hands on my waist, his thumbs skimming the underside of my breasts.

"Whoa!" From outside the tent, Bailey clears her throat. "If you don't want us to see the silhouette of everything you're doing in there, you should probably turn off that lantern."

Chris flinches, and I laugh. "Thanks, Bail."

"Any time, chica. Now get yours."

Chris hits the switch, and the tent goes dark. "One of these days, I'm going to touch you in the light of day so I can fully appreciate how fucking beautiful you are." He pulls back the covers and slides down into our makeshift bed. "Come here."

I swallow hard before fumbling in the darkness for my bag. I unzip it and find what I'm looking for before joining him under the covers.

Outside the tent lanterns are snuffed out, and Bailey calls, "Goodnight. Sebastian and Mason won't have a threesome with me, so we're all off to our tents *alone*."

I bite back my laughter and feel Chris's chuckle against my neck. "She doesn't mean it," he says. "Mason and Sebastian both know that."

"I know." I sigh in the darkness.

"I think she feels like she can't be with Mason because of how their relationship started, but I don't think I've ever seen him as infatuated with anyone as he is with her."

"It's not infatuation," I say softly. "It's love. He loves her, and she can't accept it because she doesn't understand how a guy like him could love a girl like her."

Chris rolls us so I'm under him and he's on top of me, his weight on his palms. I can't see his face in the darkness. "She needs to stop doubting her own worth and accept what he's offering," he says. He presses small kisses to the side of my neck, both teasing and restrained.

I shift under him, parting my legs and bending my knees and bringing them to either side of his hips. He's hard, and the weight of him between my legs causes a physical ache to tangle with the emotions in my chest. "Maybe she's scared he'll realize she's not good enough for him. Maybe she believes he deserves better."

"Better is irrelevant when your heart belongs to someone else." He cups my face and kisses me, long and sweet. "You know I'm not talking about Mason and Bailey anymore, right?"

"I was hoping," I whisper. It's as if he's opening his cupped hands to show me my own heart, proving it's still intact, showing me he can be trusted to protect it. "You don't know who I am."

"Then show me."

"I lost my virginity when I was thirteen."

He kisses my neck. "That doesn't change how much I want you now."

"I've slept with six guys since then. I'm safe. I mean, I've been tested, but . . . yeah, six."

"Six guys foolish enough to lose you."

I'm Easy Gee-Gee and when I was fourteen, you said you'd never put your dick near me. I will my lips to say the words, but I can't. I don't want to be Gee-Gee anymore. I don't want to invite her into this tent or let her be a part of this moment.

His lips sweep down the side of my neck. "I don't need you to be perfect. I just need you to be mine. You're the only thing I want." He slides down my body in the darkness, kissing his way over my belly with a hot, open mouth, then kneeling between my legs and pressing his tongue against my center, licking at me through my panties. I arch into that wet heat, wanting closer, more, again. When he pulls back, he skims over me with his knuckles. "Let me kiss you here."

After feeling his mouth on me, I couldn't refuse him if I wanted to. I lift my hips, and he pulls off my underwear before settling his face back between my thighs.

His touch is tender at first. The stroke of his fingers over my clit, the slide of his tongue around my heat. He unfurls something inside me—with his tongue, with his touch, with his patience. He's the heat of the sun coaxing the flower to turn her head and open her petals. He's the rich soil beneath my feet, keeping me rooted in this body and this moment. Bit by bit, I come unraveled, and he seems to as well. His tastes turn greedy, his licking and sucking more demanding before he finally slides his fingers inside.

I have to bite my lip to keep myself from moaning, but sounds slip through anyway, and as I squeeze around his fingers, he covers my body with his again and kisses me to silence my moan.

"Tomorrow," he whispers in my ear as he slides his hand from between my legs. "I'm keeping you in bed with me, and I'm finally going to see your face when you come."

I feel around on the blanket beside me until I find the condom I retrieved from my bag earlier. "Here," I whisper.

He's silent for a breath, and I hear the crinkle of the wrapper as he tries to figure out what he's holding. "Is this . . .?"

"I'm ready."

His sudden, ragged intake of breath is so damn satisfying I can't help but smile. "You're sure?"

I want to be brave but I'm scared. Not scared of the sex, but scared of what it means. And terrified that what I feel for him is so strong I'm willing to ignore that fear. "So sure."

I watch his silhouette in the darkness as he sheathes himself and then lowers over me. He hisses through his teeth as he settles between my legs, and maybe I do too because it feels so good, and I've been wanting this for so long.

His strokes are slow and steady and he kisses me while he moves—my mouth, my neck, my shoulder—his hands sliding everywhere, touching every part of me they can.

He whispers in my ear, telling me I'm beautiful, that it's so good, that he's thought about this so much. He moves and whispers and kisses and touches.

At first, I don't want him to be so tender. I don't need him to treat me as if I'm as fragile as blown glass. But every second that passes under his tender touch, I become that fragile. His sweetness sweeps away my shell and makes me breakable.

And then he shifts his hips and bends to take my nipple between his teeth, and I'm not just breakable, I'm shattering, a thousand glittering pieces on the blankets until he kisses, strokes, and praises in quiet whispers, and puts me back together again.

When he comes, his face is buried in my neck, his hands tunneled into my hair.

It occurs to me that after all the guys I've slept with and all the times I've let a man inside me, this is the first time I've made love.

CHAPTER 33
GRACE

On Monday morning, I wake up to the sun slanting in the bedroom window, the sheets tangled around my legs. I'm alone in Chris's bed but not lonely. This summer is turning out okay after all.

I need to get up, get dressed, brush my teeth, and grab something to eat before I head in to BHU to hear Mr. Gregory's thoughts on my play. I'm on such a high from the weekend that it numbs my nerves about getting his feedback.

I grab some clean clothes and rush to the bathroom for a shower. I make it quick, dry off, pull on my clothes, dry my hair, and brush my teeth. Chris is meeting me back here for lunch, and when I catch myself fussing with my hair in the mirror, I want to smack my own hands. I'm not gonna be that girl. Chris can like me as I am or not at all.

I'm such a liar.

I get to campus with plenty of time to do my morning coffee run before Mr. Gregory's arrival, but when I return, I freeze just steps inside the office.

Mr. Gregory is sitting at his desk with my play in front of him. I recognize the black-and-pink folder I used when I gave it to him before the holiday weekend. But he's scowling at it. That's ... not good.

"Mr. Gregory? I have your coffee." I force myself to walk over to him and keep my eyes off the notes scribbled onto my play.

He takes his coffee in one hand and with the other, he picks up my play and tosses it over his desk. It lands on the floor, and papers scatter everywhere. "Do me a favor," he says. "Go burn that drivel."

My stomach clenches, and my whole body goes statue still. I couldn't have heard him right. He wouldn't have asked me to write for him if he was going to say something so cruel. "What?"

"Burn that crap. Don't cling to mediocrity because you're scared of something good."

"You didn't like it?" *Stupid question, Grace.*

"It's a waste of everyone's time. Mine. Yours. Anyone with enough brain to know there are better ways to spend their time. There is absolutely nothing remarkable about that play."

I can't decide if I want to crumple into a ball and cry or scream at him for being so cruel.

I don't know what to say, but it doesn't matter because after that series of blows I can't catch my breath anyway. It hurts too much to draw air into my lungs.

He pulls a bottle of whiskey from his bag and adds some to his coffee. "Try again," he says, not looking up at me.

Why? What's the point? That play is the best I could do. The best I had to give. And his reply was that I should "burn it." I'm kidding myself. What's the point in trying again?

I stare at him. I was really proud of what I created, and his reaction doesn't just hurt—it has my dreams by the throat. It's scary to stand here and know I'll never write something good enough to impress him. It's terrifying to know that my very best is still mediocre.

Maybe all I have going for me is a pretty face.

He snarls, as if I've insulted him. "Quit looking at me like I just kicked your puppy, and get to work." He waves a hand toward the door, dismissing me.

As I leave, I want to tell myself that he's a stupid old drunk, that his ego is getting in the way of him seeing my talent, that he's putting me down to make himself feel better about his own inability to produce.

I want to tell myself those things, but I don't believe them. I want to believe that the pride I felt for that play came from my confidence in it and not from naïve *hope* that hours and hours at my keyboard would be enough. I knew all along that my play lacked the magic that brought me to playwriting to begin with, that there was nothing particularly remarkable about what I created. There's nothing particularly remarkable about me.

I leave his office and rush down the stairs, out of the department, and straight home. All I want is to see Chris. He'll pull me into his arms and quiet this ugly voice in my head.

But when I get to the door, I hear three voices inside the apartment. He's not alone.

The door's unlocked, and when I step inside, I find three guys are sitting around the coffee table. Mason's in the chair and Chris is on the couch. Another guy is beside Chris, his back to me.

Chris looks up first, and I love how his face softens when he looks at me, how the corner of his mouth draws into a crooked smile. "Good morning."

My cheeks heat because that smile makes me think of last night, the way his hands moved over me, the way he moved inside me. "Morning."

"How'd you sleep last night?" Chris asks.

Mason clears his throat. "Not much, from the sound of things."

Chris narrows his eyes at Mason. "Seriously?"

Mason holds up his hands. "Got it. Not another word."

The other guy looks up at me, smiling and extending a hand, then his smile falls away and so does mine. "Gee—"

"Grace," I say, shoving my hand into his, and I plead with my eyes for him to keep his mouth shut. All the happy warmth I felt under Chris's smile fizzles away.

"Yeah. Jewel told me you were living with Montgomery." He grimaces. "I don't know if you've heard, but we're together now. She's been fucking beside herself knowing you and I would be in the same town this summer. She's a jealous one, all right."

That's why she's been harassing me all over again.

Isaac shifts his eyes back and forth between Chris and me. "Are you two . . . ?"

Fuck. Fuck. Fuck. Fuck.

I want to curl into a ball. I want to run away. Hide under the covers, under the bed, in the back of a cold, dark cave. At the beginning of the summer, I told myself that I didn't care if Chris knew who I was. I told myself letting go of the past meant I didn't have to tell him, that I was strong enough to bear the burden of the memory so he wouldn't have to. But here I am, seconds away from him discovering the truth, and I don't feel strong at all. I want to hide.

"You two know each other?" Chris asks. He shakes his head. "Right, high school. Grace remembers me, and I feel like such a dick because I don't remember her."

I swallow hard and bow my head. I can't look Isaac in the face.

Isaac clears his throat and laughs awkwardly. "Yeah, I remember Grace. I'm surprised you don't remember, Chris."

Why is he here? Is this some kind of joke? Did Jewel send him to make sure I couldn't escape my slutty past?

I can't bring myself to look up to see either of their facial expressions. Is something clicking for Chris? Is he remembering?

I set my jaw and stride toward the coffee pot. I grab a travel mug from the rack, fill it, and slam the lid on with more force than necessary.

"What's wrong, Grace?" Chris asks.

"I have to get back to work," I lie. I don't need to be there again at all today unless Mr. G summons me. "Can't do lunch."

"Okay."

I dump some cream and sugar into my coffee and push out the door only to find Chris on my heels. He closes the door behind me and grabs one of my wrists, then the other. He tugs me back to him.

"I'll let you go, I just . . ." He cocks his head and studies my face. "What's wrong? Is this about this weekend? Please don't freak out." He cups my jaw. "We can slow down. Back off. Whatever you need."

No. It's not about what we did this weekend. It's not about how special he made me feel or how sweet he was when he touched me. "I'm just in a bad mood," I say, stepping back. "Why would you assume it's about sex? I'm not some fragile girl who's just lost her innocence and is going to cling to you now." *I'm not Olivia.*

He frowns, still studying my face like there might be answers there, and I do everything I can to make sure he finds none.

I feel terrible. My words are ugly and it's all because I'm scared of how he'll feel about me when he sees me for who I am. "I've gotta go."

He releases me. "Okay. Have a good day and call me when you get off, all right?"

"I have plans," I say. "I'll text you or something."

I turn on my heel and leave. I'm running and I hate myself for it, but I have no idea what the alternative is.

CHRIS

I watch her walk away and have no fucking idea what I did. It's not like she's always warm and fuzzy, but things have been different between us. She's softened in my arms. And I liked seeing that side of her—vulnerable and open. I liked having a minute when it felt like she wasn't throwing up a bunch of bullshit to keep the world from finding out who she is. Or maybe I only wanted to believe she was letting me see the real Grace.

When I go back into the apartment, Mason gives me a hard look and nods toward Isaac. "Maybe you two should talk?" he says, and then he excuses himself to the bathroom. Seconds later, the shower kicks on.

Isaac leans back on the couch, his dark eyes steadied on me, and I take a seat in the chair. "What's going on?"

And then it clicks. When Grace's mood changed, when that softness left her face, it was when she saw him. He's part of Dad's staff, a recent athletic training graduate who interned with Dad and will make the move to BHU. The guy always rubbed me the wrong way, but we played ball together for a few years in Champagne, and when he invited himself over today I didn't feel like I could say no. I would have found a way if I'd realized how much him being here would upset Grace.

Shit.

"How well do you and Grace know each other?" I ask. I don't want the hardness to be in my voice, but there it is, showing my irritation, making me sound like some jealous boyfriend who can't handle the idea of his woman having ever slept with another guy.

"You really don't remember her from high school?" Isaac asks.

"No. But obviously you do."

"She's hard to forget." He holds up his hands. "Sorry. You probably don't want to hear that if you two are, like, together now." He pauses a beat and cocks his head to the side. "*Are* you? Together, I mean?"

I don't know what we are, but I certainly don't want to get into it with this guy. "Does it matter?"

He laughs and stands, sweeping a hand through his dark hair. "Interesting. It's not that difficult of a question. But I guess that's the way she is, isn't it?"

My gut churns, but I don't let myself reply. I hate the idea that this asshole might actually know Grace better than I do.

"Coach is going to watch the team practice tonight. Don't be late. If negotiations go well and he signs, nobody can take their position for granted."

I set my jaw and hear it crack. "What's that supposed to mean?"

He lifts his palms. "I'm just trying to be a good friend."

CHAPTER 34
CHRIS

My father watched the team practice tonight, just as Isaac said he would, and I swear I could feel his eyes on me the whole time—evaluating, judging, calculating. The idea of him being anywhere near my team, let alone in charge of it, makes me want to throat-punch every member of the administration who's working so hard to woo him to Blackhawk Valley. It didn't help that my heart wasn't in it and I kept screwing up plays. Sebastian was inexplicably missing, leaving me with a sophomore idiot at running back who couldn't remember when to block and when to take a shuffle pass.

When I get to the locker room, the indicator light on my phone is blinking, and I reach for it, hoping for a message from Grace.

Before I can read it, someone grabs me by the shoulders and spins me around. I see Sebastian's face for a split second before he throws me against the lockers and swings. His fist meets my jaw with a *crack* that sends pain reverberating through my face and all the way down my neck.

"Whoa!" Keegan wraps his arms around Sebastian's chest and pulls him back. "What the fuck?"

Sebastian's dark eyes blaze, his nostrils flare, and anger rolls off him like heat off a bonfire. "I thought you were better than that. I fucking trusted you."

My hand goes to my jaw. *Son of a bitch.*

Keegan meets my eyes over Sebastian's shoulder, and it clicks. This is about Olivia.

I swallow hard and stand up straight as I rub my sore jaw. "I'm sorry I didn't tell you, but she didn't want me to."

Sebastian charges for me again and makes it a few steps before Mason helps Keegan pull him back. "She's my sister."

"I know," I mutter. "I'm sorry." Behind the guys, I see the locker room door open, and my dad meets my eyes before leaving. What the hell was he doing in here?

"Are you? Are you sorry enough to do the right thing now?" He lunges for me again but doesn't get far with the guys holding him.

"It's over, Sebastian. It's been over for weeks."

"Yeah, I knew some asshole hurt her. She's been moping around with a broken heart and refused to tell me who hurt her. I thought you were supposed to be a good guy, Montgomery."

Keegan's blue eyes are locked on mine. He's waiting for me to throw him under the bus, but I won't do it. Sebastian will only be pissed at us both, and it will tear the fucking team apart. It won't help anything, and now that I have Grace, I'm glad Keegan did what he did. Olivia and I were never going anywhere. Her insistence on secrecy aside, we didn't have the connection I once thought.

"You have every right to be mad at me, but I swear to you it's over." I don't have the patience for this shit tonight. Sebastian's reaction is unnecessarily dramatic for something that ended almost three weeks ago and was never much of anything to begin with. I turn to my locker and throw my gear into my bag.

"It's not over," Sebastian says behind me. His voice is softer now, some of his anger gone. "Not if she's pregnant."

GRACE

I stare into my lukewarm latte, searching for answers in the foam that I know I won't find. I don't want to go back to Chris's apartment. It's not that I thought he'd never find out or that he'd be happy about who I am. Honestly, I didn't let myself think about it at all. I was enjoying being *his Grace*.

I can't stop imagining the look on his face when he finds out. Will he turn pale? Will disgust make him run for the bathroom? Maybe he'll shudder, knowing he touched someone as used and vile as me.

So here I am, hanging out in a coffee shop with a cup of coffee

I won't drink, avoiding my bed, my room, and my roommates.

My stomach is a clenched fist, free falling and lurching into my throat all at once. My phone started buzzing a few minutes after I left and hasn't stopped since. He's texted five times to ask if everything is okay.

I can't do it. I can't face the fact that it's time to tell him the truth. I want to remember the way he looked at me this morning, the softness in his eyes. I want to remember the way he held me in his arms last night and whispered in my ear. How could he look at me the same way after learning the truth? I'm such a coward.

I feel so helpless that I want to scream. It's like when the villain in the movies sets a bomb and you know at any second everything's going to be blown to bits. Isaac's arrival is going to destroy the little life I've made here in Blackhawk Valley, and instead of figuring out how to cut the wire at the last minute, I want to run.

"Grace?"

I look up and see Olivia standing in front of my table. Her eyes are red-rimmed and puffy. "Hey."

She gestures to the seat across from me. "Mind if I sit here?"

"Knock yourself out." I don't want to be rude, but in this moment, Olivia is the last person I want to see. Isaac's presence has forced me to look in the mirror and acknowledge who I am. Since I know that person isn't good enough for Chris, it's hard to sit across from someone who threw away her chance with him for nothing.

"Are you gonna drink that coffee or stare at it all night long?"

she asks.

"I'm actually enjoying staring," I admit. I can't look her in the eye, so I study my coffee instead. "It's short a couple of shots of Baileys Irish Cream."

"I didn't cheat on Chris."

I lift my head. "What?" *Why is she telling me this?*

She sniffles and shakes her head. "Oh my God, it was so stupid. Keegan kissed me. I let him, but I didn't sleep with Keegan while I was with Chris." She shakes her head. "I wish I could go back, but I can't, and now . . ." She shifts her gaze from side to side before bringing it back to me. "Sebastian says now Chris is with you. Is that true?"

I squeeze my eyes shut. I don't know how much longer we'll be together. My omissions hang over me like a rumbling storm cloud.

"It's not my business. I know it's not. I lost him." She draws in a ragged breath. "And now he's with you while I . . . I haven't had my period in seven weeks."

I clutch my coffee and draw it against my chest as if its heat could save me from what she's saying. Mentally, I calculate the timeline. Seven weeks ago, Chris was still with Olivia. And they were five weeks ago too, which means that two weeks after her last period, they were still sleeping together. Mathematically speaking, if she's pregnant, it could be his.

"Everyone loves you." Tears roll down her pink cheeks. "They're not going to love me when this comes out. I'm going to tell Chris tonight because I know he'll want to know. Would you tell the girls that I told you first? I don't want them to hate me."

My words are clutched in a vise at the base of my throat, so I can only nod and watch as she stands from the table and leaves.

When I'm alone again, my mind races through the implications of what I just learned. Chris's goodness, his insistence on always doing the right thing, his disappointing past with his absent father. His world is about to be turned upside down, and all I can do is make sure I don't add to the wreckage.

CHAPTER 35
GRACE

The Gossamer Inn isn't just the nicest hotel in town—it's the only decent hotel within walking distance of the university. It doesn't take a genius to guess this is where Colt and his staff are staying while they're in negotiations with BHU administration.

When I step into the lobby, I go straight to the reception desk. I smile at the petite blonde behind the counter. "I'm here to see Isaac Owens. Could you call him and ask him to come down?"

She arches a brow, and her gaze drifts to my bare shoulders. She takes in my tattoos before she picks up the phone. "Your name?"

"Grace Lee." I grip the edge of the desk. I'm not going to turn around. I'm not going to let my fear of facing the past rule me.

She puts the phone to her ear and dials. "Mr. Owens? This is the front desk. There's a Grace Lee here to see you." She smirks at me. "Okay. I'll send her up." She hangs up and points down the hall toward the elevators. "Third floor, room 308."

I freeze. I'd envisioned having this conversation in the lobby.

"Is there a problem?" she asks.

I know Isaac really well. Not only did we grow up next door to each other, and I spent a lot of time in his bed when I was young, but I also have a history of really bad judgment where he's concerned.

You're not that girl anymore.

"No problem." I turn to the elevator and jab the button to go upstairs before I can lose my nerve. I have to think about Chris.

When I step off the elevator, Isaac's standing with his door open, and my squeezing, lurching stomach turns sour. I've been so naïve. By relocating across the country, Dad didn't save me from my past. He only removed me from it. And I couldn't run from it by coming here this summer. It might not be who I am now, but it's part of what made me who I am.

"Hey, Isaac."

"Gee-Gee." He rakes his gaze over my pink dress, making me wish I'd changed into something less flashy.

"It's Grace."

"Right. You're sophisticated now. A sophisticated name to go with your sophisticated football player boyfriend." He grins. It's a good-looking grin on a good-looking guy—nothing compared to Chris, of course, but he's still the cute boy from next door I always wanted to impress, the one all the girls at school thought was so charming. This is a guy who's known me forever. He doesn't look at me and have any illusions about who I am. "Damn, you're a sight for sore eyes. Your hair looks great that color. I liked you as a redhead, too, but the black is nice."

I ignore the compliment. Isaac has a way of leaving a trail of compliments that lead right down a rabbit hole, and I'm not making that mistake again. "We need to talk."

He arches a brow and folds his arms, leaning against the doorjamb. "I thought that's what we were doing?"

"No. I want to talk about Chris, and about . . ." I wave a hand between our bodies. "About our past."

He motions into his room. "After you."

I straighten my spine and step into the room, setting my purse down on the table by the door.

Behind me, I hear a male voice in the hallway. "You staying in tonight, Owens?"

"Oh yeah," Isaac says. "An old friend came to visit. I'll see you in the morning." He steps into the room, letting the door swing shut behind him.

The hotel room is a decent size—a suite with a couch and a big-screen TV. There's a kitchenette and a tiny refrigerator, and Isaac kneels in front of it as he mixes drinks into two glasses.

"I won't stay long," I say when he hands me a tumbler of brown liquid. "I'm not here to drink."

"Suit yourself," he says, and takes a drink from his.

I sniff it. From scent alone, I'm guessing it's Coke and some sort of whiskey. "What's in it?"

"A dash of happy and a shot of don't-give-a-damn." He raises his glass. "Cheers."

"Just what the doctor ordered," I say. I bring it to my lips as he drinks. When it touches my tongue, I hesitate and lower my glass without swallowing. Isaac's turned into a decent guy, but I'm here to keep him from making Chris's life any more difficult, not to hang out with an old drinking buddy. I take a seat on the couch and rest my glass on the end table. "You didn't tell Chris who I am, did you?"

Isaac takes the spot beside me, sets his drink on the coffee table, and turns to face me. "It wasn't my story to tell," he says softly.

"He doesn't remember me from high school."

"Or he won't let himself."

I frown and try to draw in a breath, but it feels like my lungs are trapped in a cage that won't let them expand. "What's that supposed to mean?"

"He doesn't want to think of you like that." He grunts. "Some guys can't handle the idea of women having experiences with anyone but them, I guess. In his case, ignorance is bliss."

"He's got some stuff going on." I pull my bottom lip between my teeth. I don't want to share too much of Chris's personal situation with Isaac. Or maybe I don't want to say it out loud because it makes it too real. *His ex-girlfriend might be having his baby.* "I don't want him to have to deal with my baggage on top of everything else right now."

He shakes his head. "Don't worry about it. I'm sure he'll get over it with some time."

Get *over* it. I don't want my past to be something Chris has to get over, but those old words haunt me. *As if I'd put my dick near that.* Five years later, and a couple weeks as the object of his affection, and the memory of those words hurts as much as ever. Maybe more. "I hope so." But maybe he won't need to find out until after I go back to New York. And maybe by then he'll be so wrapped up in Olivia that he won't care anymore. "It doesn't really matter."

Isaac rakes his gaze down my body slowly before bringing it back up to meet mine. "You're special, Grace. And if Chris can't see that because of something you did years ago, that's his loss." I want to defend Chris and explain that it's not that simple, but before I can get out the words, Isaac continues, "I always hoped you'd give me a chance someday. Not just a chance to mess around, but something real." He shakes his head and ducks it. "But I kind of fucked that up last summer, didn't I?"

"I never intended to sleep with you," I tell him. I feel courageous for bringing it up. I've always avoided talk of that night, as if silence could erase the mistake.

"I shouldn't have let it go that far. You were all over me, though, and . . ." He sighs and lifts his palms. "I wish I could say I was a better man. Fuck, Grace, you're gorgeous."

"I was *drunk*."

"I guess I didn't realize how much you'd been drinking. I was pretty wasted, too. Sadly, I can't even remember most of that night." He grimaces. "Can you forgive me?"

"I never blamed you." It's true. When rumors started

circulating the next day, Dad gave me the speech I knew well. I shouldn't have had so much to drink. I shouldn't have gone out looking for trouble.

He cocks a brow. "So if you get over your broken heart, you'll keep me in mind?"

"You're with Jewel now," I remind him.

He sighs heavily. "Jewel. Yeah. She's great, but she's no Grace Lee. What about you and Chris?"

"It's complicated."

"Because he's your brother?"

If he asked me this yesterday, I would have rolled my eyes. Instead, the question reminds me that in Chris's mind, that's the only thing that's kept us apart. He doesn't know the half of it. "I promise you that's not it."

He'll be better with Olivia. They can have a normal relationship and a normal life, and she won't have a crazy past that'll haunt them both.

The idea leaves me hollow. Stepping away from Chris is emotional suicide, a sacrifice of the girl I want to be for the sake of the life he deserves.

"It's something," he says. "There's something that brought you here instead of going straight to him to tell him your secret." He skims his knuckles over my bare knee in a touch that might be friendly or might be more. "I don't think we're going to have a problem, though. You've always been good to me. I'm happy to return the favor."

Confused, I move my leg away from his touch and press my

knees together. "That's not why I'm here." If he thinks I came here for sex, that's my fault, isn't it? He learned from my patterns.

"Come on, Grace. You don't have to worry," he says, his voice low. "I won't tell Chris. I won't tell him anything you don't want me to. About the past or about tonight." His hand slides up my skirt. I scoot back on the couch, away from his touch, but his big fingers wrap around my thigh and he shifts onto his knees so he's looming over me, a knee on either side of my hips. "Shh. It's okay. It'll be our secret. Fuck, you're gorgeous. I'm so fucking glad you came over."

A burst of adrenaline hits my blood and I shove him off me and roll over in one quick motion. He hits the floor.

"Fuck!" He grabs the back of his head. I recognize the anger in his eyes, but I don't care. It's not my job to make him happy, and I couldn't give two shits whether or not he likes me. I'm so far beyond that. "What was that?"

I hop off the couch, look around, and grab my purse. "Jesus. Do you think it's okay to touch girls whenever you want? Fucking seriously?"

"You came up here looking for it." He rubs the back of his neck. "Why the fuck else would you be here, Grace? You and I both know what you're looking for any time you get around me."

Does he really believe that? Is that what I made him believe? The idea makes me sick to my stomach and feeds this festering wound of guilt and self-loathing. I shouldn't have come up here. I should have said my piece downstairs and left.

Dad sent me to therapy for a few years after what happened in high school. One of the therapist's biggest goals was to convince me I always have the right to say no and put a stop to a situation. She made it sound so simple, like social expectations and what people will think of you don't factor into our lives or choices in any way.

I try to harness that simplicity of taking control. Right here. Right now. Regardless of what I said or did tonight or any night before, I don't want his hands on me.

I shake my head. "I didn't want you to touch me, and it's not okay." I head for the door.

"Jesus, Grace. Why are you being such a bitch about this? What happened to Easy Gee-Gee?"

I freeze with my hand on the knob. "Easy Gee-Gee was never real. She never existed. You assholes only wanted to think she did."

"You could show a little gratitude, you know." He practically spits the words. "I didn't have to keep your secret. Just like I didn't have to give time to the stupid stuttering girl next door who followed me around. You've never fucking appreciated me. I should tell your perfect boyfriend exactly who you are and the things you've done."

I turn slowly, rage filling me from my toes to my eyeballs. Isaac is tall and broad and works hard to maintain his physique, but as I study him, I realize he's the smallest man I know. He's shallow and self-centered, and he's spent his life manipulating people into doing what he wants. "Tell him whatever you want, Isaac. Maybe he'll never be able to look me in the eye again, and if so, that's something I'll have to live with. God knows I've always blamed myself and my own bad choices. *I* fucked the high school boy next door when I was thirteen; *I* went to that party at fourteen; *I* drank too much, and *I* went into that basement."

"Don't forget last summer," he says, his voice cold. "You were practically dry-humping me in the middle of that party."

"Maybe that's the way Chris will see it. Or maybe he'll see what I'm starting to see. Every time I screwed up, every time I did something that made me feel cheap and dirty, *you* were the common denominator. You were four years older than me. What kind of seventeen-year-old sleeps with a thirteen-year-old? What kind of eighteen-year-old talks a drunk fourteen-year-old girl into going to her knees for six guys? And what kind of guy fucks a girl so drunk she doesn't remember it the next day?" I open the door, my body vibrating with anger and grief for the girl I once was. "Maybe I'm a slut, but you're something worse."

I slam the door behind me and run to the stairwell so I don't have to wait for the elevator. When I reach the ground floor, I realize that I walked here while the sun was setting and now it's dark outside.

I grab my phone and see I have missed texts from Chris and Bailey. I dial Bailey.

"Hey, sister."

"I'm at Gossamer Inn, the one just off campus. Can you come pick me up?"

"Damn, I'm stuck at work. I'll call Mia. She'll be there." She doesn't ask questions, just steps up to help. Can she hear the panic in my voice? How did I get so lucky to make such amazing fast friends?

CHRIS

When I knock on the door to Olivia's parents' small ranch, Sebastian opens it with a scowl.

"I'm sorry I didn't tell you when we were together." My voice is as rough and raw as my emotions. Sandpaper would be softer. "She didn't want you to know."

"She's my *sister*," he says in a low whisper.

"Yeah. I'm sorry." I draw in a deep breath. "I need to talk to her."

His nostrils flare, and his jaw goes tight. "She's fragile right now."

I hold up my hands. "Yes, but I think she needs to know that she doesn't have to do this alone."

His shoulders sag as he exhales. "You mean that?"

"My dad wasn't around for me. I won't do that to a kid. If she's pregnant and there's any chance it's mine, I won't walk away."

"What about Grace?"

My stomach cramps, and I can only shake my head. "I don't know. I'm just trying to take it one step at a time right now. I'm not saying I'm going to marry your sister, but I promise you Olivia won't have to do this alone."

Nodding, he steps back and motions me in. "She's in her room."

The house is small and modest but meticulously clean. The old hardwood floors look freshly polished. There's a well-loved old sofa in the living room, and Olivia and Sebastian's school pictures hang over it.

I follow him to the back hallway, where he knocks on a door.

Olivia pulls it open. Her eyes are bloodshot, her face pale and tired.

Sebastian studies me, and I can tell he's trying to decide whether he can trust me with her before he leaves us.

Olivia turns back into her room and sinks onto the side of her bed, burying her head in her hands.

My chest feels too tight with a tangle of conflicting emotions as I stare at her. The pity for what I know she must be feeling is nearly suffocated by my regrets. We did all the right things and used all the right protection, and yet here we are.

"I took a test," she says. She releases a puff of air that might be a laugh in a different moment, but in this moment it's just a sound full of disgust. "Actually, I took four tests. I have a doctor's appointment next week." She sets her jaw. "And before you ask, yes, it's yours."

There are so many thoughts going through my head that I'm not sure where to start. *Why are we so damn unlucky? Why didn't you tell me sooner? Have you told your parents? How did this happen?*

She lifts her head and wipes tears from her eyes. "I didn't

want to end up pregnant, but I'm going to have this baby."

Stepping forward, I pull her into my arms, squeeze my eyes shut, and take a deep breath. Before this moment, it never crossed my mind that she might get rid of the baby, and the possibility is as terrifying as the possibility of becoming a father before I even finish college. "Good."

CHAPTER 36
GRACE

Five minutes after I hang up with Bailey, it's not Mia who pulls up but Mason. He looks at the hotel then to me. "Bailey called me because she knew I could get here faster than Mia. Get in. I'll take you home."

"I don't want to go back to the apartment." I don't think I can look at Chris, knowing what Olivia told me tonight. Knowing I need to let go will hurt too much. "Take me to Bailey's?"

His gaze shifts to the hotel again. There are questions in his eyes, but he doesn't ask them. "Whatever you want."

I climb into the car, and he drives me to Bailey's apartment complex, where he parks, turns off the ignition, and turns to look at me in the semi-darkness.

"Do you want to talk about it?" he asks.

I shake my head.

"Are you okay?"

I nod. "I'm fine. Everything's fine. I just wanted to get out of there."

"Were you with Isaac?"

"We were just talking. No big deal." I know those words are poison. *No big deal.* They're the poison we feed ourselves over and over again. We kill ourselves slowly in order to protect ourselves from the truth.

"Do you want me to walk you up?" Mason asks.

I shake my head. "I know where she keeps the spare key. I'm okay from here." When I open the door, the dome light floods the car. I swing one foot out and hesitate. "Are you going to tell Chris where I was?"

He draws in a sharp breath and swallows. "I won't lie to him if he asks."

I nod, staring at the asphalt beneath my feet. "I understand."

"Wait. Grace?"

I stop but keep my back to him.

"You need to understand how torn up Chris is about you right now. I've never . . ."

I look over my shoulder, needing to hear the end of the sentence he cut off.

"You need to start taking his calls, okay? And just be honest about what happened tonight—whatever it was."

"Nothing happened. We were talking."

"Have you been drinking?"

Would that excuse me? If I'd bought his lies and excuses and let him touch me? Would alcohol excuse my actions? "No."

What if I had been drinking? What if I'd drunk for courage before facing Isaac? Would I have let him touch me? Would I have bought into his manipulations?

I'm different now. I'm stronger, and I know Chris played a role in that. But the girl who would have felt she owed Chris something isn't so far away that I can't see an alternative ending for this night.

"You know about Olivia, don't you?"

I swallow hard. "Yeah. She ran into me tonight and told me."

Mason rubs the back of his neck. "I know it sucks, but it doesn't change how Chris feels about you. Talk to him. Tell him how you feel about him. I honestly don't think he knows."

I laugh. "Look at us. Pot and kettle."

"What's that supposed to mean?"

"Have you told Bailey how you feel?"

He sighs. "She knows."

"She knows you don't just want to be fuck buddies, but I'd bet money she has no idea that you're in love with her."

He sets his jaw and turns away from me. Maybe we both miss the darkness. There's no hiding our feelings in this light.

"It's not that simple, see?" I say.

He exhales slowly. "Be careful. Text me when you're locked inside."

I nod and walk up to Bailey's apartment, use the key she keeps hidden under the mat to let myself in, and lock the door behind me. When I look at my phone, I have a new text from Chris.

Where are you? I need to talk.

I take a deep breath and type in my reply. *I'm at Bailey's. I'm staying here. I need some space.*

CHRIS

My room felt too empty without Grace in it last night, and I didn't sleep at all.

"Has she called?" Mason asks. He sinks onto the couch next to me and nods to the phone in my hands.

"No."

He rubs the back of his neck. "Shit. Do you think this is about Olivia?"

"Maybe," I mutter. For the last twelve hours, I've felt as if I've been walking along the crumbled floor of a reality that'll give way beneath my feet at any moment.

Everything is so surreal I can hardly process it. The bomb Sebastian dropped in the locker room, Olivia's tears when I held her last night, and then Grace's text declaring she needed space.

Space? Does that have something to do with Isaac or with Olivia? Logic tells me it's reasonable for her to back away with Olivia's pregnancy announcement, but somehow I believed her feelings for me were strong enough to allow her to stand by me through this.

When I got home, all I wanted was to talk to Grace. She'd understand why I'd be so screwed up by the possibility of an unplanned child in any capacity, but especially one with a girl I'm not involved with anymore. She'd say something that would help me feel less trapped. She'd make me laugh.

"Are you sure she wasn't with someone else?" Mason asks.

Sleep deprivation is getting to my brain, because at first I think he means Grace last night, and I immediately think of her reaction to Isaac. When I realize he's talking about Olivia, I just shake my head. "She kissed Keegan, but that's it. She said it's mine."

"You'll figure it out," he says.

Then why do I feel so trapped and confused? "I know."

"We need to get to practice."

I nod. I've never struggled to do what I'm *supposed* to do, but this morning, the thought of following Mason to his car and riding to practice is a struggle. I don't want to do what I'm supposed to do. I want to find Grace and demand to know what's going on in her head. I want to pull her into my arms and kiss her so hard I stop feeling like the world is crumbling under my feet.

But I can't do that until I figure out what to do about Olivia. She's afraid she's going to end up a single mom, and she's freaking out. To be honest, so am I. Jesus, I can't do to a kid what my dad did to me. I can't, and I won't, and if Olivia's having my kid, I don't know how Grace will fit into that picture.

By the time Mason and I get to the field, I'm caught up in my thoughts. It's as if someone's punched me in the chest and left their fist inside me, and now my heart has to learn how to beat all over again, figure out how to pump around this foreign object.

When Isaac Owens passes us on his way to observe with the rest of Dad's team on the bleachers, I grab his arm to stop him. Frustration has me wrapped in its fist, rendering me so damn powerless. I tell myself that Grace's silence is his fault, that her not coming home when I needed her most has something to do with him. Everything changed when he showed up, and I just want to know what their history is.

"How do you know Grace?" I ask.

He chuckles. "I told her you didn't remember her because you didn't want to." He shrugs. "But she asked me not to tell you, so my lips are sealed."

"She asked you not to tell me what?" Were they an item? Why wouldn't she want me to know that?

"It's not like I'm real proud of that night anyway."

That night? I scan my memory for a night Isaac might be ashamed of. A memory floats to the surface, and my stomach lurches with it. I stumble backward, and Mason steadies me.

I shake my head.

It was a party at Isaac's house. We were all hanging out back around the bonfire, and autumn was coming in full force. I remember the girls complaining about being cold and Isaac telling them they couldn't go inside because his mom had said the party had to stay out back. Then it seemed like a bunch of the guys disappeared all at once.

Isaac's mom had come home early from her shift at the

hospital. She was dead on her feet and wanted to talk to him. I told her to stay put in the living room, and I'd get him for her.

I went into the basement to find him, but instead found a circle of guys—all upperclassmen, maybe six or seven of them including Isaac, all with their pants unzipped and their dicks out—and one red-haired girl on her knees in the center of the circle. Her mouth was on Isaac and the others were cheering her on quietly, some laughing nervously while they waited their turn.

"What the fuck do you guys think you're doing?" I hadn't even known when I said the words that it was a freshman they'd talked into their little game. It was bad enough that they'd pass any girl around like that, but when I found out she was some kid, a freshman who lived next door, it made me sick. I never regretted what I did that night, never regretted breaking up what Isaac had started in the basement, or having his mom call the girl's dad.

"You do remember," Isaac says, watching my face. He sighs. "For the record, I didn't tell you."

Mason's still holding on to my arm. "Are you okay?"

I shake my head. I'm not okay. I know it's irrational, since it happened five years ago, but I'm going to crawl out of my skin if I have to give her any space at all. She's my Grace, and that girl in the basement was so vulnerable and lost. I don't know how I didn't make the connection before, but in this moment, with that memory searing itself onto my brain, I just want to wrap her in my arms and protect her from the whole damn world.

I'm already reaching for my phone. "I have to get out of here."

I call Bailey and Mia, but neither has seen Grace. I check the drama department and the library, but she's not at either place. I decide to check Bailey's and find her on the little playground outside the apartment complex. She's swinging, her gaze fixed on the grass sliding beneath her feet.

"Grace?"

She looks up and sighs when she sees me, as if she knew I'd come to find her but she wasn't ready.

"That night. In the basement." I have to get it out there, have to speak her secret so it can't wrap her in chains anymore.

She flinches. "I should have told you. I should have told you who I was."

"Does it change anything?" There's a fist in my gut that says it does. Her past matters more than I want it to, but I'm not willing to let it change *us*. We can figure this out. If we can figure out the pregnancy, her past is a speed bump in comparison.

"It changes everything." She bites her lip and grips the chains tighter in her hands. A cardinal lands on the beam over her head, and she follows it with her eyes as it flies away. "For a couple of weeks we were just Chris and Grace." She swallows.

"I'm sorry I didn't remember."

"I'm not," she says. The color is gone from her cheeks. Even her lips are pale, and everything about her, from her voice to her slumped posture, speaks of complete exhaustion. "I can't even make myself regret not telling you, because the reward for my omission was those weeks. I *liked* not being Gee-Gee to you. I liked our days where you were just Chris, not the guy who stopped everything that night, not the sweet guy who swooped in right when I needed a hero the most."

"The way I feel about you hasn't changed." It almost feels like a lie, but I won't let it be. Her past doesn't matter. I won't let it get in my head, and I won't let it get between us.

"You're wrong." She tucks her chin to her chest, hiding her face from me. "You don't want to believe it changes anything because you're good and kind. But it does. Now the truth is out there."

"What can I do to make this better?" Desperation draws my words tight, makes them snap the air like flames instead of wrapping around her like the comfort she needs.

"Did you ever buy a lottery ticket?"

"Can't say that I have."

She releases a dry laugh, but she doesn't smile while making the sound, and it's empty and hollow. "Of course you wouldn't gamble."

I wince. That hits too close to home after what the sports analysts had to say about my play, and I wouldn't expect Grace to hit so low.

She's focused on the ground, seemingly unaware she's just landed a blow to my gut. "I have a few times. You know, when the Powerball gets really high." She shrugs. "It's fun. There's this period of time when I have the ticket but don't know the winning numbers yet, and I can pretend I'm going to win. I can pretend

I'll get the carefree life of the independently wealthy, that I'll always have time to write and can make my dreams come true with my checkbook. I can buy the theater and pay for the actors. In those moments, the odds don't matter. I can tell myself I didn't just throw away ten dollars on stupid lottery tickets, because until I know otherwise, there's still a chance."

"I can understand that."

She doesn't look at me. It's almost as if she's talking to herself. "The second I look at the numbers and compare them to mine, it's over. The dream is gone. Snatched away. And I can't go back. But that's why I buy the tickets—for those minutes between when I buy them and when I find out I didn't win. Sometimes I don't look at the numbers for days, weeks, even. Because once you look, it's over."

Over. I hate hearing that word in the context of us. And more than that, I hate that I understand what she means. "It's not the same thing."

"We can't go back. We can't go back to who we were before you knew."

"We're the same people we were yesterday."

A tear slides down her cheek, and she shakes her head. "No. Because now I'm the girl who got drunk and dropped down on her knees for six guys."

The words make my chest ache. She's confirming what I already knew, but my brain wants to go to war with the information, find any way it can to prove it's not true. My Grace wouldn't do that. She's not that kind of girl. And yet she's never pretended to be any other kind, has she?

I clench my fists as I try to chase the thought from my mind.

"And now you're the guy who'd never touch her. We can't go back."

"Why do you say I'd never touch you?"

"That's what you said that night." She lifts her head, but she won't meet my eyes. "You were my hero. I was drunk and I'd never fit in, and I just wanted all these popular, cool guys to like me. First, when they took me down there, I felt special. They were flirting with me, giving me all sorts of attention I'd never gotten before. I didn't realize what they had planned, and then everything happened so fast, and I knew I couldn't get out of it without them all laughing at me. I was on my knees and terrified, but more terrified that if I ran away, they'd go back to making fun of me, go back to calling me Juh-Juh-Gee-Gee. And then there you were, and I didn't have to do it. I don't think I ever could have come back from that night, but I didn't have to. You made it stop."

I want to reach for her and pull her into my arms, but I know she wouldn't let me. The most important thing I can do right now is listen. So I swallow hard, trying, like I have all day, to stomach the idea of the woman I love being cornered and manipulated into that horrible position, trying to bite back the rage I feel toward those idiots and the protectiveness I feel for the girl she'll never be again.

"I always liked you." She releases the swing's chains and wraps her arms around herself. "I had *such* a crush on you, and then that night you saved me."

How self-centered was I that I never noticed her? I was so caught up in my world, and my only memory of that redhead at the party is what happened at the party itself and people talking about "Easy Gee-Gee" after. She'd had a crush on me and I hadn't even known who she was. And this is my punishment for being so blind. "I wish I could have stopped them from taking you down there at all. If you'd have spent the night hanging out with *me*, it wouldn't have happened." *And we wouldn't be going through this now.* I wouldn't be standing here so close to her and unable to shake this feeling that she's out of my reach.

"You wouldn't have wanted me with you."

"I didn't know you. I wish—"

She tilts her head and finally meets my gaze. The tears in her eyes are a knife ripping through my gut. "Do you remember what you said about me? After?"

I scan my memory over and over, but the night's a bit of a blur. I remember what I saw in the basement, and I remember the guys being pissed at me for weeks after, telling me I was jealous they hadn't included me, or that I must be a faggot. I don't remember anything about Grace. "I'm sorry. I don't."

She shakes her head. "I was in the dining room, waiting for my dad to pick me up, and you were in the living room with Isaac. He asked you if you stopped them so you could have me for yourself."

The memory slams into me. It's like having a mirror shoved in front of me that shows me only the worst of myself, and I squeeze my eyes shut. My stomach churns. It wasn't the first time

I'd been asked, or the last. "Grace—"

"You said, 'As if I would put my dick near that.'" She speaks the words without emotion, as if she's reciting a grocery list.

The dull knife in my gut yanks up hard and fast and saws into my heart. "I was an idiot kid. I was a fucking immature asshole who was thinking of himself, trying to do some damage control because they hated me for what I did. All those guys were pissed at me. Anything I said had everything to do with me, and nothing to do with you. I'm sure I didn't even mean it."

"But didn't you? I wasn't the kind of girl you dated. You *weren't* interested in girls who'd suck six dicks in one night just so the boys would like her." A tear rolls down her cheek. "In that moment, I wished you hadn't come down there. I thought that maybe enduring the horror of what they'd planned for me might be less painful than knowing how you felt about me."

"Don't say that. I'm sorry. I'm so sorry for what I said."

"Thank you," she whispers. "I didn't want you to find out. I asked Isaac not to tell you because I knew once you found out, you'd feel like you couldn't let me go. You're so honorable, and right now that honor shouldn't be wasted on me."

I shake my head, scrambling for footing. "It's not a waste. Come home. Don't let that night destroy what we have."

"And if Olivia's pregnant, what *do* we have?"

My stomach knots because I don't have an answer. I still haven't figured out anything other than that I want Grace by my side through whatever's next.

"Bailey said I can stay with her for a while."

"Is that what you want?"

She dries her cheeks with the back of her hand. "Yeah. I think that's best."

"I don't understand." My words are a series of broken syllables strung together by sheer will. I'm desperate to put this back together, but mostly I just want to return to how we were yesterday morning, with her in my arms and the past far from our minds. "Maybe I didn't remember that night, but you did. You knew who I was. How does this change anything?"

"Because now you know, too." She shrugs. "And you're a nice guy, Chris. You're far too nice of a guy to learn the truth about the girl you've been screwing around with and allow yourself to back away. I'm not going to let you trap yourself in this"—she waves a hand between our bodies—"whatever this is when you have something so much bigger happening."

CHAPTER 37
CHRIS

With the memory of the night in Isaac's basement burning holes in my gut faster than battery acid, and Grace not returning my phone calls, I'm in no shape to face anyone tonight, so I'm fucking lucky our mandatory team meeting was canceled. I'm already in deep enough shit for leaving practice this morning.

When Mason gets home, I'm on the couch with a beer, wishing I were the type of guy who could drink his problems away. Since I'm not, I've only made it through a quarter of the bottle, and might not bother finishing it.

Since he gave me a lift to practice, I didn't have my car with me, and he refused to give me his keys so I could track down Grace this morning until I told him what was wrong, so I told him about the night in the basement, about the girl I hadn't thought about in years. I told him about the drunk high school freshman girl, and the rowdy upperclassmen. I told him so he'd give me his damn keys, but I also told him because I know I can trust Mason with anything, and it was tearing me apart inside.

Now he gives me a long, hard look. I can't tell what he's thinking and don't have the emotional fortitude to care. I stay silent.

He drops into a chair and leans forward, his elbows on his knees. "Listen. I get that it's weird. But does it really change who she is? Look at me. I'm in love with a *stripper*. I fucking hate that she shows her body to anyone who pays the cover to walk into that club, but it doesn't change who she is. It doesn't change the way I feel about her. Grace just made a mistake when she was a kid." He sighs and shakes his head. "Okay, and maybe another, if what Isaac said is true and she really stooped low enough to sleep with that douchebag last summer."

I flinch. "He told you that?"

"Yeah." He tilts his head to the side, studying me. "But it shouldn't change how you feel about her."

I blink at him. For being one of my best goddamn friends, I'd think he'd know me better than that. "You think I'm sitting here because I feel differently about her tonight than I did when I woke up this morning?"

Mason lifts his palms. "I don't know. You were kind of freaking out."

"Mase, I'm in love with her. And if I'm *freaking out* right now it's because she's not returning my texts or my calls. It's because when she saw Isaac here, she was so afraid I'd remember that she wouldn't look me in the eye. It's because I never blamed that girl for what happened that night, and I can't fucking *stomach* the idea that they used her like that. If I'm *freaking out* it's because I'm trying not to find Isaac, finish what I started, then fly back to Texas and beat the shit out of the other motherfuckers who took her to that basement." I draw in a long, ragged breath. I feel like I'm being sawed in half. "I'm freaking out because Olivia's pregnant and I should be glad that Grace is walking away, and instead I'm desperate to figure out how to get her back."

"Jesus. You need to go out. *I'm* depressed just walking into the same room as you." When I shake my head, Mason holds up a hand. "I'm serious. You had one hell of a week, and I get that this is all really fucking heavy, but I'm not going to let you sit here and stew. Everyone's getting together at Arrow's tonight, so you can't just sit around here licking your wounds. It'll be good for you to be around your friends."

GRACE

Bailey sits in the chair beside me and clears her throat. "Chris is here."

And that's exactly why I didn't want to come tonight. Where there's one Blackhawk boy, there are more, and I can't look Chris in the eye and pretend I don't want to be with him. I can't pretend the idea of him having a baby with someone else doesn't break my heart, even if I know I did the right thing.

She squeezes my wrist. "Keegan's acting nuts since the news came out."

"Because he's in love with her," I say, my throat thick. "It sucks to be the odd man out when the person you love is about to have a baby."

She hums. "Maybe. Or maybe he thinks it could be his."

Something too much like hope surges in my chest. "She said she never slept with Keegan."

"That's what she said." She grabs my hand and squeezes. "Just don't give up on Chris yet, okay?"

I love my friend, but I wish she wouldn't try to give me hope. What I need now is someone who can help me cut it off with Chris. "Maybe this was for the best." God, the words break my heart, but it's what I keep telling myself. "I'm going back to New York next month, and breaking it off now means nobody gets hurt."

Bailey releases my hand and sighs heavily. "Does it?"

I can't help it—I follow her gaze across the pool, even knowing what I'll see. My chest goes tight at the sight of him. I can see the hurt all over his face. He can't hide his feelings for shit.

He tips a bottle to his lips and drains it, and when he brings it down, his eyes lock with mine. There's an achy pull in my chest where my heart's been cracked open. He tosses his beer bottle into a recycling can and stalks toward me, and when he stands by my chair, his legs wide, his hands tucked into his pockets, his eyes searching my face, I want to throw myself at him.

"We should talk," he says.

I swallow. "What else is there to say?"

He sets his jaw and looks away for a breath, then takes my hand and pulls me out of the chair. "Come on."

"Chris—"

"Please." There's too much pain in his eyes for me to deny him, so I follow him through the house and he leads me into the back hallway, only letting go of my hand to press me against the wall.

His head is tipped forward, his hands on either side of my head, his mouth close to mine. "Why?" he asks.

I'm playing with fire by letting him this close to me, but I don't have the strength to push him away. He's warm and smells good, and I just want him to kiss me. "Why what?"

"Why are you running from me? From this?" I watch his Adam's apple bob as he swallows, and then one of his hands comes off the wall and strokes my jaw.

I lean into his touch, loving the heat of his hand and the shivers he sends through me. "I'm not running. I'm stepping back."

"Then why does it feel like you're so far away I can't reach you?" He slides a hand into my hair and twists it, but he might as well have taken my heart in his fist. "I know we're complicated and maybe just got more so, but I'm all in, Grace. I had no idea how much I needed you until you walked into my life."

"Don't," I whisper. Can't he understand how hard this is? Can't he see that hope is only going to hurt me more in the end?

"Don't make this harder."

"I'll give you whatever you need." He steps closer. "Ask me for space if I'm not what you want, ask for it if I don't make you happy or if I'm hurting you, but don't ask because you're afraid we can't figure this out. I'm not walking away from you."

My throat is thick, and my heart is raw. The last two days on top of our intense weekend together—it's all just too much. "I can't, Chris." He may deserve better than Olivia, but he definitely deserves better than me. "You're off the hook. I'm not who you thought I was."

"No." He tugs lightly on my hair, tilting my face up to his. "You're more. I want to know all of you, and I've only just gotten started."

I close my eyes. "Let me go."

I'm not strong enough to look into those blue eyes and tell him to walk away from me. So I close my eyes and keep them squeezed shut until I feel him release my hair, until the air cools as he steps away, until I hear the click of the back doors opening and closing.

Down the dark hall, I hear someone draw in a ragged breath and hiccup.

I wipe at my cheeks. "Who's there?"

The lights flick on, and Olivia stares at me with red eyes and tear-streaked cheeks. She rubs her bare shoulders and shakes her head. "What he said to you just now? He never fought for me like that." Her words are so shaky they bounce off the walls. "Not once."

She walks away, and I know I should go back out with the others, but instead I stay inside where I don't have to be tempted by what I can't have.

CHRIS

I grab another beer and drink half of it without thinking.

"Slow down," Mason says quietly. "The answers aren't in there."

Sebastian locks eyes with me and lifts his chin. I nod. I'm not off the hook with him. I assured him I'd do right by Olivia—but with Grace keeping me at an arm's length until we know for sure, I'm just not sure what *right* is.

"You okay, Montgomery?" Arrow asks.

I wish people would quit asking me that. I'm not fucking okay. "I'm fine," I grit out through my teeth.

"We heard this was where the party was!"

We all turn to see Isaac and a few of his cronies from my dad's staff entering Arrow's backyard through the gate. I take a deep breath and my fists clench involuntarily. I can't deal with this asshole tonight.

Arrow shifts his gaze to Isaac and company, and then to me.

"It's okay," I say softly. If my dad is our new coach, sending these guys away puts Arrow on the shit list from the start, and he's already going to be at a disadvantage by missing half the season.

"Sorry to crash the party," Isaac says to Arrow as they walk toward us. "We were sick of being stuck in the hotel."

"It's not a problem," Arrow says. "Make yourself at home."

"Is Grace here?" Isaac asks.

His buddy chuckles. "Since she can't stay away from you, she will be soon if she isn't already."

My blood chills. "What?"

Isaac draws in a breath through his teeth. "Hey, Chris. Didn't see you there."

"Chris." Mason comes to stand beside me. "Come on, man. Let's go add some wood to the fire." He reaches for my arm, and I shake him off, glaring at Isaac.

The guy on the other side of Isaac grins. He's another one of the staff members here with my father, so I hate him by association even before he starts speaking. "Is Grace that hot chick in the pink dress who came to your room?" He lowers his voice in a false show of class. "You hit that?"

"She came to my hotel room last night. Her signals weren't that hard to read, ya know?" Isaac grins. "Probably not the best place to talk about it." He nods toward me and adds, "If you know what I mean."

Grace was in Isaac's hotel room?

I stiffen. Arrow comes to stand by my side.

"I don't think we do know what you mean," he says, taking a step closer to Isaac.

The hackles standing on end at the back of my neck must be visible from the entire backyard, because the other guys are filing in around me.

"Don't take it personally," Isaac says to me. "Easy Gee-Gee is just the kind of girl who needs more than one man to keep her satisfied. You can't change that." He chuckles as if this is the world's most fantastic joke. "Though I think I must do a pretty damn good job, since she keeps coming back for more."

"Just shut your mouth, Owens," Mason growls.

Isaac looks around and seems to realize what he's gotten himself into. All these guys would throw a punch to protect Grace. He holds up his hands. "She came to my room last night. Showed up uninvited. It's not my fault." He shrugs. "That's all I'm saying about it."

Arrow shifts to the balls of his feet and asks under his breath, "Can I introduce this asshole to my fist?"

I swallow hard and shake my head. Grace was at Isaac's last night. *That's* why she never came home. She didn't stay at Bailey's like she said. She wasn't licking her wounds over Olivia or worried about our relationship. She was with Isaac.

Keegan steps to my side and glares at Isaac. "He's a fucking liar."

I want to agree with him, but my mind flashes to the redhead on her knees in the middle of that circle of guys. What kind of girl does that?

I hate myself for doubting her, but at the same time I wonder if I'm a fool for not heeding her warnings.

"Come on," Mason says, grabbing for my arm again. "Let's go check on that fire."

I turn to him because he's the only one not defending Grace. "What do you know?"

He shakes his head. "I don't know anything. She just needed a ride home last night, and I picked her up."

"A ride home from where?"

Mason's eyes shift to Isaac, then back to me.

Isaac smirks. "I told you already. She came to my hotel."

I'm making myself crazy trying to figure out how we can make it work when Olivia's having my baby, and she went to his hotel room last night? I think of my first night with Grace this summer, when I thought her name was Morgan. How easily had that lie come to her?

Maybe Grace was right. Maybe she's not who I thought she was.

CHAPTER 38
GRACE

I'm hiding in Mia's room when Bailey rushes in.

"Shit just went down outside. What are you doing in here?" She's out of breath, as if she's been running all over the house looking for me.

"What happened?"

"Isaac ran his mouth about you being in his room last night." Grimacing, Bailey wraps her arms around her middle as if she's nursing a stomachache.

"I went up to his room to ask him not to tell Chris about my past. While I was there, he tried to start something and—he's a fucking asshole, to tell you the truth. I left before anything happened, and that's when I called you."

"Isaac implied you went to his room to hook up. Another staff member saw you there last night and it just . . . it looks bad."

I swallow hard. "Chris thinks I slept with Isaac?"

"For what it's worth, all the guys think Isaac's a piece of shit."

I feel numb as I walk to the bed and sink into it. Chris believes Isaac? He believes him because of who I used to be. *Who I am?*

"Chris is looking for you. What do you want me to do?" Bailey asks.

Go back in time and tell me not to go to that party. Enroll at Champagne Towers and be my friend when I needed one the most. Teach me that I'm worth more than a blowjob, that I'm worth liking for more than an excellent set of fourteen-year-old tits.

"I'll talk to him," I say. "It's time for me to face this."

"Do you want me to stay with you?"

I can only shake my head, squeeze my eyes shut, and hope this is all a bad dream. I sit on the bed, my eyes closed, waiting. I hear the front door and then the click of the bedroom door before I have the courage to lift my head and open my eyes.

Chris is standing in front of me, anguish written on his face. My stomach churns and twists like someone is trying to wring a stain from a wet rag.

He believes what Isaac said. I can see it all over his face, in the way he's looking at me.

"Why didn't you tell me?" he asks. "Why make me find out from him? Why make me find out in front of everyone? And now all my teammates are talking about it. Everyone fucking knows that you showed up at Isaac's room last night like . . ." He shakes his head and laughs bitterly.

"Like Easy Gee-Gee?" I wrap my arms around my chest and squeeze tight, as if these arms could protect the heart he's had in his hands from the beginning. Bile rises in my throat, hot and thick, and I have to take a fistful of Mia's bedspread to keep myself grounded.

"Don't put words in my mouth." He shakes his head, takes a step forward, and then stops and shoves his hands into his pockets. I blink and pinch my bare arm, focusing on the sharp pain from my nails so I don't have to think about the dull ache consuming my entire core. "Do you know the first thing I thought about when I found out Olivia might be pregnant? I thought about you. I thought about how I was terrified I was going to lose you, and I needed to figure out a way to make it work. But what did you do? You went to *him*."

I try for a deep breath, but it doesn't help. Tears fill my eyes, and the pain in my core seeps into my limbs until every inch of me aches. Five years ago, Chris broke my heart, but today he broke all of me. Somehow, I walk to the door and open it without collapsing. Somehow, I lift my chin and meet his gaze, facing all the hurt and betrayal I see there. "I'd like you to leave now."

He puts his hand over mine and his eyes search my face, and I'm not sure what he's looking for, but I don't think he finds it because he drops his hand and cuts off the contact. "I loved you."

I don't even know where to start with the series of gut punches he delivered. Loved. He *loved* me? Loved. Past tense. Gone before I knew it was there. Because maybe he could love Grace, but not even a man as sweet and understanding as Chris could love a slut like Gee-Gee.

He walks through the door and stops on the other side of the threshold, his back to me. "What am I supposed to do, Grace? Tell me how I'm supposed to make this mess okay, because I can't figure it out."

"Just let me go," I whisper, and he hangs his head. "You have to now. Because, you see, this *is* about what I did when I was fourteen. You said it didn't change anything, but you were lying to us both. If it hadn't been for that night and the mistakes I made then, you might have *asked* me what happened last night." His shoulders stiffen, but I push forward. "But instead of giving me a chance to tell you that nothing happened, that I didn't sleep with him, that I threw him off me when he tried to put his hand up my skirt, you believed an asshole who thought it was his right to put his hands on me just because I was in his room."

He turns, but I shut the door before I can see his face and sink against it, my head in my hands, body shaking. I close my eyes tight and listen to the sound of his feet on the stairs.

I roll to the side, curling into a ball as I cry.

I don't realize Bailey's come back into the room until she wraps her arms around me, stroking my hair, whispering in my ear. "You have to breathe, Grace. I know it hurts, but you have to breathe."

I open my mouth and fill my lungs and wonder how I'm still in one piece, still whole when I've been broken right through the middle. "Why did he have to make me believe in the fairytale?" I whisper. "Why did he have to make me believe a girl like me could have a happy ending?" I don't even recognize the sound of my voice. It's tortured. The cry of a wounded animal.

"He just needs time," Bailey says, dragging me back to reality, which is the last place I want to be. She smooths my hair. "Just give him time."

I shake my head and take another breath. Time won't change who I am or what I've done, and it won't change that when I needed him to have faith in me, he believed the worst.

CHRIS

For three seconds, I stare at the closed door. I don't knock or breathe or hope. I just stare, horrified at what I've done.

"I thought better of you," Bailey says. She pushes past me and into the room, closing the door behind her, but not before I see Grace on the floor in tears.

My feet take me down the stairs and into the backyard before my mind can catch up. "Owens," I say as I come up behind him.

"Hey, Chr—"

He doesn't get to finish because I punch him in the face. My fist lands just right, and blood pours from his nose. It's damn satisfying.

"Fuck, man." He lunges toward me just as Mason steps between us. Mason grabs Isaac, pulling his arms back so he can't swing at me. "Jealous much?" Isaac asks, blood dripping onto the patio.

Everyone is watching—my friends, my team. I feel like I'm

on fire and the only way to put it out is to swing. "You're a piece of shit. You were a piece of shit when you took a drunk girl into your basement to pass around, and you're a piece of shit now."

"Get out of here." Mason shoves Isaac toward the gate.

Arrow steps around them to open it. "I'm afraid you guys are going to have to find another party."

Isaac flips him off and stumbles away, holding his bloody nose with his other hand. "Fucking assholes think you rule the world. Just wait until Colt gets a hold of your team."

Only when Arrow swings the gate closed behind him with a clang do I realize my hands are shaking, and the fist I threw into Isaac's nose is screaming in pain.

"He works for your new coach," Mason says. "Regardless of how you feel about your father, that's not gonna fly."

"Good to see you do something with passion," a deep voice says from the door. My dad steps out onto the patio, Arrow's dad by his side. "It's a relief, honestly. I wasn't sure you felt that strongly about anything."

I flex my aching fist. "Your boy's an asshole."

"Cosign," Mason says with a nod, and Arrow and Keegan nod, too.

Sebastian shudders and tilts his head to each side as if stretching out his neck. "I wanted to punch him myself when he was sitting down here calling her *Easy Gee-Gee*."

Pain knifes up my arm, and I wince. "I need some ice."

"Shit." Keegan's eyes go wide as he takes in my swelling hand. "Did you break your throwing hand?"

I open my eyes and meet his horrified gaze. "It was worth it."

My father pulls me into Mr. Woodison's office and paces, his hands on his hips. "Mr. Woodison's a big donor to the university, and he's had me in here trying to talk me into making the move to BHU. He almost had me convinced before your little temper tantrum out there. Is this what it's going to be like if I take this job? You're going to act up like a little boy desperate for attention?"

I'm too hot and too raw, and I can only sneer at him. "I don't want your attention."

"That's the second fight you've been in since I arrived, and I know that's not your style. You want to try again, with some honesty this time?"

Oh, fuck this bastard. "Honesty? You're an asshole." In our limited exchanges over the years, I've bit my tongue and kept myself from saying those words, but I don't regret saying them now. Not at all. Now I'm grateful that I get the opportunity to say it to his face. "When I was a little boy, I worked so hard because I wanted to make Mom proud, but also because I knew you were out there, and I wanted to make damn sure I wasn't a disappointment. Do you have any idea what it's like to be a ten-year-old boy who just wants to make his absent father proud? To believe that if I'd been better—stronger, faster, smarter, cooler—maybe you would have come home?

"Then by the time I started high school, I started getting

angry with you. I'd imagine someday you'd come and try to have a relationship with me, and I'd get to tell you to fuck off.

"But even then I hoped that when you saw me and what I'd made of myself, you'd be proud of me. Impressed." I shake my head. "I had it all wrong. I don't care whether or not you're proud of me. It doesn't matter. Because I'm disappointed in you."

He stares at me, his face blank, and whether he's waiting for me to say more or trying to figure out an appropriate response, I don't know.

"I don't want your attention, and I don't want your approval. And I sure as fuck don't want you coaching my team." I clench my hands and step back to resist the violence still simmering in my blood. "You've never given two shits about what I want, but I'm going to tell you anyway. Don't take the job. I don't ask anything from you, but I'm asking this. Turn them down and go back to Texas."

I'm shaking as I push out of the office and head upstairs to find Grace. I've fucked up and I don't deserve a chance to apologize, but I'm hoping she'll give me one anyway.

Mia's room is empty, and I can't find Grace anywhere in the house.

I head out the front door. Bailey's in the driveway talking to Mason.

"Where is Grace?"

Bailey turns her glare on me, and if looks could kill, I'd be roadkill right now. "Don't. Just don't. Give her space and take care of your own problems."

Mason flashes me an apologetic wince and shrugs. I guess everyone knows how much I fucked up. "Let's go home, man. It's been a long fucking day."

CHAPTER 39
GRACE

Wednesday morning, I drag myself out of bed and force myself to shower and dress. Bailey's made coffee and is sitting at the kitchen table. I pour myself a cup and take the seat next to her, wondering if the coffee's warmth might fill this emptiness inside me.

"How are you holding up?" she asks.

"It doesn't even hurt anymore," I say. "It's just . . ." I look away, not sure how to describe what I'm *not* feeling. "It's like he shattered everything inside me and then it all evaporated."

When I meet her gaze, she acknowledges me with a soft smile. "It comes back in waves. Sometimes they're bigger and sometimes they're smaller, but they'll take you off guard."

I pull my mug against my chest, grateful for her constant understanding. "Did Mason hurt you?"

She shakes her head. "No, but I'm afraid I hurt him. I loved him, but I was *in love* with Mia's brother, Nic." Her smile grows shaky and she swallows. "And then Nic died. After, it felt like I couldn't breathe, and then it felt like I wasn't alive at all. I don't know which was worse. I'm just saying, grief comes in waves. Just try not to get pulled under."

"I don't know what to do." I put my mug on the table. It says DIVA on the side, and I trace the letters with my finger. "I've always run away when things got bad, and I keep feeling like I want to go home, but I don't know where that is."

She grabs my hand and squeezes. "You're already home. I know you'll go back to New York in a little over a month, but Blackhawk Valley is your home just like it's mine. You're one of us now."

Her words settle against my heart and click into place. "I don't know if I can handle seeing him. I don't know if I can . . ." There it is, the wave she warned me about. This one comes with the image of Olivia and Chris with a baby and slaps me in the face. I have to close my eyes and concentrate on my breath before I can speak. "He needs to focus on her anyway. Her and the baby."

"Don't give up on him just because it hurts."

"It was already over," I say, staring into my coffee. "I was with him on borrowed time, living a fairytale when I know I'm no princess."

She squeezes my hand, and I welcome the emptiness that returns to my chest. After long minutes of silence, Bailey gets up from the table and washes her coffee mug. I'm faintly aware of the ticking of the second hand on the kitchen clock and the sound of the shower running in the bathroom before she returns to the table dressed in jeans and a pink tank.

"I have to run some errands," she says. "Do you want to come?"

I shake my head. "I have some things to take care of too."

Half an hour later, I find myself in Mr. Gregory's office. He's sitting in a chair by the window, a book in his lap, staring off into the distance. I don't bother knocking or announcing my presence. "I'm quitting."

He startles, then narrows his eyes as he turns them on me.

"Thank you for giving me a chance to work with you this summer."

"But you're quitting, so obviously you don't mean that."

"No. I do. I'm grateful." I swallow hard and draw in a long, slow breath. My eyes burn, and I feel tears rise in my throat. I don't want to cry, but I have as much power over my tears right now as I do over the waves rolling onto the shore. "I needed to hear what you had to say, even if it wasn't easy. But I think the worst part is knowing you're right. Wanting to write doesn't make me any good at it."

"You're going to quit? Just like that?" His brows are drawn together, and his gaze is steadied so intently on me that I don't have the strength to hold it. Not after today.

"I don't want to waste my time anymore. I don't want to believe in something I can't have." My voice hitches on the last words, and all I can do is look at the ceiling and will my eyes to dry.

"Do you know what it's like to be a writer who can't write?"

"Apparently I do."

"Fuck your self-pity. You are capable of writing. I'm asking if you have any idea what it's like to be a writer and have *nothing* inside you to give."

I shake my head and tears spill from my eyes. I wipe them away with my palms. "You can write. You're just not letting yourself."

"That's like telling a man with a half-hard cock that he can *fuck*. Maybe he could get it in there, but it's a waste of time and bloody embarrassing. Creative impotence is the fucking worst, and you stand there, fully capable of writing and creating, and tell me you're quitting?"

"You told me I wasn't good enough."

He throws his book onto the floor and glares at me. "Don't put words into my mouth. I told you that shit you gave me to read wasn't good enough."

"What's the difference? I *tried*."

"You *tried* to write something that fit in the box. You're wasting everyone's time with the words you think people want to read. Be brave and write the goddamn play that's ripping from your chest. Stop giving your brain the pen when writing is a job for your heart."

But my heart isn't up for the job. It's been pulverized. "I'm sorry." I back out of the office. "I'm not good enough."

CHRIS

For two days, I've been going through the motions with everything—football, workouts, time with my friends. Even the news that my father declined the position didn't bring the relief it should have. Every minute I'm swamped with exhaustion and everything seems futile.

Everyone was relieved to find out I didn't break my hand the night I broke Isaac's nose. There was some legitimate concern that the whole fucking team was going to be unable to hold a ball by the time the season rolled around. Personally, I'd take a broken throwing hand over this shattered thing I'm toting around in my chest.

Tomorrow morning, I'm supposed to go to the doctor's office with Olivia. They're going to do an ultrasound to determine her due date, and all I can think is that when I see my baby for the first time, Grace is supposed to be by my side. Grace is supposed to be the one with the baby growing inside her. And it's supposed to happen in years, not now.

I've been hiding out in Arrow's basement watching old game film, but Mason's been texting me and telling me it's time to join them out back, and I don't have the energy to fight him, so I turn off the projector and head up.

When I get to the top of the stairs, I'm stopped in my tracks when I hear Keegan's voice in the kitchen.

"Don't shut me out when there's a chance the baby could be mine."

My gut clenches, and my skin goes tight and cold.

"Shut *up*," Olivia says. "I just know, okay?"

"It can't be his. You had your period the week after he broke up with you." Keegan's whisper grows louder and frustration sharpens the edges of his words.

"It could still be his."

"It's mine, and you know it. Stop. Lying. This is about the draft, isn't it? You forget that you told me you were determined to land an NFL player. You forget that I *know* you. So now you're lying to him thinking he'll take you back."

I can't listen anymore. I walk into the kitchen, and Olivia's jaw goes slack when she sees me.

I look to Keegan and then Olivia. That sweet, innocent face, and all of her speeches about how this isn't what she wanted. She's been playing me. "It's not mine." It's not a question—not when the truth is written all over her face.

"I didn't get pregnant on purpose," she says.

Even as relief pulls a thousand pounds off my lungs, my jaw is tight with anger. "But you did lie to me on purpose?"

"I had to think of the baby's future."

Keegan's arms are crossed and he looks as angry as I feel, maybe angrier. And of course he is. The poor bastard is in love with a liar.

CHAPTER 40
GRACE

"Grace, can I talk to you?"

I turn away from the half-caff mocha I'm making to see Olivia standing at the register. The last time I saw her in this coffee shop, she was telling me she was pregnant with Chris's baby. This time, I'm here as an employee, not a customer, and Sebastian is standing behind Olivia with crossed arms. Oh, and I know the baby is actually Keegan's. Chris called with the news as soon as he found out—and left it in a voicemail, since I'm still not taking his calls. Minutes after he left the message, I had texts with the same information from Mia, Bailey, and Mason. Everyone except Bailey expected me to go back to Chris after that, but she seemed to understand that I needed time and space to sort myself out.

I nod to Olivia and finish the mocha for the customer.

"Do you mind if I take a break?" I ask Ned, the forty-year-old hipster manning the register.

"Go for it," he says.

I wash my hands and go around front to join Olivia and Sebastian. "Want to sit out front?" I ask, pointing to the tables on the sidewalk.

"Sure." She draws in a deep breath and glances at her brother. "You can go now. I'm apologizing."

He lifts his chin. "You better." His expression softens when he turns to me. "I'm sorry too. You deserve better than everything that's happened."

"Thank you," I tell him. "But you don't owe me any apologies."

The truth is, some parts of my life in Blackhawk Valley didn't actually go to shit last week. For instance, Bailey has proven herself to be a standup friend. She's let me stay at her apartment without paying rent, and has watched more sappy chick flicks to get me through this heartache than anyone should have to suffer.

I haven't been back to Mr. Gregory's office, but I've been thinking a lot about what he said to me, and since I always write a lot when I'm hurting, I've given myself permission to work on my secret project—the one that wants to rip from my chest. I don't know if it'll ever go anywhere, but it feels good to get it out.

And then there are the guys. Mason pulled some strings with a friend of a friend to get me this job at the coffee shop, and he and Keegan stop by regularly to check on me.

Chris texts me about once a day, checking in, apologizing for being an idiot. That's the problem with falling so hard for a good guy. You truly don't know if he wants you or if he's just trying to do the right thing. In this case, the guy is so good, I'm not sure even he knows.

Sebastian leaves and Olivia and I settle into the wooden chairs on the sunny sidewalk.

"How are you feeling?" I ask her. She looks tired. Dark bags pull on her eyes and her hair is in a sloppy bun instead of her typical sleek ponytail.

"Like an idiot." She keeps her gaze on her hands. "I guess you know that I lied."

I take a breath. "That was pretty shitty."

"I'm so sorry. It wasn't right, and I was selfish, and I know it screwed up everything between you and Chris. I've told him how sorry I am, and I hope you can accept my apology, but I understand if you hate me, because I would absolutely hate my guts. My mom got knocked up young and I was scared I was going to end up like her and stuck here, and I know Chris is going to be drafted—an NFL quarterback, and that's a ticket out of this town—not that any of that makes what I did acceptable, but—"

"Olivia?" I wait until she lifts her eyes to meet mine. "I forgive you."

She blinks at me. "Really? Even though you and Chris still aren't back together? Even though I screwed up everything?"

I tug my bottom lip between my teeth, suddenly wishing I'd brought a cup of coffee out here with me. I could use the comfort right about now. "Your pregnancy isn't what broke me and Chris. We have other issues we need to sort through—*I* have other issues *I* need to sort through. I appreciate the apology, but I think the biggest apology you need to deliver is to Keegan."

A tear slips from her eye and she wipes it away. "He's so mad at me."

"Can you blame him?"

"No." She closes her eyes and tilts her face up to the clear blue summer sky.

I try to imagine what she must be feeling—the tangle of fear and hormones. I don't get it. Honestly, I still don't understand what would drive a woman to straight out lie about the father of her baby, but I understand being confused and scared.

She exhales slowly and looks back at me. "Chris is so mature. I knew he'd take care of me and the baby. Keegan isn't together like that. I was afraid . . ." She drops her hand to her stomach. "I guess I thought he might suggest I get rid of it."

"Did he?"

She shakes her head. "No. I underestimated him. I always do."

"I get the impression that a lot of people underestimate Keegan. It's time to stop being one of those people. He needs that from you. Especially now."

"Why are you being so nice to me?"

It's my turn to look up to the sky, but I don't close my eyes. As I watch the puffy white clouds take their slow ride across the horizon, something clicks into place inside me. "We all make mistakes. I've made my fair share. That doesn't mean we don't deserve kindness."

"My brother says Chris is bonkers in love with you." She grins, and it's the first genuine smile I've seen from her today. "I guess I can see why."

I swallow hard and try my best to return her smile. "Now I just need to see it."

CHRIS

"*Yes, sir,*" I repeat into the phone, cringing at the ceiling as Grace's father starts in on another tirade about how he sent Grace to stay with me so I could look out for her and not so I could break her heart.

I'm the one who told him what happened. I'm pretty sure Grace would have taken it to her grave where our parents were concerned, but then, she thinks we're done, and I'm not convinced.

"I'm disappointed, Chris," Edward says. And thank God, he's slowing down, as if maybe he's nearing the end of his lecture. "If you were going to get involved with her, you needed to do a gut check and make sure you could do it without hurting her. She's been through enough."

"I agree," I say, the words snagging in my throat. "And I don't blame you for being angry with me. You're her father and that's your right, but you need to know that I'm in love with her. I'm going to fight for her."

"How are you going to do that?"

"I don't have it figured out just yet, but I have some ideas."

He's silent for a breath. "Don't disappoint me. Grace needs someone who will give her happiness and believe in her."

"I know, sir. And I can only say I want that someone to be me."

We end the call, and I decide now is as good a time as any to put my plan into action. I text Bailey.

> ***Me:*** *I need a favor. Do you have access to Grace's laptop?*

CHAPTER 41
GRACE

I throw my keys and purse onto the counter in Bailey's apartment, and grab a bag of potato chips before heading to the living room. "My dogs are *barking*." I laugh. "God, where does that phrase come from anyway? How are feet dogs?"

"You're the writer," someone says from the couch, but it's not Bailey, and my breath catches when I hear the voice. I rush around the couch to see Willow stretched out on it, her arms above her head, her feet propped up on a pillow.

Then I cry. Because oh my God, *Willow* is here. It's as if I've been standing alone in the cold and suddenly someone has shown up with blankets fresh from the dryer. I haven't gone through this alone, but no one can stand in for my best friend. "What are you doing here?"

She rolls her head to the side. "At the moment, I'm suffering from some pretty wicked jetlag, but in about three seconds, I'm gonna be hugging the shit out of you." She stretches, then hops off the couch and wraps me into her long-armed hug.

"I can't believe you're here," I blubber into her shoulder.

"My girl needed me. So here I am. And anyway, I had the week off while the family goes on holiday in Spain."

I step out of her embrace and attempt to pull myself together, taking a deep breath and wiping dry my wet eyes. "Still. Best. Surprise. Ever."

She grins. "Thanks. Your friend Bailey helped."

"How was your flight?"

"It was good," she says, plopping back onto the couch. "There were no children asking me for juice boxes, and I got to read a book that didn't star Sofia the First or Jake and the Never Land Pirates as protagonists."

"Sounds like the basis for a fantastic flight."

"You have no idea." She grins, and I know she's only half serious. She really loves kids.

"How's the sexy boss?"

"Maverick?" She tugs on her long ponytail and moans. "I think I literally go into heat when he looks at me. You know, like animals do with the conspicuous mating calls and all that? Yeah. Except I try to hide it and just walk around red-faced all the time. My first week with them, his wife kept asking me if I was coming down with something."

I snort. "Oh my God, that's glorious."

"And get this," she says, "Maverick's *brother* is visiting after they return from Spain."

I bite my lip, trying to remember if I know anything about the famous actor's brother, then I sit up straight. "*Hunt?*"

"Yep."

"Willow, I've seriously watched ten movies starring Hunt in the last two weeks."

She rubs her hands together, and I swear there's a twinkle in her eyes. "And Hunt is *single.*"

"Oh my God, are you seriously going to hook up with the uncle?"

She shrugs. "I'm open to the possibility."

I laugh hard, and it feels so good after so many days of so much sadness that I sit right next to her, wrap my arm around her shoulders, and squeeze. "Thank you for coming."

"How are you?"

"I'm in love with Chris Montgomery." I close my eyes. It's the first time I've admitted that to myself, let alone said it out loud. To be fair, I think all my friends here know. The pity-fest I've indulged in during the last week should have tipped them off.

"Have you thought about forgiving him?"

"It's not just that he believed Isaac—it's why. I can forgive it because it's understandable, but that doesn't mean we're right for each other or that we could ever work together."

She sighs heavily. "Okay. So tell me everything I've missed since I left for London."

Smiling, I start at the beginning. There's nothing that heals hurt faster than sharing it with a friend who would save you from it if she could.

When my phone rings, I almost ignore it, since I have Willow right here, but I look at the caller ID on impulse and frown when I see the call is coming from Drew Gregory's office. "Hello?"

"Grace," Mr. Gregory booms through the line. "Your boyfriend dropped off your play, and I love it. This is the one. We'll start casting next week. I assume you'll be back in the office by then?"

"My boyfriend?"

"Yeah, yeah. Tall boy. Football player, I think. What's his name? Christopher. Yes, anyway, he dropped it off, and I about shit myself it's so damn good."

Willow's eyes are wide. Mr. Gregory is talking so loud she's probably heard every word.

She looks excited. I, on the other hand, am just confused. "Um, which play did he drop off?"

"*Diary of an Angry Slut*. Do you have another one like this you're hiding from me?"

My chest goes tight. How did Chris get it, and *why* did he give it to Mr. Gregory? I'm confused and elated all at once. "You liked *Diary*?"

"Liked it? Fuck, I'd have babies with it if such a thing were feasible. Are you going to let me put it on stage this summer or not? It's *Vagina Monologues* meets *Sex and the City*, or that's what I'm having marketing put on the audition bulletins. Tell me your boyfriend didn't screw up and we can move forward."

"Ye-yes. Yes, I'll be there for auditions." *Auditions*. For my play. I pinch my leg, and it hurts, but maybe I'm still dreaming.

"Great. In the meantime, do me a favor and write the ending. It's just kind of abrupt as it is."

That's because I haven't written the ending. "Okay. I'll work on it and bring a draft on Monday."

"Fucking fantastic. Bring it with my coffee. I've been drinking this department shit, and I think it's giving me dysentery. See you Monday, girl."

Then, just as abruptly as the conversation started, it ends, and I'm staring at Willow with wide eyes.

"I told you you were talented," she singsongs.

"You have to say that. It's in your job description as my best friend."

She grins. "And what about that boyfriend of yours? He's pretty sneaky." She hops off the couch and opens my bedroom door. "You can come out now."

I swing around, and my breath catches because Chris is in Bailey's apartment, walking out of my bedroom and toward me, his hands tucked into his pockets, his shoulders impossibly broader than the last time I saw him.

"I think he rolls in radioactive slime when I'm not around," I whisper to Willow while keeping my eyes on Chris.

I see her nod out of the corner of my eye. "Totally explains the sexy Tarzan chest thing he has going on. And you understand I couldn't refuse his request to hide in your bedroom when he pointed those dimples at me."

Chris sinks to his knees in front of where I'm sitting on the couch, and only then do I notice that he's carrying a stack of papers in his hands. The page on top has my title in a loopy font. *Diary of an Angry Slut.* "I hacked into your laptop to find this," he says.

My skin tingles at his nearness, and I'm so giddy I want to jump off the couch and dance. "That's against the law."

He nods. "Yeah, and I knew you might hate my guts for doing it, but I had to, and then I read it and I knew what I needed to do." He swallows hard and his blue eyes search my face. "I know I hurt you, and maybe you can't love me after what I did, but I needed you to know that I'm in love with the woman who wrote this. She's smart and brave, and she makes me laugh. So I took a chance." He takes a breath. "You said once that you wanted to win the lottery just so you could buy a playhouse and pay the actors to bring your plays to life, but you don't need to win the lottery for that to happen. You just needed to believe in yourself. You're talented. So I did it. I took a gamble, a big-ass risk, because if you didn't want anyone to read it then I'm just an asshole. But it's so intense and funny and moving and all the things that you are."

"You're saying it was fourth down and fifteen, and you were down by six so you needed to take a chance and run it in yourself."

His lips twitch into a hesitant grin. "Yeah, something like that."

"It was a good call. Ballsy as hell, but I'd say you scored." Warmth fills my core and slides over my limbs. I slide off the couch and down to the floor so I'm sitting in front of him. I want to be closer. I want to wrap myself around him and stay there for days, and then I want to run around in circles cheering. Because

Chris is here. Because Chris believes in me. Because Chris knows exactly who I am and what I've done, and he still did this for me.

"I love when you talk football." He places the manuscript to the side and cups my face in his big hands. "I'm so sorry I hurt you. Please let me make it up to you. I'll be brave and take chances every day to prove to you that I want this to work and that it can."

"Shut up and kiss me, rule breaker."

"As you wish, football lover."

We're both grinning when our lips touch. My smile stretches from the kiss all the way down into my chest, and happiness radiates out my fingers and toes.

Until Willow clears her throat. "I'll just be out front taking up smoking if you need me."

I laugh against Chris's mouth, unwilling to break the contact just yet. Then I hear Bailey, who I didn't even know was home, say, "Hell, after that, I need a cigarette, too."

When the door clicks closed, Chris breaks the kiss and strokes his thumbs down my cheeks. "Wanna lock the door and christen Bailey's guest bed before she gets back?"

I laugh. "She'd be disappointed in us if we didn't."

EPILOGUE
GRACE

When I applied for the summer playwright program at Carson College last year, I imagined wrapping up my summer while seeing one of my dreams unfold before me—someone else speaking my words on the stage.

It didn't work out as I'd planned. Instead of being in New York, we're in Blackhawk Valley, and instead of the family drama I thought would grab someone's attention, my secret just-for-me play, *Diary of an Angry Slut,* is being performed.

As I watch the final curtain fall from the back row, my heart is in my throat, and my eyes are filled with tears. The audience laughed at the right times and gasped at the right times, and I don't know if a lot of people cried, but the ladies in front of me definitely wiped away tears. Watching people engage like that with something I wrote is so overwhelming, I can hardly breathe.

Chris squeezes my hand, leaning over to whisper in my ear,

"They loved it."

I'm too full of gratitude to trust my voice, so I tilt my head up to kiss him. Next week, I leave for Carson College. We've taken full advantage of every moment of our summer together, and we're prepared to do the long-distance thing. That doesn't mean it's not going to suck when we have to part ways, but it beats not having each other at all.

Chris leads me into the hallway, where I shake hands and feel my cheeks blaze with heat as people praise my play.

"Grace."

My breath catches. *That can't be . . .*

I turn toward the sound of my father's voice and see him and Becky crossing to us from the atrium. "Why aren't you in Italy?" I ask.

Dad smiles softly. "We cut the trip short by a few days to see your play. It was worth it." My chest fills, and I might float away from the weightlessness of my happiness.

"Your play was so amazing, honey," Becky says, wrapping me in her arms. "I almost peed my pants laughing, and then you had me crying." She draws in a ragged breath. "You're so talented."

When I step out of her arms, Dad wraps me in his before I get a chance to speak. "I'm so proud of you," he says into my hair. "And I'm glad I saw this play. I . . ." He swallows and, wrapped tightly against his big barrel chest, I can feel his shaky inhale. "What the girl on stage said? I *never* saw you as the sum total of your mistakes. I see those mistakes as my own. I wasn't around enough. If I could go back and change the way I reacted, I would.

I was always more disappointed in myself. I failed you."

I squeeze my eyes shut. My father is a proud man. He thinks through things before acting, and as a result, it takes a lot for him to believe he did wrong. "You didn't fail me. You picked me up and took me somewhere to start over." My voice cracks. Why is it that on the outside I'm falling apart when on the inside I'm finally being put back together? "And I turned out okay."

"Better than okay," he says gruffly.

I step back, and Chris takes my hand, bringing it to his lips briefly before meeting Dad's eyes. "It's been a long day, and our writer needs some sleep. We'll see you two at breakfast."

Becky grins, her gaze glued to our joined hands as if it's the best thing she's ever seen. "See you then!"

Chris leads me outside and we walk toward the apartment hand in hand, the moon glowing overhead.

"It's a beautiful night," I say. "I feel so happy and full of good things and sad all at once."

He frowns. "Sad?"

"Only a week until I go back to New York."

"Oh, the city, your other love. I forget about that bastard."

I sigh. We've talked about our options, and it doesn't make sense for me to give up the city to transfer to BHU when he's entering the draft in the spring.

"The Giants are in the market for a new QB after this season," he says, watching me.

"The baseball team?" He winces, and I laugh. "I'm joking. I know who the *football* Giants are. I just can't let on how much I know about football in public, or you might jump me."

He chuckles. "I might. Your secret football knowledge is pretty hot."

I try to smile, but it falls away. "Are you worried? I mean, about us being apart so much?"

"I'm worried I might lose my mind," he admits, opening the door to the apartment complex for me. "And I'm worried that missing you might be the toughest thing I've ever had to do, but I'm not worried about us. The longest month waiting to see you is better than the shortest moment when I thought I'd lost you."

My heart tugs sideways in my chest as if it has a mind of its own and is trying to get closer to him. "You took the words right out of my mouth."

"Are you sure?" He turns me against the stairwell and slides his hands into my hair. "Let me make sure I didn't miss any." Then he lowers his mouth to mine and treats me to a kiss so long, and deep, and sweet that I can feel the beat of my mended heart, safe and secure, and tied up in his. I'm not more vulnerable for loving him. I'm stronger.

THE END

Thank you for reading *Rushing In,* the second book in The Blackhawk Boys series. If you'd like to receive an email when I release Sebastian's story in book three, *Going Under,* please sign up for my newsletter. If you enjoyed this book, please consider leaving a review. Thank you for reading. It's an honor!

RUSHING IN
Playlist

"Joyful Girl" by Ani DiFranco
"Slut Like You" by P!nk
"Hurt" by Nine Inch Nails
"I Try" by Macy Gray
"Madness" by Muse
"Shut Up and Dance" by Walk the Moon
"You & I (Nobody in the World)" by John Legend
"Close" by Nick Jonas and Tov Lo
"Hands to Myself" by Selena Gomez
"Fix You" by Coldplay
"Gratitude" by Ani DiFranco
"Unsteady" by X Ambassadors
"Stay With Me" by Sam Smith

Other Books
by LEXI RYAN

The Blackhawk Boys
Spinning Out (Arrow's story)
Rushing In (Chris's story)
Going Under (Sebastian's story coming late 2016)

Love Unbound
by LEXI RYAN

If you enjoyed *Spinning Out*, you may also enjoy the books in Love Unbound, the linked series of books set in New Hope and about the characters readers have come to love.

Splintered Hearts (A Love Unbound Series)
Unbreak Me (Maggie's story)
Stolen Wishes: A Wish I May Prequel Novella (Will and Cally's prequel)
Wish I May (Will and Cally's novel)

Or read them together in the omnibus edition,
Splintered Hearts: The New Hope Trilogy

Here and Now (A Love Unbound Series)
Lost in Me (Hanna's story begins)
Fall to You (Hanna's story continues)
All for This (Hanna's story concludes)

Or read them together in the omnibus edition,
Here and Now: The Complete Series

※

Reckless and Real (A Love Unbound Series)
Something Wild (Liz and Sam's story begins)
Something Reckless (Liz and Sam's story continues)
Something Real (Liz and Sam's story concludes)

Or read them together in the omnibus edition,
Reckless and Real: The Complete Series

※

Mended Hearts (A Love Unbound Series)
Playing with Fire (Nix's story)
Holding Her Close (Janelle and Cade's story)

Other Titles
by LEXI RYAN

Hot Contemporary Romance
Text Appeal
Accidental Sex Goddess

Decadence Creek Stories and Novellas
Just One Night
Just the Way You Are

ACKNOWLEDGMENTS

Even on the hardest, most exhausting days, I am filled with gratitude for the countless people who keep my head above water. I'm so grateful to my husband. He doesn't just keep me from drowning, he reminds me I need to breathe. I married a man who believes in me and my work, who understands (or at least quietly accepts) my drive to tell *all the stories*, and who makes the sacrifices necessary when I need to work sixty hours a week to get a book done. Brian, you rock, and I'd very much like to keep you.

I'm surrounded by a family who supports me every day. To my kids, Jack and Mary, thank you for making me laugh and giving me a reason to work hard. I am so proud to be your mommy. To my mom, brothers, and sisters, thank you for cheering me on—each in your own way. I'm so grateful to have been born into this crazy crew of seven kids.

This book is for my sister Kim, who wears the cape of Super Mom and wears it proud. My sister Deb wears that cape too, but Kim was my inspiration for Becky, Chris's mom. Kim, I know being a single mama isn't easy, but you couldn't have done it better.

My thanks to my nephew Kai, who doesn't complain about my random texts with football questions, or even make fun of me when I ask him about slang terms. Thanks for not making me feel as old as I am, and for working out with me. I will never keep up, but it's fun to try.

If my family is my rock-solid foundation, my friends are the laughter that fills the rooms. A special shout-out to Mira, my book bestie. Maybe we don't *need* to spend two hours on the phone a week, but those calls energize me so much; they feel necessary to #livingthedream and enduring its really effing stressful moments. To my lifting buddy Kylie, my coach Matt, and the entire CrossFit Terre Haute crew. Thank you for teaching me to love picking up heavy things and giving me an outlet I needed more than I ever realized. I've been blessed with so many amazing people in my life. You encourage me, you believe in me, and you know how to make me laugh.

To everyone who provided me feedback on Chris and Grace's story along the way—especially Annie Swanberg, Heather Carver, Janice Owen, Mira Lyn Kelly, and Samantha Leighton—you're all awesome. Thank you for helping to make this idea in my head into something worth reading.

Thank you to the team that helped me package this book and promote it. Sarah Hansen at Okay Creations designed my beautiful cover and did a lovely job branding the series. Rhonda Stapleton and Lauren McKellar, thank you for the insightful line edits. Thanks to Arran McNicol at Editing720 for proofreading. A shout-out to all of the bloggers and reviewers who help spread the word about my books. I am humbled by the time you take out of your busy lives for my stories. You're the best.

To my agent, Dan Mandel, for believing in me and staying by my side through tough career decisions. Thanks to you and

Stefanie Diaz for getting my books into the hands of readers all over the world. Thank you for being part of my team.

To my NWBs—Sawyer Bennett, Lauren Blakely, Violet Duke, Jessie Evans, Melody Grace, Monica Murphy, and Kendall Ryan—y'all rock my world. I'm inspired by your tireless work and always encouraged by your friendship. Thank you for being a part of this journey.

To all my writer friends on Twitter, Facebook, and my various writer loops—especially to the Fast Draft Club and the All Awesome group—thank you for keeping me company during those fourteen-hour work days.

And last but certainly not least, a big thank-you to my fans. I've said it before and I'll continue to say it every chance I get—you're the coolest, smartest, best readers in the world. I owe my career to you. You're the reason I get to do this every day, the reason I *want* to, and the reason I push myself to better my craft with each book. I appreciate each and every one of you. You're the best!

~Lexi

CONTACT

I love hearing from readers, so find me on my Facebook page at facebook.com/lexiryanauthor, follow me on Twitter and Instagram @writerlexiryan, shoot me an email at writerlexiryan@gmail.com, or find me on my website: www.lexiryan.com

Printed in Great Britain
by Amazon